'Tell me about the man who died. What manner of man was he?' Amy asked.

'I know nothing of him. He boarded the coach with you, and your tickets were in his pockets, so one supposes he was looking after you,' James replied.

'So I was totally dependent on him,' she mused.

'It would seem so.'

'How did I get from the overturned coach to the inn?' she wanted to know.

'I rode one of the coach horses with you in front of me. Have you no memory of that?'

'None at all,' she said swiftly. But that *was* her memory. A slow ride, cradled in front of him on a horse with no saddle. She had felt warm and protected, with his arm about her and his coat enveloping them both. She did not remember arriving at the inn, so she must have drifted into unconsciousness again. 'How difficult and uncomfortable that must have been for you.'

He noticed the colour flood her face and felt sure she had remembered it. How much more was she concealing? He would have it out of her, one way or another, before another day was through.

Born in Singapore, **Mary Nichols** came to England when she was three, and has spent most of her life in different parts of East Anglia. She has been a radiographer, school secretary, information officer and industrial editor, as well as a writer. She has three grown-up children, and four grandchildren.

Recent novels by the same author:

TALK OF THE TON
WORKING MAN, SOCIETY BRIDE
A DESIRABLE HUSBAND
RUNAWAY MISS
RAGS-TO-RICHES BRIDE
THE EARL AND THE HOYDEN
CLAIMING THE ASHBROOKE HEIR
  (part of *The Secret Baby Bargain*)
HONOURABLE DOCTOR,
  IMPROPER ARRANGEMENT

THE CAPTAIN'S MYSTERIOUS LADY

Mary Nichols

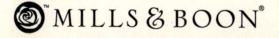MILLS & BOON

First published in Great Britain 2010
Large Print edition 2010
Harlequin Mills & Boon Limited,
Eton House, 18-24 Paradise Road, Richmond, Surrey TW9 1SR

© Mary Nichols 2010

ISBN: 978 0 263 21155 9

Harlequin Mills & Boon policy is to use papers that are natural, renewable and recyclable products and made from wood grown in sustainable forests. The logging and manufacturing process conform to the legal environmental regulations of the country of origin.

Printed and bound in Great Britain
by CPI Antony Rowe, Chippenham, Wiltshire

THE CAPTAIN'S MYSTERIOUS LADY

Chapter One

Early spring 1750

A breathless James arrived at the Blue Boar in Holborn just in time to see the stage disappearing out of sight. He stood and watched it go and swore roundly in several languages.

'Dammit, Sam,' he said at the end of this tirade. 'The devils have slipped through our fingers again. They're as slippery as eels, the pair of them.'

'Yes, sir. Do you think they knew we were on to them?'

'Couldn't fail to, could they? We have been hounding them for two years. But they need not think this is the end of it, for I will not give up while there is breath in my body.'

Captain the Honourable James Drymore turned from the sight of the back of the stage disappear-

ing from the end of the road and went into the inn
to enquire about its passengers. He did not expect
to be given names; they would have meant little if
he had. Those two, whose real names he had ascertained were Morgan Randle and Jeremy Smith,
would have used aliases and probably disguises,
too. If his informant had been right, they were
finding his pursuit of them too close for comfort
and had decided to leave London for the provinces.
He did not know their destination, but he had
learned, only that morning, that they had arranged
to meet at the Blue Boar at nine in the morning
with the intention of boarding a coach north. He
had rushed home to pack a few clothes, put some
money and his pistol into his pocket and, with
Sam in tow as he always was, made all haste to the
inn.

'Two men travelling together,' the proprietor
repeated, when James finally persuaded him to stop
rushing about issuing orders to his servants and
speak to him. 'Well, there were two, clerical men I
should say. Dark clothes, bob wigs, shallow hats.'

'And was one a spidershanks, without an ounce
of fat on him, and the other a beefy fellow with a
bulbous nose?' James asked, mentioning attributes
it would be hard to disguise, even if their clothes
and wigs were changed.

'You could so describe them, sir. What might I ask is your interest in them?'

'I am empowered by the Bow Street magistrate to arrest them for theft and murder, so if you know anything of them you should tell me at once.'

'I don't ask the passengers for their histories when they board one of my coaches, sir. I'd never do any business that way.'

'I understand that, but perhaps you could tell me their destination.'

'They bought tickets to Peterborough. Where they were going from there I cannot tell.'

'And when is the next coach going in that direction?'

'To Peterborough? Not until tomorrow, but there's one going to Lynn in half an hour. You could leave it at Downham Market and find your way to Peterborough from there.'

'That will have to do.'

He bought inside tickets for himself and Sam, his friend as well as his servant, and went into the inn's parlour to wile away the thirty minutes they had to wait. There was a good fire in there and they sat warming their frozen toes on the fender and drinking mulled wine.

James had every reason to want to see Randle and Smith brought to justice. The victim of the murder he had spoken of had been his own wife. Poor, innocent Caroline had simply been in the wrong place at the wrong time when those two had run into the silversmiths' to rob it at gunpoint. According to the shopkeeper, she had been buying a silver cravat pin as a present for him. She appeared well and happy and had told him she was looking forward to having her husband home again after two years at sea. The thieves had waved their pistols about and when he had been too slow in obeying their commands to hand over everything of value, one had fired and the ball had ricocheted off the wall behind Caroline and mortally wounded her.

She had been carried to Colbridge House, the family home in Golden Square, but in spite of the best care his father could obtain for her, she had died the same day. 'She passed away with your name on her lips,' his father had said, giving him the pin that had been in her hand. 'She charged me to give you this.' James had taken it and wept over it, wept over her grave, too, but when his tears dried, he had been miserable, angry and guilty by turns.

He had been a poor husband, had not told her often enough how much she meant to him, and now it was too late. If he had not been away so much, they might have had children; he knew she had wanted them, as he had. And poor, innocent darling, she was thinking of him when she went into that shop to buy him a coming-home present. The anguish was unbearable and his temper was something dreadful to behold. Only his patient and loyal Sam Roker put up with him.

A visit to Bow Street had followed, where he had raved at the watchmen and constables for their lack of action. It was unfair of him, he supposed; they were not employed to investigate, but simply to arrest wrongdoers when they were brought to their attention. There seemed no one prepared to spend time on detective work. It was slow and laborious and nearly always futile. James had resolved to catch the pair himself, come hell or high water. It was a quest he had been pursuing for the best part of two years and had involved putting on some strange disguises and mixing with the rogues who inhabited London's underworld. News of his pursuit seemed always to precede him because, whenever he followed up a lead he had been given, the quarry had decamped. The lure of a reward had eventually brought information that the two men were leaving London from the Blue Boar, but, once again, he had arrived too late.

He sat drinking his spicy wine, while musing on his life with Caroline. He had been away at sea a great deal of the time, but when he was at home, they had been happy together, delighting in each other, sometimes dining in, sometimes going to the theatre, meeting friends, going for walks, planning the family they hoped to have, until it was time to leave her again. After his last leave, he had, for her sake, resolved to quit the service, settle down to domesticity and become a doting husband and father. He had been torn apart with guilt to think she would never know of that promise. The plans he had made for going back to his small estate near Newmarket and becoming a gentleman farmer meant nothing without her to share them. He could not bear to stay there and left his steward in charge while he set about tracing the murdering thieves. It had become a crusade from which he never wavered.

In so doing he had been instrumental in uncovering other crimes which he had reported to the appropriate magistrate, earning him the name of thieftaker, a soubriquet he hated. Thieftakers had a bad reputation with the public for frequently faking evidence to obtain a conviction in order to claim the reward. He did not need the money. True, he was only the second son of the Earl of Colbridge and not his heir, but he had been left an annuity by his maternal grandfather that, together with his pay and his share of prize money, meant he was of independent means. Anything he was offered for his services to law and order he gave to charity. 'What we need,' he was fond of telling Sam, 'is an independent police force paid for out of taxes, a body of astute, incorruptible men whom everyone can trust.'

'And pigs might fly,' Sam would say. 'Folks'd never agree to pay for it.'

They heard a horn followed by the rattle of a coach coming into the yard and went to join their fellow passengers. Apart from two or three men who climbed on the roof, which was cheaper, there were three inside besides themselves. A parson in a black suit of clothes, a full wig and wide-brimmed hat, and a man and a young woman who appeared to be travelling together. James, settling himself in the seat opposite, found himself covertly studying her.

She was so pale there was hardly a vestige of colour in her face and even her lips seemed blanched. Her eyes were blue, but they were clouded by worry. Her clothes, though not the height of fashion, were nevertheless of good quality. Her simple unpadded open gown was in a blue-and-white striped material with an embroidered stomacher. She had a cloak, but no hat or gloves and her shoes were flimsy, not intended for out of doors. Her fair hair hung about her shoulders in a tangle, as if she had left home in a great hurry. Had she been coerced into making the journey? Or even abducted? She did not look as if she would fetch much in the way of ransom.

She noticed him looking at her and quickly looked away. Was she ill? Was she nervous because she was unused to travelling by public coach? She would not look at her companion and when the man put a hand on her arm, she flinched as if she had been struck. He wore a black suit of clothes, shiny with age, and a beaver hat with a wide crown crammed on to a grimy scratch wig. Not on the same social plane, James concluded. A servant, perhaps, but not one she trusted.

Sam, sitting in the corner, was looking out of the window at the darkening sky. 'We'll have snow afore long,' he said to no one in particular.

The man with the girl simply grunted in response. 'Are you and the lady going far?' James asked him pleasantly.

'That's our business,' the man growled and James noticed the young woman imperceptibly shake her head as if warning him not to pursue his questioning.

He turned to the other occupant of the coach. 'What about you, sir? Do you have far to travel?'

'To Cambridge, God and weather permitting,' the parson said. 'I never knew winter to last so long. We should be seeing the shoots coming through the cold earth by now, but not a sign of them yet. And what with earthquakes and suchlike I do not doubt we are being punished for our wickedness.'

'What, all of us?' James queried. 'Surely the righteous should not be punished along with the wicked?'

The man paused to look at him and then went on as if such a remark were too foolish to merit an answer. 'I would not have travelled if it could have been avoided. I abhor London with its smoke and grime and stink. Full of thieves and cutthroats. Why, I had my pocket cut while walking in Hyde Park yesterday.'

'I am sorry to hear that.' James answered him, but he was looking sideways at the young woman. She had not moved, was staring straight ahead and did not appear to be listening. What was going on in her head, for clearly something was? He wondered how to draw her into the conversation and then asked himself why he wanted to. If she wished to sit silent, then so be it. 'Did they take much?'

'Several guineas, sir. I do not know what the country is coming to, when a man of the cloth can be blatantly robbed in daylight.'

'You reported it, of course.'

'Yes, but the judiciary are more concerned with rooting out Jacobites, than protecting honest citizens.'

'Yes, I heard tell the Young Pretender is about to

make another bid for the crown,' Sam put in. 'Everyone is in a fever over it. He is here, he is there, he is everywhere.'

'He would surely not make another attempt without French backing,' the parson added, looking worried. 'He would not dare, would he?'

''Tis all rumour,' James said. 'You may be sure the Scots won't come to his aid again, not after the way Butcher Cumberland put them down after Culloden. And without them, where would he get the money to pay troops and buy supplies and armaments? It is common knowledge his pockets are to let and he has to resort to begging from his friends.'

'The Arkaig treasure,' Sam said. 'I reckon someone knows where it's been hid.'

James noticed the man beside the girl sit forward and show an interest in the conversation for the first time. James smiled to himself, wondering whether to speak of what he knew. He had been on board one of English ships sent to intercept the French vessels taking supplies to the Scottish rebels in the last battle of the '45 rebellion off the shore of Loch Nan Uamh. Before they had chased the French vessels off, everyone on board had witnessed the Highlanders hauling large quantities of cargo up from the shore to the woods, some of it extremely heavy, and it was common knowledge that there had been several thousand *louis d'or* in barrels. There was brandy, too, and many of the rebels had been paralytic with drink. He could not believe they had not appropriated at least some of the gold. Their captured leaders had talked of it and tried to account for it all, but a large proportion had never been found.

'I hope nothing comes of it,' he said. 'It would mean war and though I do not doubt we would be victorious, I should not like to see another monarch executed.'

'Are you a Jacobite sympathiser, sir?' the parson demanded.

'No, indeed not. I serve my king and country and armed rebellion has to be put down. That does not mean I approve of some of the measures taken to achieve it, nor that men should be persecuted for sincerely held beliefs. This is a free country, after all.'

'Free!' the young woman's companion scoffed. 'Free from what, I should like to know. 'Tis only the likes of you and the parson there can call themselves free.'

'Please,' the girl said suddenly. 'You are all speaking too loudly and I have the headache.'

James, surprised that she had spoken in the

refined accents of a lady, bowed towards her and spoke softly. 'I beg your pardon, madam. When we stop to change the horses, I will obtain a tisane for you.'

'Thank you,' she murmured and turned to look out of the window, presenting her profile to him. She had good bone structure and there was a tilt to her jaw, which might have been an indication of courage or perhaps stubbornness. But even so, he noticed a silent tear spill over one eye and roll down her cheek. Before he could stop himself he had reached forward and scooped it up on his finger. She turned startled eyes on him and he smiled reassuringly without speaking. He took off his coat and rolled it up to make a pillow and propped it behind her head. 'Why not lean back and close your eyes? It might help.'

She did as he suggested, though her companion's look was enough to fell an ox. James, sitting back in his shirt sleeves and waistcoat and ignoring the chill air, pretended to shut his eyes, but between half-closed lids he could see she was still tense, still far from relaxed. But she had effectively silenced all conversation. Something was wrong, he could feel it in his bones, and it was not simply a headache. He wondered whether he ought to do something about it, but then told himself it was not his business and perhaps he was allowing his imagination to run away with him.

That was it; she was running away, possibly from her family or an unwanted suitor or perhaps from the fear of another earthquake. A second one exactly a month after the first had set the citizens of London deserting the capital in droves. But if that were so, she had chosen a singularly ill-bred escort, and why, if she was gently bred, did she not have a female companion with her? But supposing she was the one in the wrong, had run away and was being taken reluctantly back home?

They had stopped now and again to change the horses, but they did not leave the coach until they reached the Feathers at Wadesmill, where they were told they had half an hour to visit the necessary and have something to eat. Once out of the carriage, the young lady returned his coat. 'Is there anything I can do for you?' he whispered as he took it from her and slung it over his shoulders.

She turned to look up at him and for the first time he saw animation in her lovely eyes. It made her suddenly beautiful and vulnerable as well. There was hope in that glance, which quickly turned to despair when her companion seized her arm and led her away to a table in the corner where he pushed her roughly into a chair and ordered food.

'They're a rum pair, ain't they?' Sam said, as they seated themselves at another table.

'Who?'

'Those two over there.' He nodded imperceptibly in their direction. James noticed she was pushing the food about on her plate, but not eating.

'Yes, there's something not right there.' In spite of a reputation he had for being hard and unbending, he could still sympathise with anyone in trouble and he felt sure the young lady was in trouble.

'You ain't thinkin' of doin' somethin' about it, are you, Cap'n?'

'And let Randle and Smith get away again?' As he had done so often before, he imagined his wife's terror at being confronted with the gunmen and his anger surfaced again. Those two were going to pay for their crimes and pay heavily. That was his true errand, not rescuing women who might or might not need rescuing. And what would he do with her if he did separate her from her escort? He could hardly take her with him. 'We still have a long way to go,' he said, as a waiter put their food in front of them and he ordered a tisane to be taken to the young lady. 'We will see what transpires.'

* * *

What actually transpired was something not even he had expected, though why he should be surprised when the coach was later held up by highwaymen, he did not know; it was a common enough occurrence. It had been fully dark by the time they reached Cambridge where the parson left them, and he had wondered if the man and the girl would stop there, but they must have been in as great a haste as he was, for they had elected to go on. The journey north through Ely had been uneventful and they were proceeding as fast as the coachman dared go along an extremely bumpy road with the river on one side and a spindly stand of trees on the other, when two men brandishing pistols appeared from the copse on horseback and commanded the driver to stop. The coach pulled up so sharply they were all flung against each other. The girl gave a little cry to find herself in James's arms, as a man with a black kerchief about his lower face opened the door and waved a pistol at them. 'Out!' he commanded. 'We'll have your valuables or your lives.'

James helped the girl to alight and put his arm about her shoulders to support her. When the pistol was waved at him, he thought it expedient to hand over his watch and a purse containing a few guineas. The robber took them and stowed them away inside

his voluminous cloak, then turned to the other occupants of the coach. Catching sight of the man
who had boarded the coach with the girl, he
promptly fell about laughing. 'Here, Jerry,' he
chuckled. 'Look who's turned up.'

His accomplice, who had been keeping his eye on
the coachman, appeared beside him. He, too, had
his face covered so that only his eyes were visible.
'Gus Billings, as I live and breathe, and the lady,
too. Now, there's an interesting turn of events.'

James felt the girl's shoulders stiffen under his
hand and heard her stifle a small cry. She was
shaking and only his arm about her was stopping
her from sinking to the ground. He gave her
shoulder a little squeeze of reassurance.

'I'm only doin' your biddin',' the man called
Billings told the other two. 'If you want to lay yer
hands on you know what, you'll allow me to get
on with it.'

'And who is this?' Jerry waved his pistol towards
James, who did not flinch, though the girl did,
quite violently.

'Dunno, do I?' Billings said.

'I am the Honourable James Drymore, Captain of
his Majesty's navy,' James told him in his haughti-
est voice. 'And I advise you to allow us to proceed
or it will be the worse for you.' It was an empty

threat; there was nothing he could do to stop them. His pistol was in his coat pocket and he could not reach it without taking his arm from around the young lady and he was afraid if he did she would collapse in a heap at his feet. Sam had no weapon.

The masked riders laughed and beckoned Billings to join them. He went reluctantly but, after a few whispered words, he came back and, taking the girl's arm, wrested her from James and pushed her back into the coach. It was then James tried to reach into his pocket for his pistol, but a shot whistled past his ear. 'Get back in the coach and be off with you,' the first highwayman ordered. 'And think yourselves fortunate I'm feelin' generous today.'

They resumed their seats, the horses were whipped up and they were on their way again.

'Madam, are you all right?' James asked the young lady.

'Leave 'er alone,' Billings said. 'Can't you see she's upset?'

'Indeed I can, but I do not think it is I who upset her.'

'Being held up by robbers is enough to overset anyone.'

'True. But I notice you were more surprised than overset. The scoundrels were known to you.'

'Please,' the girl pleaded. 'I thank you for your concern, sir, but I am perfectly well.' Which was very far from the truth, but she evidently did not want him taking the man to task.

He looked across at Billings, who was eyeing him warily. If the fellow were to drop his guard, he might be able to overpower him with Sam's help. But if he did, what in God's name would he do with the young lady? And how could he be sure those two highwaymen were not following them? The coachman must have had the same idea, because he was driving at breakneck speed, relying on the moon and a couple of carriage lamps to light his way. Further conversation was almost impossible as they all hung on to the straps and endeavoured to stay in their seats.

When they stopped for a change of horses at Downham Market, he would endeavour to part Billings from the young lady long enough to interrogate them both separately, James decided. Whatever he discovered he would report to the local constable, though it would be impossible to give a description of the robbers, considering the night was dark and they were masked and shrouded in cloaks. No one was safe on the roads while men like those two waylaid travellers. He was glad he had had the foresight to hide his precious cravat pin and most of his money in a belt about his waist and keep only a little in his purse. It was a common practice and he wondered why the thieves had not known it, or, if they did, had not searched him. He supposed they had been taken aback to find an acquaintance on the coach and their exchange with him had put it from their minds.

His musings came to an abrupt halt as the coach wheel dipped into a particularly deep pothole, seemed to right itself and then lurch off the road. In spite of the coachman's heroic efforts, he could not bring it back on course and it went over and slid down the embankment, accompanied by the sound of frightened horses and splintering wood. The coachman yelled, Sam swore loudly, Billings screamed and then was silent. The girl uttered not a sound, as the vehicle came to rest on the steeply sloping bank only inches from the river.

James, who was thankfully unhurt, climbed out of the wreckage and turned to help the young lady. She was unconscious, which accounted for her silence, but was mercifully alive. He picked her up and laid her gently on the grass, then turned to the others. Sam was climbing out, looking dazed but otherwise unhurt. Billings must have broken his neck; his head lolled at an unnatural angle and he was clearly dead. The coachman, who had been flung into the river, was climbing out, dripping wet weeds in his wake.

James went to help him while Sam and the guard saw to the horses.

One was clearly dead, another had struggled free and was in the river, swimming strongly for the other side. As soon as the other two had been released from the traces, one scrambled to its feet and galloped up the road in the direction from which they had come. The fourth, though clearly terrified, was unhurt and allowed itself to be led up on to the road. Once that was accomplished, everyone stood and surveyed the wreck. It was certainly not going to take them any further.

'Do you think those devils are behind us?' the coachman queried, as James bent to tend to the young lady. She had a nasty bump on her temple, which would account for her passing out, but he could detect no broken bones. She would undoubtedly be bruised and sore when she regained her senses.

'No tellin', is there?' Sam said. 'And they'd be no help, would they?'

'No, but the sooner we get away from here the better.' He was trying to wring the water out of his wig, but it was a sorry mess and he gave up the idea of replacing it on his head and stuffed it in his equally wet pocket.

'How far is it to the nearest village?' James asked, glad he had given up wearing a wig. Opportunities for having one cleaned and dressed were few and far between while he was chasing criminals all over the country, and now his own hair was so long and thick no wig would stay on it. Usually he tied it back with a narrow ribbon, but if he was dining out, he allowed Sam to roll a few curls round some stuffing and powder it.

'Highbeck's four mile or thereabouts,' the coachman said. 'We'd ha' bin calling there in any case.'

'Right, then I'll ride the horse and take the young lady up in front. The rest of you can walk.'

'She's out cold, she'll not be able to hold on,' Sam put in. 'And the 'orse ain't exactly quiet, is 'e?'

'I can steady it with one hand, if you tie her to me.'

As no one had a better idea, this was done. He replaced his hat, which he had found in the wreckage of the coach, and mounted up, stilling the horse's protests with calm words and firm knees. Sam fetched a strap from the boot and tied it round the lady's waist and lifted her up to him. He slipped the loop over his head and put his arm through it, cradling her to his side, inside his coat. 'Right, she is secure enough. I'll see you all at the inn.' He picked up the reins and set the horse to walk.

He could feel the warmth of her body through his

shirt and realised it was the closest he had been to a woman since he had last held Caroline in his arms, the day he had waved her goodbye to go on his last voyage. He stifled the half-sob, half-grunt of anger that rose in his throat and looked down at the slight figure in his arms. Her head was nestling on his chest as if she knew she was safe, but her face was paler than ever. She should have started to come round by now, but she was still unconscious, though every now and again she gave a low moan and he prayed she had come to no lasting harm. He dared not make the horse hurry.

Her escort was dead and could not be questioned now. Did that mean she was free of trouble? When she came to her senses, he would have to find out what was going on, who she was, where she came from, then restore her to her family. If she had a family. She had no means of identification on her, no luggage, no purse, nothing but the clothes she wore, now filthy and torn. He had been through Billings's pockets, but he'd had nothing either, except a few shillings and two coach tickets, destination Highbeck. That was the name of the village he was heading for. Did that mean she was nearly home? Or was it Billings's roost? The questions plagued him as he clopped onwards, cradling the unconscious beauty in his arms. For she was beautiful, he realised, and her skin, except where it was bruised by the accident, was smooth and creamy. Her scarf had come loose and he could see the top of her breasts peeping from her stomacher. They rose and fell with her even breathing and for the first time in an age, he felt a *frisson* of desire. He pulled himself together, wishing she would regain her senses, but if she did and realised where she was, she would be mortified. Would she be as frightened of him as she had been of Billings? he wondered, not liking the idea.

It was dark by the time he reached the village. A dog barked loudly from a farmhouse on his right; another answered from the churchyard on his left. He clopped on. A few cottages straggled along the road until he came to the crossroads and here there was light spilling from the open door of an inn. He reined in, slipped the strap from around his neck and called for the landlord to come to his assistance; he could not dismount until someone took his burden from him.

A man came out carrying a lantern. 'Make haste, man,' he told him. 'The lady has been injured. She must be put to bed. Is there a doctor hereabouts?'

'Not before Downham, sir. My wife will see to her.'

James gently lowered the girl so that the inn-keeper could take her, then he dismounted and took her back to carry her inside.

The innkeeper's wife hurried forwards. 'What has happened?'

'The coach overturned four miles back,' James told her. 'There's a dead man and a dead horse. The coachman, the guard and my servant are following on foot. They will all need bruises and cuts seeing to and sustenance when they arrive, but first a room and a bed for the young lady.'

'This way, sir.' She led the way up a flight of stairs where she pushed open the door of a bed-chamber. 'Will this suffice?'

He looked about him. Although it was small, the room and the bed hangings were clean. 'Yes, thank you.'

'Do you need anything else? Hot water? Food and drink?'

'All of those things when the lady regains her senses. Unfortunately she has been unconscious for some time and I do not even know her name.' He put his burden on the bed.

'My goodness, I know her,' the lady said, peering down at the unconscious woman. 'She used to live at Blackfen Manor, hard by here, when she was a child. I disremember her name—it was some time ago, you understand—but I know the ladies at the Manor, Miss Hardwick and Miss Matilda Hardwick.'

'Then send for them at once. They will know what to do.'

The girl on the bed stirred and moaned and opened her eyes. 'Where am I?'

'At the King's Arms in Highbeck,' James answered. 'You had a nasty knock on the head when the coach overturned.'

'Coach?'

'Yes, you were travelling on it. Don't you remember?'

'No. Where was I going?'

'Coming here, I think.'

'Why?'

'You have kin at Blackfen Manor,' the innkeeper's wife put in. 'I expect you were coming on a visit.'

'I don't remember.'

'It is hardly surprising,' James said. 'You were knocked out.'

'Who are you?' she asked him.

'Captain Drymore, at your service,' he said. 'I was travelling on the same coach. Now you must rest. We are going to send word to Blackfen Manor for someone to take charge of you. I will leave you in the care of our hostess and come to see you again later.'

The innkeeper's wife accompanied him to the door. 'Was she travelling alone?' she asked.

'She had an escort, but he's dead,' he whispered. 'I don't know whether to tell her that or not.'

'We should tell the ladies when they come.'

He left her to tend to the girl's bruises and went downstairs again to find the others had arrived and were making themselves comfortable in the parlour with a quart of ale each, while food was prepared for them. 'What now?' Sam asked when he joined them.

'She is known to the innkeeper's wife. It appears she has kin close by and someone is going to fetch them to take charge of her,' James told him.

'Thank the Lord for that, for a moment I thought we were going to be saddled with her.'

James realised, with a jolt, that her predicament had driven the main purpose of his journey from his mind, but it was time he began to think of it. 'And you wouldn't want that, would you, my friend?'

'To be sure, it would put a spoke in the wheels. Has she got her senses back?' Sam asked.

'Yes and no. She is conscious, but still too dazed to know what has happened to her. No doubt the sight of her relatives will be all that's needed.'

'Then we go on?'

'To Peterborough?' James queried vaguely, his mind still half with the mystery of the girl.

'Yes, had you forgot where we were going and why?'

'No, I had not and I'll thank you to mind your manners.'

'I beg your pardon, Cap'n sir, but you must admit you can't be worrying about that one upstairs when we are so close to success.' Sam was almost as determined on catching those two as he was, knowing what it meant to him.

'How do you know we are close to success?'

'We know they were on that coach and going to Peterborough, don't we?'

'Just because they paid the fare to Peterborough, does not mean they meant to travel all the way there. They could have left the stage anywhere to put us off the scent again. Or they may have gone on somewhere else,' James pointed out.

'And they might have been held up by those two highpads. That would have delayed them, don't you think?'

'Very true, but in the absence of evidence to the contrary we will head for Peterborough.'

'I took the liberty of making enquiries, Captain, and there's a coach coming through at first light which will take us on to Downham Market. And there are connections to Peterborough.'

'Good. We can't do anything more here.'

* * *

After they had eaten, James went up to speak to the young lady and take his leave of her. She had swallowed a little supper, he was told, but she was still dazed. 'She'll be fine as ninepence when the Misses Hardwick come to take care of her,' the innkeeper's wife said, as they stood outside the bedchamber talking quietly.

'You have sent word to them?'

'Yes, but they are maiden ladies and will not venture out at this time of night. They will be here in the morning.'

'Are you sure of that?' He was torn between staying and leaving. It was curiosity mixed with pity and a feeling of responsibility that made him want to stay and see her safely with her kin, while the determination to find his wife's killers and see them hanged drove him relentlessly.

'Oh, yes, indeed. Lovely ladies they are, always pleasant, always have a kind word for everyone and they do a deal of good in the village. I reckon she must be a niece or something of the sort. It's a mystery, though.'

'What is?'

'No baggage, no money, nothing, according to the coachman.'

'I will recompense you for her food and lodging.'

'I did not mean that, sir, indeed I did not. I am sure the Misses Hardwick will see to that. I was thinkin' what a mystery it was.'

'Yes, to be sure. But no doubt when the lady recovers her senses she will be able to enlighten you. In the meantime, can I leave her with you?'

'Yes, of course. You must be anxious to continue your journey.'

'I am.' His mind was made up. 'Pressing business, you understand. We shall go on the early coach, but a bed for the rest of the night will be welcome.'

'Certainly, sir. I'll see to it.'

He took several coins from his purse and handed them to her, enough to cover his and Sam's stay and the young woman's. 'I will go in and say my farewells. I doubt I shall see her in the morning.'

He opened the door and stepped into the room. The invalid lay in the bed, staring at the ceiling, lost in thought.

'Madam,' he said, moving over to stand beside her. She looked small and frail in the big bed.

She turned towards him. 'Captain Drymore. That is right, is it not? I have remembered your name correctly?'

'Yes, that is my name. Can you tell me yours?'

A tear found its way down her cheek. 'I must have had a really bad bang on the head, for I cannot remember it. I have been lying here, racking my brain, and it just will not come.'

He sat down on the edge of the bed. 'Do not distress yourself. When you are with your relations again and in familiar surroundings, everything will come back to you.'

'I expect you are right. But I must thank you for what you have done for me. The landlady has told me and it seems I am in your debt.'

'Not at all. I did nothing.' He stood up. 'I came to say goodbye and to wish you well. I am leaving very early in the morning to continue my journey. Mrs Sadler has assured me I can safely leave you in her care until your relatives come for you.'

'Then goodbye, sir. And again my gratitude.'

He gave her a small bow and left the room. He did not like leaving her, but Sam was right, he could do nothing more for her. They were strangers who had passed a few hours in each other's company, that was all. But she was a courageous little thing and he hoped she would make a full recovery. One day, perhaps, after he had seen justice done for Carrie, he might call at Blackfen Manor and enquire after her.

Chapter Two

Amy was walking across the fields surrounding Blackfen Manor, stopping every now and again to watch a butterfly flitting from flower to flower, or a skylark soaring, or gazing into the water of the river at her own reflection. It was like looking at a stranger. The image gazing back at her was unknown to her. She saw a woman in a plain unpadded gown, with fair hair tied back with a ribbon, a pale face and worried-looking eyes. It was the same when she looked in the mirror in her bed-chamber, a stranger's blue eyes looked back at her. 'Who are you?' she would whisper. Teasing her woolly brain about it only brought on a headache.

'Do not fret, it will come to you, my dear,' Aunt Matilda had said. She was the rounder and softer of the two ladies who had come to the King's Arms to fetch her after the accident. The other, Aunt Harriet, was taller and thinner, more practical and down to earth. Both wore gowns with false hips, though nothing like as wide as those worn in London, and white powdered wigs. They were, so they told her, her mother's sisters and their surname was Hardwick, none of which she could remember. She didn't remember her own name, let alone that of anyone else.

'You are Amy,' Aunt Harriet had told her, when Matilda could not speak for tears. 'And once we have you home, you will soon recover your memory. It is the shock of the accident that has taken it from you. You will be chirpy as a cricket tomorrow and then you can tell us what happened.'

'I am glad I have found someone who knows who I am,' she had told them. Lying in bed in the inn with no recollection of who she was, or how she had got there, had been frightening.

'Of course we know who you are. Did we not bring you up from a child? You were coming to visit us, no doubt of it, though why you did not send in advance to say you were coming, we cannot think.'

They had brought her to Blackfen Manor in their gig, put her to bed and sent for their physician. He had said she had no broken bones and her many bruises would fade in time. And he confidently predicted her memory would return once she was up and about surrounded by familiar things and people she loved and trusted. She had to believe him or she would have sunk into the depths of despair.

But after two months, she could remember nothing of her life before that coach overturned, and very little of the immediate aftermath of that. Her aunts were kind to her, fed her with beef broth, roast chicken, sweetbreads and fruit tarts, saying she was far too thin, and provided her with clothes, having assumed her baggage had been stolen from the overturned coach. They fetched things to show her in an effort to jog her memory, saying, 'Amy, do you remember this?' Or 'Look at this picture of us and your mama our papa had painted just before she married Sir John Charron.'

'Amy Charron,' she murmured.

'No, not Amy Charron, not any more,' Matilda had told her. 'You are wed to Duncan Macdonald, have been these last five years.'

'Married?' This had surprised her, though why it should she did not know.

'Yes.'

'Where is he? Why was he not with me?'

'We have no idea, though if he knew you were coming to visit us, he would not worry, would he? When he learns what has befallen you, he will come post haste.'

'Did I deal well with him? Were we happy together?'

'Only you can know that,' Harriet said. 'You never complained of his treatment of you, so one must suppose you were.'

'Do we have children?'

'No, not yet. But there is time, you are still very young.'

'How old am I?'

'Five and twenty.'

Twenty-five years gone and all of them a mystery!

She had written to Duncan to tell him what had happened, which had been difficult since she knew nothing about him except what her aunts were able to tell her, did not even know the address to write to until they told her. He was an artist, they had said, though how successful he was they did not know. He was of middling height and build, was careful of his appearance and always wore a bag wig tied with a large black bow, which did not tell her much. In any case, she had had no reply.

It was all very frustrating. She could not remember her husband. What did he look like? Did she love him? She supposed she must have done or she would not have married him, but if he turned up would she know him? How could you love someone you could not remember? Why had she left him behind when she made the journey? Why had he allowed her to travel alone? But she hadn't been alone, had she? By all accounts there had been a man with her and he had died of a broken neck. Who was he? She wasn't running away with him, was she? Oh, that would be a despicable thing to do! But how could she know whether she was a wicked person or a good one? When she asked the aunts, they were adamant that she had the sweetest temperament and would not hurt a fly. 'Goodness, have we not brought you up to be a good, law-abiding Christian?' they demanded. 'If anyone is wicked, it is certainly not you.'

'Why did you bring me up?'

'Because your mama is an opera singer and is always travelling about from one theatre to another and that was not a good life for a young child, so we offered to rear you,' Aunt Matilda said. 'We wrote immediately to tell her you are here safe and sound. I am sure she would have come to see you if she were not in the middle of a season of opera at Drury Lane.'

'And my father?'

'He lives abroad.'

'Why?'

They had shrugged. 'Heaven knows.' But she thought they did know.

'Did I love him?'

'Of course you did,' Harriet said. 'You were especially close and very downpin when he went away.' They had showed her a portrait of him, a cheerful-looking man with grey-green eyes and a pointed beard, but it did nothing to help her recall the man himself.

She stopped walking to turn back and look at the Manor. It was a solid Tudor residence, with a moat about it and a drawbridge with twin turrets on either side of the gate, which led to an enclosed courtyard. She found it difficult to believe she had spent most of her childhood there. In the last two months she had explored every inch of its many nooks and crannies, but nothing reminded her of anything. It was like being born, she supposed, with no history behind you and everything new.

She had strolled about the gardens both within and outside the moat and climbed the tower on the edge of the estate that had been built as a look-out and from which she could see the countryside for miles around: the river, the road, the village with its church and inn, all things she had known and loved in her childhood, according to her aunts. The people she met in the village would speak to her, ask how she did, address her sometimes as Mrs Macdonald, but more frequently as Miss Amy, and she would reply, hiding the fact she could not remember their names.

She could not even remember Susan, much to that good woman's sorrow. Susan was in her middle thirties and had been with the family since she was twelve, moving up the hierarchy of the servants from kitchenmaid to chambermaid and from there to lady's maid. But she was more than that, she was a valued companion to both old ladies and had known Amy since childhood, had watched her grow up and helped her dress, scolded her when she was naughty and praised her when she was good. Susan had added her efforts to get her to remember, all to no avail.

Her aunts were worried, she knew that. They had tried everything they could think of to jog her into remembering, but nothing seemed to work. 'I fear something dreadful occurred before the accident that occasioned your loss of memory,' Matilda had said only the day before.

'Something so dreadful I have blotted it from my mind, you mean?'

'Perhaps. If only Duncan would come, I am sure the sight of him would effect a cure.'

'Then why has he not answered my letter?'

'We cannot tell,' Harriet put in. 'Unless something has happened to him, too. I have written to ask your mother to make enquiries.' Her mother, so she was told, had an apartment near the theatre, not far from Henrietta Street where Amy and her husband had their home. That was another thing Amy could not remember. Racking her brains produced nothing. By day she was calm, though worried, but her nights were beset by violent dreams in which she was running, running for all she was worth, knowing there was something evil behind her.

Only the week before, her mother had written to say she had not seen Duncan and their house was unoccupied. Lord Trentham had come to see the opera and had taken her out to supper afterwards and she had asked him to help uncover the mystery. Lord Trentham, Aunt Harriet had explained to Amy, was a lifelong friend of the family and a man of influence. Whether he would succeed Amy was not at all sure, but he seemed her only hope.

Sighing, she began to walk slowly back to the house, trying, as she did every day, to remember something, anything at all, that would shed some light on the life she had led before the coach overturned. She knew she had been rescued by a gentleman who had apparently been another passenger, but she had been so dazed by her experience she could not remember his name or what he looked like. And he had not stayed to see her handed over to her aunts, so they had no idea who he was. Had he known her before that journey? Was he part of the mystery?

James was on his way to Bow Street to pay Henry Fielding a visit. He had not caught his wife's murderers thanks to that coach overturning and the delay in arriving at Peterborough, where the trail had gone cold. He had returned to London, along with thousands of others who had decided the threat of more earthquakes had been exaggerated and the world was not about to come to a violent end. Rather than go to his Newmarket estate, he decided to stay with his parents at Colbridge House, expecting Smith and Randle to return to the metropolis as soon as they thought the coast was clear but, in two months, none of his contacts had seen or heard anything of them. London's Chief Magistrate had been a great help to him over his quest in the past and he might have heard something of them.

The street was crowded with people going about their business, jostling each other in their hurry to reach their destinations: city men, gentlefolk, parsons, hawkers, women selling posies, piemen, street urchins. James hardly spared them a glance as he made his way on foot to the magistrate's office, where he found him in conversation with Lord Trentham, a one-time admiral, whom he had known from his years of naval service.

'Now, here's your man,' the magistrate said to his lordship, after greetings had been exchanged and a glass of brandy offered and accepted. 'He can help solve your mystery.'

'Oh, and what might that be?' James asked guardedly, assuming they wanted to inveigle him into more thieftaking.

'A man has gone missing and his lordship wants him found.'

'Men are always going missing,' he said. 'I know of two myself I should dearly like to find.'

'Still no luck?' Henry queried.

'Afraid not. I have been chasing them all over the country. What we need is a paid police force, one that investigates crime as well as arresting criminals, a body of men in uniform that everyone can recognise as upholders of law and order.'

'I agree with you,' the magistrate put in. 'I am working on the idea and one day it will come about, but in the meantime I must put my faith in people like you.'

'That has come about because of my determination to see Smith and Randle hang.'

'Bring them before me, and they will,' the magistrate told him. 'In the meantime, will you oblige Lord Trentham?'

'I assume the missing man is a criminal of one sort or another?' James enquired.

'We do not know that,' his lordship put in. 'Might be, might not. His wife's family want him found.'

James laughed. 'An absconding husband!'

'We do not know that either.'

'It is a mystery,' Henry Fielding said. 'And you are a master at solving riddles and can be trusted to be discreet.'

'That is most kind of you,' he said, bowing in response to the compliment. 'But I am not at all sure I want to solve this particular riddle. Coming between husband and wife is not something I care to do.'

'Let me tell you the story and then you can decide.' Lord Trentham said.

'Go on.' He was availing himself of the magistrate's best cognac and politeness decreed he should at least hear his lordship out.

'The wife in question is the daughter of a very dear friend, Lady Sophie Charron—'

'The opera singer?'

'The same. Two months ago she was on a coach travelling to her relatives in Highbeck, in Norfolk, when the coach was held up by highpads, only for it to be overturned half an hour later. She has recovered from her injuries, but cannot remember anything leading up to the accident. Her memory is completely blank. And her husband has disappeared. The house where they lived is a shambles. We are of the opinion something happened.'

James had begun to listen more intently as the tale went on, realising they were talking about his mystery lady. He had often wondered what had become of her, had not been able to get her out of his mind, even after he had been to Peterborough and back. Her pale, frightened face haunted him. How could he be sure he had left her in good hands? Was this another occasion for guilt that he had done nothing to help her? Was his pursuit of Smith and Randle robbing him of his common humanity? He had toyed with the idea of calling to see how she fared, but Highbeck was remote and not connected with his own search and he could not be sure she was still there so he had put off doing so.

'I met the lady,' he said quietly. 'I was travelling on the same coach.'

'You were?' Lord Trentham leaned forwards, his voice eager. 'Then you know more than we do.'

'Not about her husband I do not. I did not know she was married.' He went on to tell them exactly what had happened and his impressions of the demeanour of the young lady. 'She was at the inn being looked after by the innkeeper's wife when I left. I was assured her relatives had been sent for and would take care of her, but I have often wondered if I was right to leave her.'

'Oh, yes, her aunts, Lady Charron's sisters, fetched her and she is staying with them at Blackfen Manor,' his lordship explained. 'But her husband has disappeared. They think if he could be found, her memory might be restored to her.'

'What do you know of him?' James asked.

'His name is Duncan Macdonald.'

'A Scotsman?'

'I believe so, though he has lived many years in England. He is an artist, though not a very successful one. He also plays very deep and I believe the couple were in financial trouble. It might be why he has disappeared.'

'A cowardly thing to do, to leave his wife to set off alone for her relatives, don't you think?' James remarked.

'Yes, if that is what he did, but perhaps he had disappeared before she left. She might have been going to look for him,' his lordship suggested.

'She chose a singularly unattractive helpmate if that was the case. A surly individual in a rough coat and a scratch wig. She seemed terrified of him. Also, he was known to the robbers who held up our coach. And I believe she recognised them as well, although I may be mistaken in that,' James said.

'Oh dear, it is worse than I thought,' said Lord Trentham. 'Did you by chance learn the man's name?'

'Gus Billings, I think one of the highpads called him, but he died in the accident. Could he have been her husband under an assumed name?'

'Unlikely. I only met Duncan Macdonald once when we attended the same opera and he and Amy came back stage to speak to Lady Charron, but he wore a bag wig and was dressed in a very fine coat of burgundy satin. He was charming enough, had exquisite manners, but there was something about him that made me wary. Amy was, is, a dear girl, certainly not a lady to consort with criminals.'

'As you say, a mystery,' James said, turning over in his mind what he had learned, which was little enough. At least he now knew the young lady's name was Amy. He thought it suited her.

'You will undertake to investigate, my dear fellow, won't you?' his lordship pleaded. 'Her mother and her aunts are all anxious about her and I promised I would do what I could to help.'

'Memory is a strange thing,' he said. 'Sometimes it shuts down simply to avoid a situation too painful to bear. One must be careful not to force it back. Mrs Macdonald might be happier not remembering.'

'True, true,' Lord Trentham said. 'But if we could discover what is at the back of it without distressing her, then we might know how to proceed.'

James was torn between taking on the commission and continuing the search for his wife's killers, but that had lasted so long and yielded so little reward he did not think it would make any difference if he set it aside for a week or two. He would do what he could to help, if only to make amends for not doing anything before. 'If you would be so good as to furnish me with a letter of introduction to the lady's aunts, I will go to Highbeck and see what I can discover,' he said. It ought not to take him long and after that he must resume his search for Smith and Randle. He would not rest until they were caught.

Lord Trentham wrote the letter; once this was done and handed to him, James returned to Colbridge House to instruct Sam to pack for a stay in the country, realising, as he did so, that once again he had unwittingly found himself embroiled in uncovering crime.

Amy was just leaving the mill next to the King's Arms, where she had gone to buy flour to make bread, when two horsemen rode into the yard of the inn and dismounted. The taller of the two hesitated when he saw her and looked for a moment as if he were going to speak. He was broad as well as tall, handsome in a rugged kind of way, with intense green eyes that seemed to take everything in at a glance, including her scattered thoughts. His tricorne hat covered sun-bleached hair, which was tied back with a narrow black ribbon. As with any gentleman who came to the village from outside it, she wondered if he might be Duncan, but when he sketched her a little bow and proceeded into the inn without speaking, she knew it was not the husband she looked for, for surely he would have spoken to her, taken her into his arms, called her by name?

The man had looked slightly familiar, as if she ought to know him, or at least was acquainted with him. Did that little bow confirm it? Or was it simply a courtesy? If only she could remember! She went on her way to make her purchase, intending afterwards to visit Widow Twitch, an old lady who lived in a cottage down a lane on the other side of the village who, according to her Aunt Matilda, had known her since she was in leading strings and was also recognised as a wise woman who had the gift of telling the future. Her advice might be worth listening to.

James had recognised Amy immediately and had been on the point of greeting her, but decided against it. He had wondered if she might remember him, considering he had held her in his arms on the ride from the scene of the accident to the inn. The memory of that had certainly stayed with him. He had spoken to her later and she had remembered his name then, but today, though she had looked at him, there had been no recognition in her blue eyes. Until he had spoken to the Misses Hardwick and ascertained exactly what they wanted of him, he would remain incognito.

He was glad to see that she looked well. Her cheeks were rosy and her hair, which had been so unkempt and tangled, was now brushed and curled into ringlets, over which was tied a simple cottager hat. She wore a striped cotton gown, a plain stomacher and a gauze scarf tucked into the front of it, an ensemble that would be decried in town, but was perfectly suitable for the country. She had filled out a little too, so that she bore little resemblance to the waif he had held in his arms. It was difficult to believe that her mind retained nothing of her past. Would reawakening her memory, even supposing it could be done, fling her back into that world of fear? She had been afraid, of that he was certain.

He did not need to eat, having dined at the Lamb in Ely not two hours before, so he left his baggage at the inn where he had booked rooms for himself and

Sam, and hired a horse to take him to Blackfen Manor, leaving his own mount to be groomed and rested. He wondered if he might overtake the young lady, but there was no sign of her as he trotted along a well-worn path bordering fields of as yet unripe barley.

He passed the tower at the gates to the grounds and proceeded up a gravel drive until the Manor came into view. He did not know what he had expected, but the solid red-brick Tudor mansion with its mullioned windows and twisted chimneys was a surprise. He half-expected the drawbridge to be raised to repel raiders, but laughed at his fancies when he saw the bridge down and the great oak doors wide open. He trotted under the arch into a cobbled yard and dismounted at a door on the far side.

He was admitted by an elderly retainer who disappeared to acquaint the ladies of his arrival and take in the letter of introduction James had been given. He returned in less than two minutes and conducted James to a large drawing room where two ladies rose as he entered. He removed his tricorne hat, tucked it under his left arm and swept them a bow. 'Ladies, your obedient.'

'Captain, you are very welcome,' the elder said. She was in her forties, he supposed, tall and angular.

The other was shorter and rounder, but both were dressed alike in wide brocade open gowns with embroidered stomachers and silk underslips. They wore white wigs, topped with white linen caps tied beneath their chins. 'I am Miss Hardwick and this is my sister Miss Matilda Hardwick. We are Lady Charron's sisters. Please be seated.'

'Glad we are to see you,' Miss Matilda said, as they seated themselves side by side on a sofa. 'You will take tea?'

'Thank you.' He sat on a chair facing them as tea was ordered. While they waited for it, he used the opportunity to look about him. The plasterwork was very fine and so were the wall tapestries, though they were very faded and must have been hanging there for generations. Some of the furniture was age-blackened oak, but there were also more modern sofas and chairs. There were some good pictures on the walls, a fine clock on the mantel, together with a few good-quality ornaments. A harpsichord stood in a corner by the window. Of Mrs Macdonald, there was no sign.

'Have you any news?' Matilda asked eagerly. 'Has Mr Macdonald been found?'

'He had not been located when I left the capital,' James said. 'The word is out to look for him, but I have come to make your acquaintance and endeavour to discover how much Mrs Macdonald remembers.'

'Absolutely nothing at all,' Matilda answered. 'We have tried everything.'

A servant brought in a tray containing a tea kettle, a teapot and some dishes with saucers, which he put on a table. Harriet took a key from the chatelaine at her waist and unlocked the tea caddy. James watched her for a minute in silence, as she carefully measured the tea leaves into the pot and added the boiling water. They were, he concluded, careful housekeepers, though whether from choice or necessity it was hard to tell.

'Tell us about yourself,' commanded Harriet, handing him a dish of tea.

He smiled. He was evidently not going to be taken on face value. 'My name, as you will have learned from Lord Trentham's letter, is Captain James Drymore. I am the second son of the Earl of Colbridge. I am twenty-seven years of age and have spent most of my adult life as an officer on board several vessels of his Majesty's navy. Two years ago I sold out and returned to civilian life.'

'Are you married?' Matilda asked.

'I am a widower.'

'I am sorry for it,' Matilda said. 'But no doubt a handsome man like yourself will soon marry again.'

'Tilly!' her sister admonished. 'You must not put the Captain to the blush like that.'

Matilda coloured and apologised.

'Think nothing of it, Miss Matilda,' he said with a polite smile—marrying again was the last thing on his mind. 'It is natural for you to wish to know all about me if I am to be of service to you.'

'Oh, I do hope you can be. Amy will be back directly and you will be able to judge her for yourself.'

'Unless I am greatly mistaken, I have already met the young lady,' he said. 'I was on the coach with her when it overturned.'

'You were?' Matilda put down her tea in order to sit forward and pay more attention. 'Then you must know all about it. What happened? Did you speak to Amy? Did she speak to you? Who was the man who died? My sister saw his body when they laid it out at the inn before burial and she is sure it was not Duncan Macdonald.'

'Ah, that was the first question I meant to ask you,' he said.

'We have no idea who he could have been,' Harriet said. 'Or what he was doing with Amy.'

He told them about the journey, the highwaymen and the accident, but left out the fact that their niece was afraid of her escort and that he was known to the highpads. He saw no reason to distress them unnecessarily. 'Will you tell me about Mrs Macdonald and her husband?' he asked when this recital was finished. 'It is necessary to know as much as possible, you understand.'

'Yes, of course,' Matilda put in. 'We raised Amy. She is like a daughter to us. She met her husband, Duncan Macdonald, during a visit to her mother in London just over five years ago. We were shocked when she said she was going to marry him. We knew so little about him, except that he was a close friend of her father. She does not even remember that.'

'He is an artist,' Harriet said. 'Or so he says, though we have seen nothing of his work.'

'But you did meet him?'

'Yes, the first time soon after they married and again about two years ago when they came to stay for a while. I am afraid I did not take to him. He was a little too charming to be sincere and he had Amy like that.' She turned her thumb to the floor as she spoke. 'But perhaps I do him a disservice. You must draw your own conclusions.'

'How can he?' Matilda said. 'The man has disappeared.'

He smiled at the lady's undeniable logic, and then turned as the door opened and Amy herself came into the room. She stopped uncertainly when she saw him scrambling to his feet. He bowed. 'Mrs Macdonald.'

'This is Captain Drymore,' Harriet told her. 'Do you remember him?'

Amy looked hard at the man who stood facing her. It was the one she had seen that afternoon at the King's Arms, but underlying that was the feeling she had experienced then, that she had met him before. How could you forget someone as big and handsome as he was, a man with a commanding presence and clear green eyes that looked into hers in a way that made her catch her breath? 'I saw him arriving at the King's Arms this afternoon…'

'Before that,' Matilda said.

'No.' She turned to James. 'Should I remember you?'

He smiled. 'I would have been flattered if you had. We were both aboard the coach that over-turned.'

Her sunny smile lit her face. 'Then you must be my mysterious saviour.'

'I did no more than any gentleman would have done.'

She sat down beside him, so close her skirts brushed his knee, and turned to face him. 'Tell me what happened. Every little detail.'

Acutely aware of her proximity and the scent of lilacs that surrounded her, he repeated what he had told her aunts, no more, no less.

'And did I tell you anything of why I was making the journey?'

'No, madam.'

'There was a man with me. I am told he died. Do you know who he was?'

'I am afraid not. Perhaps he was a servant, someone your husband trusted to see you safely to your destination?'

'Perhaps. But, you see, my husband has disappeared…' She stopped. 'Now, why should I bother you with my concerns when you have been so kind as to come and enquire after me?'

He bowed in acknowledgement, deciding not to set her straight on the reason for his visit. He felt he could learn more by not appearing an interrogator. 'I have often wondered what became of you and, as I have business in the area, I decided to pay my respects. Are you fully recovered from your injuries?'

'Indeed, yes, they were only a few scratches and bruises. The worst of it is my lack of recall, but my aunts assure me that is only temporary.'

'I am sure it is,' he murmured.

'And is it not strange that the Captain is known to Lord Trentham?' Miss Matilda put in.

'Ah, then perhaps had we met before through his lordship?' she said, turning to James.

'I do not think so,' James said. 'I am sure, if we

had, I should have remembered it. Someone as charming as you would not be easily forgotten.' He had been so long out of polite society that he surprised himself with the ease with which the compliment rolled off his tongue.

'Thank you, kind sir.' She gave a tinkling laugh, which seemed to indicate she was not overburdened with memories of her fear and again he wondered if it were wise to interfere.

'Where are you staying, Captain?' Miss Hardwick asked him.

'At the King's Arms, madam. It is convenient for my business.'

'If your business is not too pressing, would you care to have supper with us? We have so few visitors, especially from the capital, I am sure we have much to talk about.'

'Thank you. I shall look forward to it.' He rose to take his leave, as she rang for Johnson, the footman, to see him out.

'Will seven o'clock be convenient?'

'Perfectly.' He bowed to each in turn, according to seniority and took Amy's hand to convey it to his lips.

She felt a shiver of memory pass through at his touch, but it was gone in an instant. That was always happening to her, a faint flicker of recollection that was gone before she could grasp it. She repossessed herself of her hand and bent her knee in a curtsy. 'Until this evening, Captain Drymore.'

After he had gone, she sat down with her aunts. 'When the Captain said he was on that coach I hoped he would be able to enlighten me a little,' she said wistfully. 'But he does not seem to know anything.'

'Perhaps we will learn a little more over supper,' Harriet said. 'He might jog your memory with some small thing that happened. I hope he is going to stay hereabouts for a little while. It is so agreeable to have visitors.'

'And such a pleasant man,' Matilda said. 'He almost makes me wish I were young again.'

'Tush, Tilly,' her sister chided her. 'You are too old for daydreams.'

'I know.' It was said with a sigh. 'But he is a handsome young man, do you not think so, Amy?'

'Yes, I suppose he is,' she said slowly, unwilling to admit she had found him extraordinarily attractive. And somewhere in the back of her mind a tiny memory was stirring, a memory that made her blush to the roots of her hair. Not only had she met him before, she had been held in his arms!

'You are a married woman, Amy,' Harriet said, making her wonder if her aunt could read her mind.

'Just because you cannot remember your husband, does not mean he does not exist.'

'Is Duncan handsome?' Amy asked.

'Some think so.'

'Did I?'

'Oh, I am sure you did.'

'I wish I knew where he was. I wish…' Oh, she had too many wishes to enumerate them all, but above all, she wished she could remember who she was. Widow Twitch had talked in riddles about trials to come and a search for treasure that would end in a death, but not her death. She was to put her trust in those sent to help her. Who they might be, the old lady could not tell her.

'Patience, my dear, patience,' Matilda said, as Harriet hurried off to confer with the cook about the supper menu. 'It will all come right in the end, I am sure of it. Now, what will you wear tonight? You must look your best.'

The question gave her another problem. The clothes the aunts had found for her were a mix of some she had left behind when she married because they were worn or outdated, some of her aunts' that had been altered to fit and some bought on a shopping expedition to Downham, the nearest town. Not wishing to be a financial burden on her aunts, she had been careful not to be extravagant. She could not understand why she had embarked on the journey to Highbeck without money or baggage. Aunt Harriet had said it must have been stolen from the wrecked coach before it had been retrieved, or perhaps the highwaymen had taken it.

That was another thing. The coach had been held up only minutes before it overturned, which must have been a frightening experience, but she did not even remember that. She would ask the Captain more about that at supper. Thinking of supper reminded her of her aunt's question.

'I think the Watteau gown we altered will do well enough,' she said. The soft blue taffeta sack dress had been one of Harriet's and was not intended to fit closely. Its very full back fell in folds from shoulder to floor and the front was laced over white embroidered stays and finished with a blue ribbon bow just above her bosom. The same ribbon decorated the sleeves, which fitted closely to the elbow and then frilled out to her wrists in a froth of lace. It had been easy to alter it to fit her.

'Yes, it becomes you well enough,' her aunt said. 'Susan will dress your hair and you may wear my pearls. They will be yours one day in any case.'

'You are so very good to me,' Amy said, jumping up to hug her aunt. 'I am not at all sure I deserve it.'

'Nonsense! Of course you do. You are my dearest niece and have been a joy to me ever since you came to Highbeck as a little girl. Now run along and take a rest before you dress. You must be in fine fettle when Captain Drymore comes back.'

James rode back to the inn in contemplative mood. He found himself going over and over what had happened on the fateful day when he and Mrs Macdonald had been travelling companions. She had behaved strangely, her face a mask, lacking animation, but the eyes were a different matter. Her distress was obvious in them. To undertake a journey of that length with no baggage and no money was reckless and foolish, and indicated she had left home in a great hurry, though whether voluntarily or not, he could not say. Lord Trentham had said the house she lived in had been a shambles and he had gone and seen it for himself before leaving London. Something had happened there, something violent. But that did not necessarily mean she had come from there when she boarded the coach. It could have happened after she left.

The man with her had been a queer sort of escort, a rough character with no manners at all, one of the lower orders, someone a lady would certainly not choose to take care of her. Where had they met?

What hold did he have over her? He was certainly known to those two highwaymen. Did she know them, too? She had certainly been afraid of them, but any young lady would be frightened under the circumstances, so that did not signify. And where was her husband? The mystery intrigued him, the more so because a lovely and seemingly innocent young lady was involved. But was she innocent? Was she perhaps an even better actress than her mother?

He had been dealing with the criminal fraternity long enough to know you could not tell by appearances. Some seemingly innocent young ladies were bigger criminals than the men, deceiving, thieving, pretending to be the victims of the crime when they were the perpetrators. He had come across such women more than once and had hardened his heart to turn them in. But was Mrs Macdonald like that? Had she been fleeing from justice when he first met her? The more he thought about it, the more he realised he would not rest until he had the answers to all these questions.

He arrived back at the inn to go over it with Sam, but his servant had no more idea than he had what had happened, and he was more wary. 'Sir, 'tis my belief you're being conned by a pair of fetching blue eyes,' he said.

'Why do you say that? Our presence on that coach could not have been predicted, nor that I should visit Mr Fielding when I did.'

'True,' Sam admitted. 'But you didn't have to say you'd come here, did you?'

'I was curious.'

'Ah, now we have the truth of it. And I'll wager my best wig you wouldn't have been so eager if she had been an old witch with long talons and a pointed chin.'

James laughed. 'Witches fly about on broomsticks, they do not need coaches.'

Sam appreciated the jest. 'So, what are you going to do?'

'I am going to have supper at Blackfen Manor. I suggest you get to know the locals. You never know what you may learn.'

'You will need your best coat, then. 'Tis as well I fetched everything out of your bag and hung it up in your room to let the creases drop out.'

'Good man. I think I will sleep for an hour or so. I am wearied with travelling. You may rouse me at six o'clock with a dish of coffee and hot water to wash.'

Promptly at seven, he was shown into the drawing room at Blackfen Manor where the three ladies waited for him. They had obviously taken trouble with their attire; Mrs Macdonald in particular looked very fetching in a gown whose colour exactly matched her eyes and, though wigless, her hair had been carefully curled and powdered. He executed a flourishing bow. 'Ladies, your obedient.'

They curtsied and Aunt Harriet bade him be seated, offering him a glass of homemade damson wine while they waited for supper to be served.

'Are you comfortable at the inn, Captain?' Amy asked. He had, she noted, taken trouble with his appearance. Gone was the man in the buff coat and plain shirt; here was a beau in a coat of fine burgundy wool, trimmed with silver braid down its front and on the flaps of the pockets. Rows of silver buttons marched in a double line from the neck to well below the waist, though none of them was fastened. His waistcoat was of cream silk, embroidered with both gold and silver thread, above which a frilled neckcloth cascaded. A silver pin nestled in its folds and a quizzing glass hung from a cord about his neck. He wore his own hair, arranged with side buckles and tied back with a black ribbon.

'Yes, it suits me well enough, thank you.'

'Where do you live? Ordinarily, I mean.'

'When I was at sea, I had no permanent home, so my wife stayed with my parents at Colbridge House in London, but just before I left the service I bought a small country estate, near Newmarket, intending to settle down there. But it was not to be.'

'May I ask why?'

'My wife died.' He spoke flatly.

'Oh, I am so sorry, Captain,' she said, noticing the shadow cross his face and the way his hand went up to finger the pin in his cravat. 'I would not for the world have distressed you with my questions.'

'Do not think of it, Mrs Macdonald. It happened while I was away at sea. I did not even see her before the funeral.'

'That must have been doubly hard for you to accept.'

It surprised him that she used the word accept and had hit upon exactly how he had felt, still felt. 'Yes, it was.'

'That is all we can do, is it not?' she said. 'Accept God's will, though we do not understand why it should be. I have to accept there is a divine purpose in my loss of memory, but for the moment it eludes me.'

He was grateful for her insight and for the way she had changed the subject so adroitly, allowing him to become businesslike again. 'I have no doubt your memory will return, perhaps suddenly, perhaps slowly, little by little.'

She blushed suddenly remembering the only memory that had flitted into her mind earlier that day, that he had held her in his arms. When and why? And had she been content or outraged? She was glad when the butler came to announce that supper was on the table, and the Captain offered his arm to escort her into the dining room behind the aunts.

It was a big oak-panelled room with heavy dark oak furniture that had probably been there since Elizabeth was on the throne. They took seats at one end of a long refectory table and were served with soup, followed by a remove of boiled carp, roast chicken, braised ham, peas, broccoli and salad, together with several kinds of tartlets.

'Do you know if those two criminals have been brought to book?' Amy asked, after they had all helped themselves from the dishes, and was surprised when he appeared startled.

'Two criminals?' he repeated to give himself time to digest what she had said. Surely she knew nothing of Randle and Smith? It was not that he wanted to keep his quest for them a secret, but simply that if she had known of them, it would give the lie to her loss of memory and set her firmly among the ne'er-do-wells.

'Yes, those two who held up the coach. My aunts are sure they stole my baggage, for I had none when I arrived.'

He breathed again. 'Oh, those two,' he said. 'No

doubt they followed us and looted the coach after we left it. It was in a sorry state and everything scattered. Unfortunately we were not able to gather anything up.'

'There, I was sure that was what had happened,' Harriet put in, busy cutting up the chicken, ready to be offered round. 'You would never have set off without a change of clothes.'

'It is strange that so momentous an adventure can have slipped my mind,' Amy said. 'You would think it of sufficient import to be unforgettable, would you not? Were they masked? How did they speak? Did they injure anyone? Were they gentlemanly?'

'Certainly not gentlemen,' he said. 'Rough spoken and in black cloaks and masks, impossible to identify. They were armed and each fired once, but hit no one. I think they took pity on you, for after they had robbed me, they let us go.' He was, he realised, being sparing of the truth. He did not want to give her nightmares.

'Did you lose much?' she asked.

'A few guineas that were in my purse. The rest of my money and valuables I had concealed about my person.'

'How clever of you!' she exclaimed.

'I do a great deal of travelling, Mrs Macdonald, and have learned to be as cunning as the criminals.'

She wondered why he travelled and if he had more knowledge of lawbreakers than he had admitted. He might even be one of them, for all she knew. Except of course her aunts had accepted him as being known to Admiral Lord Trentham, who had sent a glowing introduction. That, of course, could be a forgery. How suspicious and untrusting she was! Had she always been like that or was that something she had learned recently?

'But you have not heard of them being appre-hended?' she queried.

'No, unfortunately I have not.'

'Tell me again about the man who died. What manner of man was he?' Amy asked.

'I know nothing of him. He boarded the coach with you and your tickets were in his pockets, so one supposes he was looking after you. He cer-tainly bought your refreshments whenever we stopped.'

'So I was totally dependant on him,' she mused.

'It would seem so.'

'How did I react to his death?'

'You were unconscious and knew nothing of it at the time,' he pointed out.

'How long was I unconscious? And how did I get from the overturned coach to the inn?' she pressed.

'I rode one of the coach horses with you in front of

me. Have you no memory of that?' he asked curiously.

'None at all,' she said swiftly. But that *was* her memory. A slow ride, cradled in front of him on a horse with no saddle. She had felt warm and protected, with his arm about her and his coat enveloping them both. She did not remember arriving at the inn, so she must have drifted into unconsciousness again. 'How difficult and uncomfortable that must have been for you.'

He noticed the colour flood her face and felt sure she had remembered it. How much more was she concealing? He would have it out of her, one way or another, before another day was out. 'It was my privilege and pleasure,' he said, lifting his glass of wine in salute to her and looking at her over its rim.

Quizzing him was making her feel uncomfortable and she changed the subject to ask him what he thought of the village and its surrounds, to which he replied he had not yet had the opportunity to explore, but intended to do so when his business permitted, and on that uncontentious note they finished their meal with plum pie and sweetmeats.

He declined to stay in the dining room alone and repaired with them to the drawing room for tea. Noticing the harpsichord in the corner, he enquired if anyone played it.

'I used to years ago,' Matilda said. 'But I have not touched it in years. Amy is the musician here.'

He turned to look at her. 'Will you play for us, Mrs Macdonald?'

She went over to the instrument, sat herself down at it and, after a moment's hesitation, played 'Greensleeves' with unerring accuracy and sensitivity. As the last notes died away, she turned towards him, eyes shining. 'How strange that I remember that,' she said. 'I know I have always loved music, just as I know I love flowers and can tell their names and recognise birds by their song.'

He smiled. 'That is a good sign, don't you think. And can you ride?'

'Oh, yes,' she said eagerly. 'I love to ride.'

'Then would you like to ride out with me tomorrow and show me the countryside? I am sure I shall enjoy it the more for having you to guide me.'

She readily agreed and, having arranged a time for him to call, the evening was brought to an end. He took his leave and rode back to the inn, feeling more benign than he had done for years.

Chapter Three

Amy, dressed in a riding habit consisting of a dark blue jacket, a tight waistcoat, a full petticoat and a broad-brimmed hat with a curling feather, was ready and waiting for him when he arrived at the appointed time next day, riding the huge black stallion on whose back he had entered the village the day before. His riding coat was the same one, though his shirt and neckcloth were fresh. His boots had received the loving attention of his servant. She greeted him cheerfully. 'You are in good time, Captain.'

'It would be a grave discourtesy to keep a lady waiting,' he said, sweeping off a tall beaver hat with a silver buckle on the front of it, and bowing from the waist. His queue of fair hair had been tied back with a narrow velvet ribbon, although a few strands, shorter than the rest, curled across his forehead and about his ears. It was a style that the elite of London would have deplored, but she had come to the conclusion he was not a slave to fashion. She rather liked it. She liked everything about him.

A chestnut mare had been saddled and brought to the door where a groom helped her to mount. 'Now, Captain, where would you like to go?' she asked, picking up the reins.

'I am in your hands, madam. I do not know the area. All I can say about it is that it is very flat and there is a prodigious amount of water.'

She laughed as they trotted over the drawbridge and down the short drive to the lane. 'Yes, but have you ever seen such skies? As a child I used to think the clouds were mountainous seas with great galleons sailing upon them. Sometimes their sails were pink and purple, sometimes golden or blood red, if the sun was behind them. I would imagine them having a great sea battle and the red ones were ships on fire. And such rainbows we have, you would never believe.'

'You remember all that?'

'I must do. How strange! I did not realise it until I spoke of it. You must be good for me, Captain— already you have helped me recall something.'

'Then perhaps, as we ride, you will remember more.'

She was more animated than he had seen her

before, as if she revelled in her returning memories, but they were of her childhood, triggered by her surroundings, not the more recent events, which, unless he missed his guess, had been the cause of the forgetfulness. Resurrecting those might bring her pain. He was still not sure that he was wise to interfere, especially as he admired her spirit and courage and would hate to see either subdued. He did not want to see her return to the frightened dejected young woman she had been when he first met her. It would serve her best to take it slowly.

They rode through the village with its church and vicarage, its inn at the crossroads and double row of thatched cottages, acknowledging the greetings called by the few people who were about. Most were at their work. Leaving the village behind, they turned off the main road along a path beside the river whose banks were lined with willows, their graceful fronds swaying in a gentle breeze. At the edge of the water yellow flags held proud heads above the duckweed. Swans and mallards sailed placidly along, ignoring the man in the rowing boat with his huge load of cut reeds. Above them a few fleecy clouds punctuated the blue of the sky.

'How peaceful it is,' she said, as they brought their mounts to a walk. 'I think I love this spot above all others.'

'But you lived in London, did you not?'

'Yes. My husband needs to be in the capital because that is where he obtains his commissions. He is an artist, you see.'

'Do you remember that?'

'No. It is only what I have been told.'

'What manner of artist is he? Landscape or portrait, or perhaps he is an illustrator or caricaturist?'

'That, I am afraid, I cannot tell you.'

He reined in to negotiate a large puddle and then drew alongside her again. 'It seems to me, Mrs Macdonald, that your loss of memory stems from your life in London. Perhaps you ought to return there.'

'I have thought of that,' she said slowly. 'But something in me rebels at the idea. I find myself shaking at the prospect and can only conclude I am afraid.'

'Oh. Do you know what you fear?' he queried, his interest flaring.

'No. The unknown, perhaps. Aunt Matilda says I must not think of going until I feel more confident. And there is no one to accompany me. Neither aunts are good travellers and they do not like London with its noisy crowds. I keep hoping my husband will arrive and the mystery will be solved.' She sighed. 'My aunts are convinced I was on my way to visit them, and I can think of no other reason why

I should have been on that coach, and I do not want to leave until I find out why. Perhaps I arranged to meet my husband here.'

'Perhaps.'

They rode on in silence for some minutes, watching the river traffic. There were several boats loaded with reeds and sedge, being towed by patient, plodding horses to Ely to be made into baskets of all kinds and for use as thatch. Other boats were loaded with produce from the black fertile soil: cabbages, carrots and turnips, a crop recently introduced, which found a ready market in London. There were also flowers and eels by the barrel load. Later in the year there would be cherries, apples and grain. He listened to her melodious voice telling him of these things and realised that her childhood was slowly coming back to her. How long before the rest of her memory returned, and would it bring with it pleasure or pain?

'Nearly everything goes by river,' Amy went on. 'Much better than the roads. They are especially bad because the peat shrinks as it dries out between the ridges of clay and causes bumps and hollows.'

He chuckled. 'Yes, I can vouch for that. The coach that brought us to Highbeck was throwing us all over the place. And as for riding bareback…'

'Especially when trying to keep an unconscious woman upright. You must have found it very difficult.'

'Not at all,' he said gallantly. 'It was my pleasure. I am glad you took no lasting harm from it.'

She laughed. 'From the ride? None at all, you looked after me very well. If only I could remember—' She stopped, suddenly recalling the feel of being in his arms, the strength and warmth of him, and felt the colour rise in her cheeks.

'Patience,' he said, echoing her aunts. 'I do not think you should try to force it.'

Her agitation was calmed as they came to a wide expanse of reed beds and water whose ripples reflected the rays of the sun. 'Black Fen,' she said. 'There were many more fens like this before the fields were drained. It was a huge undertaking and in some areas is still going on, with men digging ditches and emptying the water from the fens into them. That is why the fields are divided by dykes, not hedges. The reclaimed land is very fertile.'

'But people still live by the water?'

'Yes, shooting ducks, gathering reeds and sedge for thatching and baskets, catching eels, which are sent to the London markets in barrels. In winter the fen floods the surrounding land and in spring when the water drains away we have excellent pasturage.' She dismounted at the water's edge and pointed to a tiny cottage on the edge of the lake that looked as if it were about to tumble in, so lopsided was it. Beside it was a landing stage where a rowing boat was moored. 'A ferryman lives there. He will take you wherever you want to go.'

He jumped down to stand beside her. 'Perhaps one day I will hire a boat to explore the water and bag a few ducks.'

'You mean to stay a while, then?'

'Yes, I think so. My business is like to take longer than I thought.'

'This is a rather remote place for a city gentleman to have business,' she said.

'It is not business in that sense,' he said, wondering whether to tell her why he had come to Highbeck, but they were getting along so well, he did not want to introduce a discordant note. He was learning more about her all the time; the more he was with her, the less he could believe she would consort with criminals. 'It is more of a personal nature…'

'I am sorry, Captain, I did not mean to pry,' she explained hurriedly. 'I am forever asking questions. Since the accident, I have been reading all I can about Highbeck and the Manor, about the artistic community in London, the news of what is happening abroad, quizzing everyone who comes to call, anything to help me to remember and understand who I am. Please forgive me.'

'My dear lady, there is nothing to forgive.' He

was saved from going on because she was turning to remount and he hurried forward to bend and offer his clasped hands, lifting her easily into the saddle when she put her foot into them. She picked up the reins and settled herself while he mounted his stallion, then they proceeded in silence until they reached the village again, but it was a companionable silence neither seemed inclined to break.

As they were passing the church, he wondered if there was anything to be learned there. 'Shall we go inside?' he suggested.

They tethered their horses and went into the cool interior of the church. Although not large, it was a beautiful building. They knelt to genuflect and then wandered about, reading the names on the memorials, many of them of the Hardwick family. 'We go back a long way in the village,' she said, pointing to a plaque commemorating Sir Charles Hardwick, who died aged forty-six in 1645. 'I wonder if he fought in the war between King and Parliament. Perhaps he died in battle.'

'Perhaps. Many did,' he said. 'But here is another Sir Charles. This one lived from 1627 to 1676. And yet another. It seems that every eldest son was Charles. No, I am in error, for here is a Sir Robert. He was born in 1660 and died in 1720.'

'I believe he was my grandfather.'

There were others, younger sons, sisters and daughters and they spent some time studying the inscriptions and figuring out who was related to whom before leaving and resuming their ride.

At the crossroads by the inn, she chose another way to return to the Manor. 'Then you will have seen all there is to see,' she told him. 'Another day you might like to ride further afield to Downham Market or Ely, which are the nearest towns. Or there is Lynn and Wisbech, both busy ports, but a little further off. You see, we are not so isolated as people from the great metropolis believe.'

He laughed. 'You are a great advocate for the area, Mrs Macdonald. I saw a little of Ely as we passed through on our way here. The cathedral looks worth a visit.'

'Indeed it is.'

'I shall endeavour to visit all the places you spoke of while I am here and if you would be my guide, I shall enjoy it all the more.' Once again he surprised himself that he still knew how to pay a compliment to a pretty woman.

She turned to look at him, unaccountably pleased by the flattery. He was undoubtedly still mourning the loss of his wife—it showed in the way he spoke of her and the way his eyes clouded at unspoken memories—but in spite of that he knew how to make himself agreeable. Was he perhaps the person Widow Twitch meant when she spoke about someone being sent to help her? But why should he? His own business would surely be more important to him. No, she decided, anyone helping her to regain her memory would be someone known to her, who knew her and could enlighten her about herself, someone who also knew her husband. Perhaps Duncan himself. If only he would come! Until he did, she found it difficult to believe she was a married woman. Why did she still feel so fearful? A tight knot of apprehension lodged itself in her stomach. Had she taken more note of Widow Twitch's words than was healthy? Whom should she trust?

In the space of a quarter of a mile, the countryside had changed. Away from the water were lanes with hedges of hawthorn, bramble, elder and climbing convolvulus, alongside fertile fields and meadows where cows grazed. There was even a small copse of trees. They passed a farmhouse and some tiny cottages. She pointed to one standing a little apart from the others. Chickens and pigs rooted in the small yard and a cat sunned itself on a low wall. 'Widow Twitch lives there,' she said, pointing with her crop. 'She is the local wise woman.'

'And have you consulted her?'

'Yes, but she spoke in riddles. She talked about a

search for treasure.' She paused suddenly. 'Oh, that is not what you are searching for, is it?'

He laughed. 'No, I have not been lured here by the prospect of riches. Tell me, what treasure did she mean?'

'I have no idea, but people are always visiting the area looking for King John's lost gold. She surely did not mean that? And what would it have to do with me?'

'I have no idea. As you say, a riddle. What else did she say?'

'She talked of trials to come and a death. I found it all very disturbing,' she confided.

'Take no note of it. I am not inclined to believe anyone can look into the future. If they did, we should all be better off, do you not think? We could avoid the pitfalls life throws at us and embrace only the good things.'

'Perhaps she was talking about something that had already happened. The death of that man on the coach, perhaps.'

'Perhaps. Have you started to remember anything of him at all?'

'No. And Aunt Harriet definitely did not know him. She has a strong stomach and peeked at him when he was laid out for burial. Aunt Matilda is the more squeamish of the two and would not look.'

'You are very fond of your aunts, are you not?'

'Indeed, yes. Since the accident I have come to know and love them all over again and am quite certain I always did. It is not Highbeck or Blackfen Manor that frightens me.'

'But you *are* frightened?'

'Yes, a little, but I think it is only of the unknown.'

'That may be said of everyone. Perhaps that is why wise women are so much in demand,' he commented drily.

'Yes, I suppose I was very silly to go to her.' She sighed.

They were clattering over the drawbridge into the courtyard. 'Will you come in and take refreshment?' she asked, as a groom hurried forwards to take her reins and help her dismount.

'Thank you.' He jumped down, threw his reins to the groom and followed her indoors.

They found the Misses Hardwick in a small parlour where one was sewing and the other reading. They rose to greet him, bade him take a seat and ordered refreshments to be brought.

'Did you enjoy your ride, Captain?' Matilda asked him.

'Yes, indeed. We have explored the village, looked upon the fen, investigated the church and talked of how people about here make their living, including…' He paused to turn to Amy. 'What was the wise woman's name?'

'Widow Twitch,' she said.

'Oh, she is harmless enough,' Harriet said as the refreshments arrived and she set about making tea and handing out little almond and cherry cakes. 'There are some who believe every word she says, but it is my contention she fabricates most of it. Every young girl would like to believe a rich handsome man is coming to carry her away and every young man dreams of finding a pot of gold. It is nonsense, of course.'

He smiled and looked at Amy, who flushed a becoming pink. 'We came to the same conclusion, did we not, Mrs Macdonald?'

'Yes,' she agreed, looking from Harriet to Matilda, who was shaking her head imperceptibly. It was Aunt Matilda who had suggested calling on the old lady and Amy supposed she did not want to be scolded for it.

'I wonder if you can tell me if there is a house to let hereabouts,' James said, addressing Miss Hardwick. 'You see, I think my business may take longer than I thought and it would be more convenient to have my own establishment. It need not be very large, I do not intend to entertain on a grand scale and I have only one servant at present.' How much of this idea was a conviction that the answer to the riddle lay in Highbeck and how much to a reluctance to go back to his own empty home, he was not prepared to speculate.

'One cannot run a house with one servant,' Miss Matilda put in.

He acknowledged this with a slight bow. 'I shall take on more as necessary.'

Matilda looked at Harriet. 'Harriet, what about the Lodge?'

Her sister looked thoughtful for a moment, then brightened. 'Do you know, I think that is a capital notion. If it is occupied, it might keep Cousin Gerald off our backs.' She turned to James. 'Our cousin has been trying to persuade us to move out of here into the Lodge. He calls it the dower house.'

'He may call it what he likes,' Matilda said hotly. 'We are not dowagers and he cannot treat us as if we were. He has no right to dictate to us. The Manor is ours unentailed, whatever he might think or say.'

'Now, now, Tilly,' her sister admonished. 'The Captain does not want to hear of our troubles.'

That they had troubles was news to Amy. She had met Sir Gerald Hardwick once, soon after the accident. He called to see how she did, which she thought very civil of him, but he had had no patience with her loss of memory and thought browbeating her would restore it in no time. Aunt Harriet had sent him on his way, saying, 'Amy will make a full recovery, no doubt of it, so you may take your rapacious self back to Ely.' Amy had thought that was somewhat harsh, but her aunt said he deserved it, a statement she had been obliged to accept, knowing nothing of what had gone before.

James bowed. 'I would not wish to cause dissent between you and your relation,' he said. 'I can look elsewhere.'

'Indeed you will not,' Harriet told him. 'You will be doing us a good turn if you move into the house.'

'Then I accept your kind offer. If there is anything I can do to be of assistance, then please tell me.' He looked from one to the other, wondering if they might satisfy his curiosity, but all the reply he received was a chorused, 'Thank you.'

'You should see the house first,' Matilda said. 'It may not be to your liking. Amy will take you, it is but a stone's throw away.'

'Of course,' Amy said. 'Shall we go now? Your horse will be looked after until we return.'

He agreed and waited while she hurried up to her room to change out of her habit into something more suitable for walking.

'I collect you have not told Amy the real reason

for your visit?' Harriet said, as soon as she was out of earshot.

'No, she has accepted me as a friend of the family. I do not want to spoil that. If you think I should…'

'No, no,' Harriet said quickly. 'You must work in your own way. I only asked so that we might know how to go on. It is important that we are in accord.' She paused before going on. 'Have you learned anything today?'

'Very little. She is, I believe, coming to remember her childhood here and that is a start, but any questions about her life in London draw a blank. I think something must have happened there before she ever boarded that coach.'

'Our view exactly,' Matilda said. 'But we are fearful of what might happen if she were to return there. We have discouraged her from attempting it.'

'I think you are right. Until we know the truth of it ourselves, she is best here being looked after by your good selves.'

'How are we to find out? We never travel to London.'

'I shall send my man back to the capital to fetch things I need. We rode here, not expecting to stay above a day or two, and I have but one change of clothes. I shall instruct him, while he is there, to try and find out who this Mr Billings was and what happened at the house. And if there is any news of Mr Macdonald.'

'He is trustworthy?'

'I would trust him with my life, madam. And he knows how to keep his tongue between his teeth. You need have no fear.'

'Good.' She paused as footsteps sounded on the stairs. 'Here comes Amy. I think we will not say anything about your man for the moment.'

'Very well.'

He rose to his feet as Amy came into the room, dressed in a cool muslin gown with a light shawl thrown about her shoulders. Her cottager hat was tied on with a ribbon beneath her chin. 'I am ready,' she said.

They set off on foot, crossing the drawbridge and turning away from the drive and the main entrance to go across a green sward and taking a path through a small copse. 'The trees were planted by one of my ancestors to protect the Manor from the prevailing east wind,' she told him. 'It can go right through you in the winter.'

'That I can imagine,' he said with a laugh. 'There is very little between here and the Arctic to stop it.'

'Perhaps that is why fen folk are so hardy,' she said. 'This path leads to a back entrance to the grounds, which is where the Lodge stands. See, there it is.' They had come out of the trees and she pointed to a squat red-brick house, two storeys high, with a door in the centre of the façade and windows either side. It was neatly thatched. Beyond it were tall gates set in the wall surrounding the estate, on the other side of which was a lane. 'It guards the Manor, just as the tower guards it on the other side. I am sure it was intended to withstand a siege.'

'Has there ever been a siege?' he asked.

'I do not know. Perhaps in the past there might have been, perhaps in the struggle between King Charles and Parliament.'

'This was strong Cromwell country, I believe.'

'Yes, but I have been told the Hardwicks were loyal to the king.' She took the key Harriet had given her from her pocket and unlocked the front door.

'Ah, then they would need strong defences.'

They stepped inside and looked about them. They were in a small hall with doors to right and left and an oak staircase going up from the middle. 'It is the first time I have been in here since the accident,' she said. 'It smells musty from being shut up and no one living here. If we open the windows, I am sure it will clear it.'

'How long has it been standing empty?'

'I do not know, nor why. Shall we explore?'

They wandered from room to room, flinging open windows just like a young couple looking for a first home, Amy thought, and smiled at her fancies. She was married and had a home, even if she could remember neither husband nor house. How did Duncan compare with the man who walked beside her? Was he as handsome, as forbearing, as amiable? Did he make her laugh? Realising her escort was speaking, she shook her foolish thoughts from her. 'I beg your pardon, I was daydreaming.'

'Remembering?'

'No, wishing I could. What was it you said?'

'I was saying I would need furniture. There is very little here.'

'Yes, I had not realised that. No doubt my aunts thought it unwise to leave sofas and soft furnishings in place for fear of them going mouldy. I am sure it can be remedied.'

'Of course. A visit to the shops to buy what I need will soon have it comfortable.'

What hard furniture there was, like a few tables and chairs, cupboards and shelves, was in good condition, though thick with dust. 'I think a cleaning woman must be your first concern,' she said, running her finger along the banister as they made their way upstairs. 'I have no doubt Aunt Harriet will know of someone.'

There were five rooms on the upper floor, all half-furnished. They looked in each and he decided which one he would take and which Sam could have. 'I shall need a cook-housekeeper to live in,' he said. 'But cleaning and laundry women can come in daily.'

She went to the window of the main bedroom and flung it open. 'Come and see,' she said. 'The view from here is better than I imagined it would be.'

The window was not large and they stood very close together, so close she could feel his warmth. It gave her a feeling of being protected, as if he would always stand at her side and keep her safe. It was a strange sensation and she came to the conclusion she was remembering that bareback ride cradled in his arms. Until that moment, she had been feeling cold and alone. Now, how did she know that? Was she truly remembering or simply making things up to suit herself?

'I can see the lane leading to the Manor, and a glimpse of the chimneys above the trees,' he said. 'And the tower on the far side. I suppose, given a siege, it would be possible to signal from here to there.'

'But we are not preparing for a siege, are we?' she said, laughing to cover her embarrassment. He had put his hand on the wall on the other side of her in order to lean out and she was very conscious that it was only inches from her shoulders. He had only to drop his arm casually and he would have her in his embrace and that was followed by the thought that she might enjoy it. She shook herself. She was a married woman and should not be indulging in such fancies.

He was suddenly conscious of how close they were and straightened up. 'No, thank goodness. Shall we go downstairs again? I should like to look at the kitchen offices and the outbuildings.'

These proved adequate, but not luxurious, but he was quick to tell her he had known worse. 'Shipboard life is very basic,' he said. 'You learn not to mind.'

'That must have been hard, considering you came from an illustrious family.'

'One can become used to anything in time,' he said, as they went round shutting the windows again. 'And the common sailors had by far the worst of it.'

'Had they been pressed?'

'Some of them. I do not agree with taking a man by force, but sometimes it is necessary. Some are ill suited to the life, but they soon become inured.'

She locked the door again and they set off back the way they had come. 'I recollect you said you had left the service.'

'Yes. I meant to settle down…'

'Instead you embarked on a life of travel of a different kind.'

'Yes,' he said, remembering Caroline and his quest for her killers. He ought to have found them long before now, but they were hardened criminals and knew how to go to ground when the pursuit became too close for comfort. He would have them in the end, even if he had to remain a thieftaker for the rest of his days. In the meantime, having taken on this commission, he would see it through.

Alerted by his sudden withdrawal, Amy turned towards him. He was looking sombre, his jaw rigid, making her wonder what it was that could change his expression so quickly. 'I am sorry,' she said. 'I did not mean to pry. It is my insatiable need to know all about everyone I meet that makes me like that. Please forgive me.'

'There is nothing to forgive,' he said, without satisfying her curiosity, and then confounded her by adding, 'But I think I may stay here for a while. The area suits me and so does the house.'

'Then we shall be neighbours.'

'Yes. I shall like that.'

'And so shall I and my aunts. They have taken a liking to you, Captain, and that is rare for them. They are usually restrained by shyness.'

'Miss Hardwick does not strike me as shy.'

'Perhaps not. Perhaps it is more of a reticence, a wariness of strangers. But you are not a stranger, are you? You are known to Lord Trentham, who thinks highly of you. It is enough for the aunts. If they approve then I do, too.'

'Thank you for that. Do you know his lordship?'

'I do not remember him, but I am told he once courted my mother, though nothing came of it and she married my father instead. She thought a sea captain, even one with a title, would be away from home more than she would like, and so she turned him down. I have all this from my aunts, you understand. It is the result of my quizzing them from morning to night in order to try to remember.'

'Do you remember your father?' he asked.

'No. He lives abroad and, according to the aunts, has done so this last four years. They could not tell me why, but suppose he and my mother did not deal well together. She is an opera singer.'

'Not used to domesticity then,' he said, mentally noting that a little over four years before the man they called Bonnie Prince Charlie was on English soil, not that many miles to the north of where they were, and causing mayhem in his bid to regain the throne for his father. Many of his English sympathisers had been forced to flee the country when the rebellion failed. Was Charron one of their number?

'No, that is why my aunts brought me up.'

They had arrived back at the house and he accompanied her inside to tell the Misses Hardwick, over a glass of Rhenish wine, that he would like to take the Lodge. The rent was agreed and they were able to suggest someone as cook-housekeeper and Harriet promised to speak to the woman herself. Then his horse was sent for and he bade them farewell and left them.

'It will be good to have the Lodge occupied again,' Matilda said after the clatter of his horse's hooves faded from the cobbles of the yard. 'And by such an amiable man. I am sure we will be able to rely on him when Cousin Gerald comes calling.'

'What about Cousin Gerald? Why does he want you to move to the Lodge?' Amy asked, silently agreeing that the Captain was an amiable man. Unusually for someone who was used to a rough life at sea, he had shown himself to be gentle and considerate. He was not obliged to look after her after the accident, nor come calling to see how she did, even if he did have business in the neighbourhood, and that was a point in his favour. What was his business? She had stopped quizzing him when it became clear he did not like it, and to go on might shatter her illusion that he was her knight, if not exactly in shining armour, then in a good quality riding coat and a fine beaver hat.

'Cousin Gerald has a bee in his bonnet,' Harriet told her. 'It is all about our father's will. Papa inherited the estate from his father, which is as it should be, considering he was the eldest son. Gerald is the son of Papa's younger brother and, when our father had no sons, considered himself next in line. He was angry when he discovered the estate was not entailed and Papa could leave it to whom he liked and had bequeathed it to us. He has been contesting the validity of the will ever since.'

'Do you think he can win?' Amy asked.

'No. We have a very good lawyer and he is adamant Gerald has no case, but that does not stop him harassing us now and again in the hope that we will give in.'

'But you will not?'

'Certainly not! We are not going to give away your birthright,' Harriet said firmly.

'Mine?'

'Naturally yours. You are the only offspring of the three of us.'

'I do hope Cousin Gerald does not cause trouble for Captain Drymore,' Amy said pensively.

Harriet laughed. 'I am quite sure the Captain is

able to look after himself. And us too should the need arise.'

Amy did not doubt it, but was it fair? Were her aunts or her mother, through Lord Trentham, using the man under the pretext of doing him a good turn? Was that his business in Highbeck, protecting the aunts from their cousin? She was not sure she liked being involved if that were the case. On the other hand she did not want him to leave. She told herself it was because he helped her to remember things, but deep down she knew that was only a part of it.

'Staying here?' echoed Sam. 'You mean it?'

'Yes, I mean it. I am taking a house close by.'

'But why? Smith and Randle ain't nowhere hereabouts,' Sam protested.

'I know that. But there is a riddle to be solved and I mean to solve it,' James said decisively.

'Very well, Captain.' It was said with a heavy sigh. 'When do we move?'

'Soon, but I have shopping to do first and staff to enlist. And I have a commission for you. I want you to go back to Colbridge House and gather up my belongings—clothes, books, sword, pistols, anything I might need—and hire a wagon to bring them hither. Then see what you can find out about a certain Duncan Macdonald. He is reputed to be an artist.'

'Mrs Macdonald's husband?'

'Yes. Go to his house, I will furnish you with the direction, and search around. You might find a clue as to his whereabouts, but do not disturb anything more than you have to. Try the coffee houses frequented by his like, the clubs…'

'I'll never get through the door of a gentleman's club, you know that,' Sam scoffed.

'No, but there are plenty of clubs for the middling sort and I do not think Macdonald aspires to anything higher. I will give you letters to take to Lord Trentham and Mr Fielding, they might have news of him. And then put your ear to the ground for anything about Mr Gus Billings.'

'Him that died in the coach?' Sam asked.

'Yes. And those two highpads because he was known to them and I have a notion Mrs Macdonald knew them, too.'

'And should I make further enquiries about the other two, Smith and Randle?'

'Yes, naturally those two must not be forgotten. When you have discovered all you can, return to me here.'

'I might be gone weeks—how will you manage without me?'

'I am not old or helpless, Sam. I can see to myself.' He gave a sudden chuckle. 'Until you send me more, I only have one change of linen, one spare coat and waistcoat and a pair of shoes. And I do not wear a wig. I am not going to need a valet, am I?'

'I ain't simply a valet,' Sam said, aggrieved.

'No, indeed you are not, you are my helpmate and friend. It is because of that I know I can trust you with this errand.'

Slightly mollified, Sam went off to order dinner for them, muttering about a pair of blue eyes turning his master's head. James heard him, but did not reprimand him. The man was a treasure and he did not know what he would do without him. But was he right? Should he have returned to London himself and pursued his enquiries there? What more could he learn about Duncan Macdonald or Gus Billings in Highbeck? On the face of it, very little, but if the lady remembered why she had fled or been forced from London, he wanted to be on hand to hear it. And though he decried wise women and their fanciful predictions, he could not help remembering what Widow Twitch had told Amy. Trials to come. And a death? Whose death? She surely did not mean Amy's; if she did, he was determined to prevent it and if that meant staying close by, then he would stay. Pair of blue eyes indeed!

He smiled to himself. Those eyes were lustrous, full of intelligence and humour when she was not worrying about her memory. But that was not all she had in her favour; there was a flawless skin and a lovely figure and thick fair hair that framed a perfect oval face. Not for her mountainous wigs, powder and rouge; you could not improve on what nature had endowed her with. He realised suddenly that he had not thought like that about a woman since Caroline had died—did it mean he was coming to accept what had happened? Certainly his obsession with finding Smith and Randle had been pushed to the back of his mind, if only temporarily. Was that a good thing or a betrayal of his wife?

Sam came back to tell him dinner was ready in the dining room and they went in together; Sam always ate with him except when James was in company or entertaining. They talked a little about Sam's enquiries in London and where he should go and then about what was needed to furnish the Lodge, some of which might be better bought in London and brought down on the wagon. After that he wrote the letters for Lord Trentham and Mr Fielding and the direction of the Macdonalds' London home in Henrietta Street. Not the address a gentleman would choose, but hadn't Lord Trentham said they might be in financial trouble? Poor Amy!

He ought not to be thinking of her in those terms.

She had a husband, a husband she wanted found. Would finding him fill her with joy or disillusion her? More than ever he was determined to get to the bottom of the mystery and that meant spending time in her company, which would be no hardship. He would buy a light carriage and suggest she accompany him to shop for things he needed for the house.

He bought a gig and a pony the very next day, taking the coach into Ely and driving his purchase back himself. He was pulling into the yard of the King's Arms when he saw Amy with a basket on her arm. He jumped down to greet her, sweeping off his hat and bowing.

'What have you got there?' she asked, nodding towards the carriage. 'It looks very smart.'

'I am glad you think so. I could not live in the Lodge without a vehicle, could I? I must be able to go out and about, shopping and making calls.'

'Making calls?' she asked with a smile. 'Have you made calling acquaintances already?'

'Yes, the ladies of the Manor are all charming and welcoming. When I am settled in I hope they will call on me.' He paused. 'Mrs Macdonald, I have a favour to ask of you.'

'Then ask it, Captain. If it is in my power it shall be granted,' she said.

'Oh, it is in your power. I would like you to help me furnish the Lodge. I have no idea what I require and it needs a lady's touch. Would you do that?'

'Gladly.'

'Then will you accompany me to Downham Market tomorrow to do some shopping?' James asked.

'In the gig?'

'Yes. I shall drive carefully, I promise.'

She laughed. 'How can I refuse? I shall be delighted.'

They parted on that note and she returned to tell the aunts of the encounter. 'Will you help me to draw up a list of things the Captain will need for the Lodge?' she asked.

'Yes, but you ought to have a chaperon,' Harriet said thoughtfully. 'Susan, perhaps…'

'But it is only a gig, there is hardly room for three people without a squeeze. And surely I will come to no harm in the Captain's company,' Amy protested.

'I am sure you will not, but it is improper—'

'I think it is too late to worry about the proprieties. Was I not travelling in that public coach with a man I did not know?'

'Perhaps you did know him,' Harriet pointed out.

'Even if I did, I did not have a chaperon. If you

insist, the Captain will think you do not trust him and that after he saved me from death…'

'Saved you from death! How is that? You were not dying,' her aunt exclaimed.

'I might have been if he had not picked me up and ridden with me to safety,' Amy insisted.

Matilda laughed at this exchange. 'Harriet, let the child go. She will come to no harm.'

'And you are as bad as she is,' her sister rounded on her. 'Filling her head with romantic nonsense. Do not think I do not know you sent her to Granny Twitch. And I'll wager the woman did not have a word to say about Duncan, but filled her head with nonsense about handsome men and pots of gold.'

Amy found herself laughing aloud and the aunts soon joined in and the matter of the chaperon was forgotten as she told them exactly what the old lady had said. 'What did I tell you?' Aunt Harriet said. 'Nothing but nonsense.'

Amy hugged them both. 'When shall we make the shopping list? Do you think it matters about how much he has to pay for things?'

'No, of course not, but let us have dinner first. We can do it after that.'

When James arrived next day, driving the gig up to the front door, Amy was ready with a comprehensive list in her reticule. He jumped down to help her up, then returned to his seat to pick up the reins. 'Do you know the way?' he asked.

'Oh, yes,' she said, then stopped in confusion. 'How do I know I do?'

'I expect it is part of your early memory, before you went to London,' he said, as they trotted along the short drive. 'And we have already decided that is returning. Quite quickly, it seems.'

'Yes, you are right. Now, go to the village and turn right at the crossroads. The road is straight from there.'

The weather was perfect as they bowled along at a steady pace. James was in no hurry; he could think of no more enjoyable way to spend a day than to be with the lovely young lady who sat beside him, pointing out landmarks, windmills and churches, the riverside staithes and brown-sailed wherries, and chatting cheerfully about the country-side and the items that he would need to make the Lodge comfortable. He was determined to make it a pleasant day for her and set aside the troublesome matter of a lost memory. He was of the opinion it would come back when she was relaxed and not trying to force it.

Amy felt entirely at ease with him. And that surprised her. Somewhere in the back of her mind was the thought that she had not always felt comfortable with menfolk. Today, she was not going to tease her memory, but enjoy the day in company with this enigmatic man. Honest and open though he appeared to be, there was something he was holding back, and that was undoubtedly the nature of his business in the area. One day, perhaps, he might tell her of it, but she did not intend to spoil their time together by asking about it. Gradually the tight knot that always seemed to be in her stomach relaxed its hold on her.

'I think we can safely leave buying the kitchen equipment to Mrs Landis,' she told him. Mrs Landis was the woman Aunt Harriet had recommended as cook-housekeeper and James had been pleased to take her on. She would already be at work at the Lodge, directing the two cleaning women who had also been employed. By the time they returned from their expedition, they expected to find a marked improvement in the state of the house. 'We will concentrate on the parlour and the bedrooms.'

'I am in your hands.'

'Aunt Harriet told me the hangings were taken down and stored at the Manor, and they should be in good condition, so a few rugs, a sofa or two, a cupboard, one or two small tables, a clock, a few pictures and ornaments. A bookcase, perhaps, though without books…'

'My man will send my books with my other belongings,' he said.

'And in the bedrooms, a chest, some drawers and a dressing table in each. Will you be content with the bedsteads that are there?'

'Yes. They will suit me well enough, but I shall need bedding.'

'It is quite a long list. I doubt we shall manage it all today.'

'No matter, there will be other days.'

She liked the idea of going out with him again and helping him to make a comfortable home of the Lodge. It made her feel useful and helped to fill days that sometimes seemed empty. Above all, she appreciated his company. He seemed to know when to talk and when she would rather not, when to laugh and tease and when to be serious, and she wanted to learn more about him. In spite of his amiability, he still managed to keep many things to himself. Was he simply a retiring man or was there some reason for it? Of course, if Duncan turned up she would have to devote her time to him. Would she know him? But she had promised herself not to worry about her lost memory today and thrust the thought from her. 'You must tell me if I am dipping too deeply into your purse.'

'Oh, I think I can manage to furnish a small house without trouble,' he said. 'Do not think of that.'

They arrived at Downham to find it was market day and the town was crowded. Leaving the pony and gig at the stables, they set off on foot. It was then he realised she was nervous of crowds; she was pale and shaking, though manfully trying to overcome it. Without speaking, he took her hand and tucked it under his elbow and put his free hand over it, to reassure her.

The feel of his hand on hers was warm and protective and she turned to smile at him, thankful that he understood without either of them speaking. She did not know what it was that made her so fearful, nor why she should experience it again now, after a perfectly relaxed and peaceful ride. 'What shall we look at first?' she asked, determined to be practical.

'Bedding,' he said. 'After all, I can manage without furniture for a day or two, but if I am to move into the Lodge tomorrow, I need to have something to cover me. And Mrs Landis too will need to be comfortable.'

'You mean to move in tomorrow?' she asked incredulously.

'Why not? There is no sense in staying at the inn when I have a perfectly good house nearby, is there?'

They found a stall selling goose-feather quilts and pillows, another linen sheets and blankets, which he paid for and arranged to be delivered, then moved on. 'I doubt we will find sofas here,' she said. 'But my aunts tell me there are warehouses in Wisbech and Lynn that will be more likely to have what you want—'

She stumbled suddenly and he caught her to steady her, wondering what had caused it. She stood still, unable to go on, and he noticed that her eyes were riveted on something or someone in the crowd. All he saw was a market square lined with stalls and thronged with people of all kinds, men, women, young and old, rich and poor. Her gaze seemed to be directed at a couple of rough-looking men, but they had turned and hurried away, disappearing in the mêlée. For an instant he was reminded of Smith and Randle, and if she had not been with him he would undoubtedly have gone chasing after them, just as he had chased after every other likely pair for the last two years. He shook himself. He had no reason to believe they were in the fens, none at all, and he was being fanciful.

'Do you know those two?' he asked, nodding in the direction they had disappeared.

'Who?'

'There were two men at the end of that row of stalls. They seemed to engage your attention.'

'No, I do not think so. But then, I cannot be sure, can I?' She was grateful he was there because she could not stop shaking. 'You must think me very foolish to start at every stranger who looks at me. I fear I have been too sheltered at the Manor since the accident.'

'No, my dear, not foolish,' he said. 'But I think we have done enough for now. Let us go home. We can shop for the rest another day.'

He took her arm and guided her back to the posting inn where he bought them a dish of coffee to drink while the pony was re-harnessed to the gig and fetched round to the front.

She was silent on the return journey, but he did not try to make her talk. Something had troubled her, a returning memory invoked by the sight of those two men. Perhaps she was thinking of the two highway-men who had held up the coach. They had been cloaked and masked, but had she recognised them in spite of that? Gus Billings had known them. The mystery was no nearer being solved, but he would not give up. It had engaged his interest to the exclusion of everything else. He gave a quirky smile; if Sam had not gone to London, he would undoubtedly have had more to say about a pair of appealing blue eyes.

Chapter Four

Amy went over to the Lodge the next day to see how Mrs Landis and her cleaning women were faring, and found them very busy. The housekeeper was dealing with a large quantity of pots, pans, crockery and provisions she had ordered and which had just arrived by carrier's wagon. The cleaning women were busy with buckets of water, mops and feather dusters. Already the difference was remarkable.

As soon as he heard her voice in the kitchen, James hurried there to see her, telling the housekeeper to rustle up some refreshments for her and bring them to the drawing room.

'Oh, no, Captain, Mrs Landis is far too busy to wait on me,' Amy protested, earning a grateful look from the housekeeper. 'I only came to see if there is anything I can do to help, not to create more work.'

'We are managing very well,' Mrs Landis said. 'But I thank you for the thought.'

'I am off to Wisbech where I am told there is a warehouse full of useful articles,' James said. 'Would you care to come with me to choose what we need?'

'Yes, I should like that. Are you going now?'

'As soon as I have harnessed the horse. Can you be ready?' he asked.

'Yes, I will go and tell my aunts and wait at the drawbridge for you.'

It was the first of several such outings, both to Wisbech and Lynn. Over the next few days they bought two sofas and a pair of elegant low tables, chairs, fire screens, a clock and candelabra for the drawing room, a desk and bookshelves for the book room, clothes presses, dressing tables and mirrors and candle stands for the bedchambers, discussing what was needed, even arguing a little about their preferences in which he nearly always let her have her way, and gradually the Lodge was becoming a comfortable home for a gentleman. Not the most elaborate or costly that could be had, certainly less than the son of an earl might expect, but James professed himself more than satisfied. On all the trips they learned a little more about each other and established a comfortable rapport, although none of it helped to restore her memory. It certainly did nothing to solve the mystery of the absent husband.

A wagon had arrived from the capital with his clothes and other personal effects, so James was able to dress according to whatever he was doing. He would come up to the Manor to dine with Amy and the aunts dressed in beautiful coats and waist-coats, well-cut breeches and snow-white shirts and always the same simple pin in his pristine neck-cloth.

He was an amiable dinner guest, an entertaining raconteur and knowledgeable about events in the capital and indeed the rest of the world, but he was still something of an enigma to Amy. In the middle of some discourse, she would notice his eyes cloud over as if he were remembering something that gave him pain and he would put a hand up to the pin in his cravat, before appearing to shake himself out of it. And sometimes his opinions about the punishment of criminals seemed hard and inflexible, but she suspected that underneath that exterior was a softer man.

This was borne out on a trip to Ely. In spite of its vast and magnificent cathedral, Ely was little more than a village, dominated by the river that was its chief means of communication. Produce imported from abroad at Wisbech and Lynn was brought by river, and the harvest of the fens—reed, fish, water fowl—came to Ely to be sold at its market. On Sundays and holy days, the people came from all over the area to worship under its octagon lantern. James and Amy had spent some hours exploring and were on their way back to the Lamb where they had left the gig when they saw a boy speeding towards them through the crowd, followed by a man, shouting, 'Stop, thief! Stop that boy!'

Not wishing to be bowled over by them, Amy stood aside, but James took two long strides and had the boy in his grasp. He was not above ten years old, barefoot and dressed in rags. His arms and legs were thin as sticks, but even so he kicked and squirmed in an effort to free himself. All in vain; James held him fast.

'Much obliged to you, sir.' The boy's pursuer, who was as plump as the boy was skinny, had reached them and stood before them, panting for breath. 'The blackguard has stolen my dinner.'

'Your dinner?' James asked mildly, though not relaxing his hold on the boy.

'Yes. A fine meat pie in a cloth. I put it on the wall by the staithe while I shook hands with a friend and asked him how he did. Quick as lightning, the pesky thief nabbed it and was off.'

'What have you done with it, boy?' James asked, giving him a little shake.

'I never had it.'

'Do not lie, you wicked boy,' the man said. 'You've eaten it.'

'How could he?' Amy felt she had to speak in the child's defence. 'He could hardly eat it and run at the same time.'

'Please keep out of it,' James told her. 'There is gravy down his shirt front.'

'I dropped it,' the boy said, and began to cry.

Amy could not contain herself. 'I have no doubt the poor child was hungry. You can hardly blame him.'

'I do blame him,' the man said. 'Hand him over to the Watch at once.'

'Captain, I beg of you not to do any such thing,' Amy said, lifting her appealing eyes to his. 'The poor boy must have imagined the pie had been left on the wall and forgotten. Can you not let him go? After all, it is not our business to arrest anyone, let alone a child.'

'Hey!' the man said. 'The boy is my prisoner. I am the injured party and I want justice done.'

'Here is your justice, sir,' James said, handing him a guinea. 'You may buy a week of dinners with that. I will undertake to punish the culprit.'

The man took the coin and strode off towards the

market place, leaving the boy with James and Amy. 'You are not going to hand him in, are you?' she asked. 'Oh, please do not.'

'Children have to learn right from wrong,' he said, then smiled suddenly. 'But I doubt he will learn that in prison.' He squatted down beside the boy. 'What is your name, boy?'

'Joe Potton.'

'Well, Joe Potton, if I let you go, will you promise to behave in future? No more thieving.'

The child nodded. James found a sixpence in his pocket, which he put into the boy's hand. 'Now, off you go and do not let me catch you stealing again.' In the blink of an eye the child was gone, disappearing down an alley before anyone could change their mind.

'You are making me soft, Mrs Macdonald,' James said, knowing perfectly well the child would steal again as soon as the opportunity arose. 'All we have taught that boy is that crime does sometimes pay.'

She laughed. 'You were the one who gave him sixpence, not I.'

'I know,' he said with a wry smile. 'But you were no doubt right. He took the pie because he was hungry and, having dropped it, was still hungry. Could I leave him like that?'

'I think you are not as severe as you would have

us believe,' she said. 'Underneath I believe you to be a compassionate man.'

'Perhaps where children are concerned. They are not born wicked and learn only what adults teach them. But grown men who steal and murder, that is a different matter.' He spoke so vehemently she turned to look at him.

She saw that clouded look in his eyes again and noticed how rigid he held his jaw, and came to the conclusion that something had happened in the past which still troubled him. She longed to ask him about it, but his demeanour did not invite questions and they returned to the inn in silence.

By the time they were in the gig and on their way home, he had recovered his good humour and was talking about the Lodge and how comfortable he felt there, which he attributed to the help she had given him. 'It is down to the excellent work of my little homemaker,' he said, surprising himself and making her laugh. And in that happy frame of mind they arrived back at the Manor.

He spent a few minutes exchanging civilities with the Misses Hardwick and then took his leave. After he had gone, Amy told them about the little boy and the way the Captain seemed to be intractable about handing him over to the Watch at first, but then gave in to her entreaties to let him go and gave him a sixpence. 'He said I was making him soft,' she said. 'And he called me his little homemaker. That was a quaint thing to say, do you not think?' They chuckled over it, but Aunt Harriet saw fit to remind her that she was a married woman and should not encourage the Captain in such familiarities, which quite took the shine off the outing.

In spite of that, Amy would not be put off her role as adviser and helpmate over the furnishing of the Lodge. It gave her something useful to do, and for a little while, choosing colours and materials and selecting a few pictures and ornaments took her mind off her troubles. She would go for several hours, sometimes a whole day, without thinking about her loss of memory, until someone said something that reminded her and then her lovely eyes would become shadowed with sorrow for a time, but then James would say something to her about the Lodge and she was herself again.

One day, about a week after their trip to Ely, she was making her way to the Lodge through the copse when she realised she was being followed. Thinking it might be some of the village children, she turned with a laugh, ready to run after them. It was not children, but two men who dodged behind the trees as she turned. She was sure they were the same two she had seen in Downham Market the first time she and the Captain had gone shopping together. She started to run, bursting into the Lodge without knocking, just as James came out of his book room.

He hurried towards her. 'Amy, what is wrong?'

She flung herself into his arms, oblivious to the fact that he had called her by her given name. He held her, not knowing what had caused her distress, but prepared to hold her in his arms until she had calmed enough to tell him. Her unpowdered hair was soft beneath his chin and smelled of lavender. He resisted the temptation to put his lips to it. 'You are quite safe,' he murmured. 'I will let no one hurt you.'

'I'm sorry to be such a ninny,' she said, drawing away from him. 'I was so frightened.'

'That I could see,' he said gently. 'Now come into the drawing room and tell me what happened.' He led her into the room and they sat together on the new sofa with his arm still about her. She did not object; indeed, she hardly seemed aware that it was there.

'I was being followed. It was those two men.'

'Which two men?'

'The two I saw in Downham Market when we went to buy your bedding.'

'Are you sure? Did they speak?'

'No. I ran.' She laughed shakily. 'What a bumpkin

I am. I should have confronted them, asked what they were doing on the estate. Sent them away.'

'No, you did the right thing. If they had turned nasty…' He did not elaborate on that prospect, but went to the sideboard to pour a finger of brandy into a glass. 'Now sit there and sip that while I deal with them.'

He strode off to the copse, which was not thick enough to conceal anyone for long, but could find no one there. He went up to the Manor without coming across a soul and then came back and searched all round the Lodge and in its outbuildings, but found no evidence of intruders.

'There is no one there,' he said, returning to Amy who was sitting exactly where he had left her, though she appeared somewhat calmer.

'I did not imagine them.'

'I am sure you did not, but knowing you had seen them trespassing, they no doubt made good their escape.'

'I was afraid they were after me.' That was her biggest private fear, that she was mixed up in something disreputable.

'Why do you say that?' Had she remembered something, something that truly terrified her? His thoughts went to the man in the coach and the two highwaymen. He was almost sure she had recognised them even though they had been masked. Could it be the same two men, and, if so, how did she know them? He did not voice his thoughts, not wishing to frighten her even more nor put memories in her head that were not real ones.

'I don't know, it was just a feeling I had. What do you suppose they were after?'

'A rabbit or two for the pot, perhaps. Or work. Or alms.'

'They were unkempt, but not ragged and certainly not half-starved. But you are no doubt right and I am being silly,' she said with an attempt at a smile.

'Not at all,' he said gently. 'After what you have been through, I am surprised you are not more timid.'

'How do you know what I have been through?' she asked sharply.

'I meant the highwaymen and the coach over-turning and the death of your escort, not to mention losing your memory.'

'Oh, that. I wish I could remember what happened before that. Why did I lose my memory? Why can I not even remember my own husband? If it had not been for the aunts telling me they had met him, I would have doubted his existence. Surely I would know, inside myself, if I were married? And yet, I do not. What is my forgetfulness hiding from me? Are those two men part of it?'

'I cannot tell,' he said. 'But it would be a wise precaution to have an escort when you go out, even to come here, though my own feeling is that they were simply ne'er-do-wells out for what they could find.' He tried to be convincing, but even in his own ears he did not sound very sure.

He took the half-empty glass from her fingers and put it on a side table, then took her hand to bring her to her feet. 'Are you feeling better now?'

'Yes, thank you.' She was still a little fearful, but his presence beside her was reassuring. Was that why she had flung herself at him in that unladylike manner? He had not batted an eye at it, but held her in his arms and comforted her. And she had allowed it! As a married woman she should feel ashamed of her actions, but somehow she did not—which was another question that needed answering when her memory returned. 'I came to help you put up the pictures we bought.'

'They will keep for another day. I think you need to go home and rest. And do not be afraid. I will come with you,' he said.

Putting his pistol in his coat pocket, he accompanied her back to the Manor, staying so close to her that if anyone should appear, he could put his arm about her and defend her in an instant, but they met no one. He had enjoyed the feeling of having her in his arms, the softness of her, the faint smell of lavender, the way she seemed to lean on him. Not since he had left Caroline to go to sea had he felt like that towards a lady. But he would do well to remember she was married, he chided himself.

The aunts welcomed him as they always did, but were concerned when Amy related what had happened and tried to describe the two men for their benefit.

'Do you think they came from the village?' James asked them. 'They might have been poachers.'

'I do not recognise the description,' Harriet said. 'And I know all the men who live hereabouts.'

'Until we know who they are, we must all be careful,' Matilda said. 'I will warn the servants. The maids must be accompanied by one of the menservants when they go out, and you, Amy, must not go out alone.'

'So I have told her,' James said, smiling at Amy and making her heart turn over. He was so gentlemanly and caring towards her, when he had no reason to be at all. But, oh, how grateful she was. 'I will make it my task to escort Mrs Macdonald when she wishes to go out and about. With your permission, of course.' He bowed to each aunt in turn.

'But what about your business, Captain?' Amy said. 'You must not neglect that for me.'

'It can wait,' he said. 'Your safety and ease of mind are more important.'

She felt her face go scarlet. Such fine compliments from a gentleman to a lady, but she should remember she was married. The worst of it was she did not *feel* married. She did not really feel anything at all. Except empty. She was like an empty jug waiting to be filled. Captain Drymore could fill it with his compliments, his kind words and secure arms, his smiles and courtly manners. What then would happen when her memory returned and there was no room inside her to receive it?

'We are very grateful,' Harriet said. 'We know Amy will be safe with you to guard her.'

'In that case,' he said, 'I should like to take Mrs Macdonald out on the fen tomorrow if the weather holds.' He turned to Amy with a smile that sent a warm glow flooding through her. 'You recall I talked of taking out a boat and shooting duck?'

'I remember that very well,' she said. 'I remember all that has happened since my aunts brought me here after the accident, every little thing. It is what went before that is haunting me like a ghost, a wraith with no substance.'

'I see,' he said, impressed by the way she expressed herself. He could almost feel her loss himself. 'Then will you do me the kindness of accompanying me?'

She hesitated only a moment, thinking of those two men, but how could they hurt her out on the fen in a rowing boat protected by a man with a gun? With Captain Drymore she felt safe. 'I shall be delighted.'

'Then will ten o'clock in the morning be convenient?'

'Perfectly.'

'I will have Cook make up a picnic for you,' Matilda said.

He thanked her, bowed and took his leave. Amy turned back to the aunts. Harriet looked a little disapproving, but Matilda was smiling.

The weather held and they set out for the river at Highbeck with James carrying the picnic basket in one hand and his gun under his other arm. The ammunition was in the pocket of his plain buff coat. Amy looked fetching in a light blue, wool round gown and a wide-brimmed straw hat tied under her chin with a wide ribbon. In her hand she carried a little case, which contained her sketch book and charcoals.

At the staithe, James hired a rowing boat for the day and they were soon making their way upstream. Amy dabbled her hand in the current and watched him as he propelled them with the long, firm strokes of a man who knew how to get the maximum distance from each pull of the oars. They fairly skimmed along, past the riverside cottages, the slow-moving barges, the stately swans that it was unlawful to kill because they all belonged to the crown, towards the open water of the fen.

Once out in the middle he stopped rowing and allowed the boat to drift, while he looked about for a duck for the pot. There were several about, but it was so peaceful, with not a sound but their occasional quack, he could not bear to shatter it with the noise of a gun going off. Instead, he sat with his hands still on the oars, his gun idle at his side, and watched her draw. Once again he was struck by her loveliness. She had discarded her hat and her hair was brushed and loosely tied back with a blue ribbon. It framed a perfect oval face whose complexion was clear, her cheeks a natural rosy pink. Living in the country was good for her.

She appeared at ease; no terror marred her lovely eyes, as it had the day before, and he was glad of it. But he ought not to forget that he had been asked to try to restore her memory, to find out why she had lost it in the first place. It was a task he was relishing less and less. If she could be content without knowledge of her past, then ought he to leave well alone? *He* did not want to know about it. He wanted her just as she was, a young, innocent girl. This thought brought him up short. What did he mean he *wanted* her? Had he forgotten she was married? Had he forgotten his beloved Caroline and his vow to exact retribution on her killers?

He had always managed to remain aloof before, to be cool and committed to the job in hand; now he was a mass of contradictory thoughts and emotions. He ought to board the first stage back to London, forget all about Highbeck and Blackfen Manor and its inhabitants, and resume his search for Smith and Randle. But how could he abandon the lovely girl beside him?

She looked up from her sketchpad and saw him watching her, a strange expression on his face, of contemplation, of anger, of pain perhaps, as if something had suddenly made him sad. It was the look she had seen once or twice before and it puzzled her. She smiled. 'What are you thinking about?'

The sound of her voice brought him out of his reverie and he shook himself, almost visibly. 'Nothing of any moment. I was enjoying the tranquillity.'

'Yes, it is peaceful here. It is a different world from the bustle of the towns, as if God meant to keep a corner of the country all to himself and allow no one to disturb it. I feel very close to Him here, even more than I do in church.'

'Then I must not shatter the peace by killing His birds.'

She laughed. 'But that is why you came out here.'

'It was only one of the reasons and the easiest to cast aside.'

'You needed to think?'

'Yes, I needed to think,' he confirmed.

'And have you reached a conclusion?'

'No, except that we cannot hurry nature and should not even try.'

'I am beginning to think like that about my memory. The harder I try to recall things, the more they slip from my grasp. Could I be happy never remembering?' she asked a little wistfully.

'Only you know that, my dear.'

She looked sharply at him; he appeared unaware of the manner in which he had addressed her, just as he had not noticed calling her Amy the day before. Ought she to discourage such familiarity? But she did not want to introduce a discordant note by standing on her dignity. Besides, had she any right to dignity? 'I don't know. There are days, like today, when I think I might be content without a past. At other times, when something upsets or frightens me, like those two men, I want to know everything and I feel angry as well. Very angry.' She stopped suddenly and hurriedly stowed away her sketchpad and crayons. 'But we do not want to talk about my problems today. Let us find somewhere to eat our picnic.'

He picked up the oars and set off for the bank on the far side, which looked inviting. It proved ideal. There was a gentle sward of grass sloping down to the water's edge, shaded by a hawthorn in full flower. He rowed in as far as he could and then jumped out, to pull the boat up into shallower water. Then he returned for Amy and, picking her up in his arms, waded the last yard or two on to dry land.

She was not heavy and he stood for several seconds, savouring the feel of her, remembering how he had picked her up after the coach crash and how helpless she had been then. She was not so helpless now, but still vulnerable, still needing protection. He set her on her feet and then he stripped off his coat and spread it on the ground for her to sit on before returning to the boat for the picnic basket and her drawing case.

They unpacked the hamper together, exclaiming at the great quantity of food that had been provided for them. 'There is enough here for an army,' she said, pulling out chicken legs and meat patties, ham, bread and butter, sugar plums and a bottle of homemade cordial. It was best to ignore the strange sensations she had felt coursing through her when he picked her up. He had only done it to keep her feet dry, she told herself firmly.

They ate well and when they could eat and drink no more he sprawled on the grass while she leaned against the gnarled trunk of the hawthorn, surrounded by its dropped white petals, and brought out her sketch book to finish her drawing. She was surprised to find she had a talent for it. The Captain came to life under her busy fingers, his firm jaw, thick blond hair, his muscular arms resting on the oars, his plain brown coat with its pearl buttons, his long legs in well-fitting breeches. He exuded strength and masculinity. But there was also a softness about him, a gentleness it was difficult to portray and she had to try several times before she managed to capture his expression. Thoughtful, sad, but steely, as if anger were only just below the surface of his gentility. Not a man to make an enemy of, but a staunch ally when in trouble, she was sure of it.

She finished the figure and began on the surroundings, the water and reeds, the ducks and swans, the great fen sky overhead. Today there were few clouds, but she added one or two like the galleons in full sail just as she had described to him, one darker and more menacing than the rest. She put a face in that, an anonymous face, not recognisable as anyone she knew. She was so engrossed she did not notice that he had stirred and was sitting at her elbow looking at what she had drawn.

'My God! What a talent!' he said. 'You have got me to a whisker.'

'Thank you.'

'Who is that?' He pointed at the cloud face.

'No one, just a face, giving the cloud a personality. I thought I'd draw another with a cherub in it, just to balance it.'

'Yes, but I think you should leave it for another day because the wind is getting up and we shall soon have real clouds and I think it might rain. Time for our idyll to end.'

Absorbed in her drawing, she had not noticed how much cooler it was becoming and quickly set aside the drawing and helped him pack the remains of the picnic away, throwing the last of the bread and pastries to the ducks, who fell on them squawking and quarrelling. She laughed as she watched them, while he put on his coat, then he picked her up and waded out to sit her in the boat, jumped in himself and rowed them back to the staithe.

They had left the boat with the hirer and were walking back to the Manor when they met the bent form of Widow Twitch, carrying a bundle of herbs she had gathered. She stopped in front of Amy. 'Good day to you, Miss Amy. You have a fine gentleman escort, I see.'

'Yes, this is Captain Drymore. He has moved into the Lodge.'

'I know. He's a-searchin' for peace o' mind.'

James laughed. 'Tell me something I do not know, good woman.'

'It'll only come to you when you stop lookin' for it.'

'I will bear that in mind,' he said, humouring her.

'And is it the same for me?' asked Amy.

'Yours is a different case. You must find what you have lost.' She pulled a sprig of one of the herbs from her bundle and offered it to her. 'That's rosemary for remembrance. Put it under your pillow when you go to sleep.'

Amy accepted the token. 'Thank you. And will that restore my memory?'

'It might help. I give no guarantee,' the old woman said.

'I'll wager she won't,' James murmured as they went on their way.

'She means no harm.'

'No, but harm can come without her meaning it.'

'Are you saying my memories might hurt me? Or perhaps other people?'

He shrugged. 'Who can tell? But the old lady had a point about finding something when you have given up looking for it. I have frequently found that to be the case. I have lost a buckle or some such thing and it has turned up after I have decided to use another pair. Have you not found that so?'

She laughed. 'Yes, often.'

'Then what the woman says is not so strange after all, and does nothing to prove she can see into the future.' He took her arm. 'I do think we should hurry. The sky is becoming very black and that is something the good Widow Twitch did not warn us about.'

It began to rain heavily as they were passing over the drawbridge. They ran the last few yards across the courtyard and dashed indoors as a great clap of thunder echoed behind them.

'You had best stay until the rain eases,' Amy told him. 'Let us find the aunts.'

The aunts repeated Amy's invitation to stay and, as dinner was about to be served, an extra place was soon put on the table and they sat down to eat together.

'Did you enjoy your day on the fen?' Harriet asked James, handing him a tureen of soup from which to help himself.

'Exceedingly.'

'And how many duck did you bring back for the pot?'

Amy laughed. 'None. He did not want to disturb the peace with a gun.'

'That is something I would have expected from Amy,' Harriet said. 'She is soft-hearted, but a grown man, and a military man at that, declining to disturb a few ducks, is indeed unusual. If everyone were like that, there would be a great deal of hunger hereabouts.'

He grinned wryly. 'I stand rebuked,' he said. 'Another time I will let pop and bring home a dozen.'

'Oh, I hope not,' Amy said. 'They are such beautiful birds.'

'And did you enjoy your picnic?' Matilda asked Amy.

'Indeed we did. We moored on a lovely spot on the other side of the fen and sat under the shade of a hawthorn. I did some drawing and the Captain snoozed.'

'I did not,' he protested. 'I was thinking. And I watched you draw.'

'Amy is an accomplished artist,' Matilda told him. 'I do not know how good her husband is, for I never saw any of his work, but I doubt he is any better than she is.' She turned to Amy. 'What did you draw?'

'The fen and the sky and the Captain in the boat.'

'After we have finished our meal, you must show it to us.'

'We met Widow Twitch on the way back. She said I must continue to strive after my memory and gave me a sprig of rosemary to put under my pillow. She also told the Captain he must stop searching for peace of mind, because it would only come once he did,' Amy told her aunts.

'All nonsense,' James said, dismissing it. 'My mind is perfectly at peace, especially here with good friends who entertain me royally.'

'Thank you,' they murmured in unison and on that note they finished their meal. The aunts went to have an afternoon nap and, as it was still raining, Amy offered to show James round the Manor. 'That is if you have nothing else you would rather do,' she added.

'Nothing,' he said. 'I should like a guided tour.'

He was already familiar with the drawing room and dining room and the wide hall with its blackened staircase, but very little else and was intrigued by the number of small rooms whose function did not seem at all clear. One was used as a sitting room for the ladies on informal occasions, one as a book room, lined with shelves of old books, another as a store room; yet another was cluttered with coats and capes, boots and old guns, some of which could not have been fired for years. In one corner a spiral stone staircase led down to a cellar where the wines and preserves were kept. To one side of this was a low door. Amy opened it to reveal a cavity in what appeared to be the exterior wall. 'A priest's hole,' she said. 'Or so they tell me.'

'Or perhaps an early privy. I doubt a priest's hole would have so obvious a door.'

'You may be right, but a piece of heavy furniture pulled across would conceal it, would it not?'

'Perhaps, but then the poor man would hardly be able to breathe.'

She led the way upstairs, creeping quietly past the aunts' bedchambers and pausing before the door of another. 'That is my room,' she whispered, and moved on. 'There are several guest rooms and dressing rooms along here and round the corner at the end is another staircase down to the servants' quarters and further along another to the upper floors. We do not use those rooms, but there are some fine views. Shall you like to see?'

'Lead on.'

The stone staircase was in one of the corner turrets and had small slit windows, which he assumed were meant for guns or bows and arrows to be used in defence. The whole place was like a small castle, though built of brick, not stone. Halfway up a corridor led to more rooms, smaller than those below and only half-furnished. At the top was a small room with windows on all four aspects. From this lofty point they could see the round tower on the edge of the estate and, moving to the opposite side of the room, the roof of the Lodge showing between the trees. Far below them the water in the moat was being pounded by rain.

'I should not like to lead an attack on this fortress,' he said. 'You can be seen coming for miles and, apart from that small stand of trees, there is no cover. The only way of overcoming the defenders would be to starve them out.'

'I had not thought of it like that. To me it is simply a comfortable home.' Amy laughed.

'That is because its occupants have made it so.'

'You have made me curious. Shall we go down to the book room? I believe there are documents there which might tell us more.'

He followed her downstairs and into the book room where she found a key in a desk and unlocked the door of a cupboard. It was packed with rolled-up parchments, some of them very old. They laid them on the floor and knelt down to go over them. There was a charter from Queen Elizabeth that was yellowing with age, which James said they should not disturb. Some, more recent, revealed that the family had been on the Royalist side during the Civil War a century before. The second Sir Charles

Hardwick was put in prison by Cromwell's men, but never charged, and was released and his estate returned to him when Charles II returned to take up his throne. 'It is that king's great-nephew who caused the recent Jacobite Rebellion,' he said, aware of how intimate they were, kneeling side by side on the floor.

'And there is talk that it will flare up again.'

'The Young Pretender does not have the money, men or arms to mount another invasion. I am persuaded it is nothing but idle gossip.'

'Can that possibly have a bearing on my loss of memory, do you think?' she asked, suddenly looking worried. 'Everyone assumed the trouble was in London and I was coming here on a visit, but supposing it had a more sinister reason?'

'I believe you are being fanciful.'

'Perhaps. But Widow Twitch was right. I have to know.'

'Then you must put the rosemary under your pillow,' he said, smiling broadly.

'You are teasing me!' she exclaimed.

'Yes, for I put no faith in the old lady's remedies. And the idea you could be involved with the Jacobites is pure fantasy.'

Her worried expression vanished. 'You are right. Aunt Harriet always used to say I had too much imagination. Lets us pack these things away again and venture out. I do believe the rain has stopped.'

They went outside and wandered round the garden paths, noticing how green the grass was and how fresh all the plants were, after which he fetched his gun from where he had left it in the hall and took his leave, striding away through the trees to the Lodge. She watched him go and wondered what Widow Twitch had meant when she said he was looking for peace of mind. He had admitted, when they first met, that he was searching for something. She returned indoors and took out her drawing to study it.

Yes, there was something in his expression that indicated he had other things on his mind besides bagging a few ducks. And it must be rooted in Highbeck—why else would he have come to such an out of the way spot? He had mentioned the Jacobite rebellion of five years before, but that was over and done with and though it must have been frightening for those in the path of the advancing rebels, they had never reached as far south as the Wash. She must have been living at Highbeck at the time because it was before she married, but she could not remember it. She looked again at what she had drawn and ran her finger over the Captain's face, just as if it were his real flesh and blood she touched and gave a little shiver. She liked the man, liked him very much, and she wished she could banish his haunting look of sadness.

She had another nightmare that night, more vivid than any that had gone before. She was in a room looking out of a window, watching for someone. Behind her there was a bag full of gold and silver coins and sparkling jewellery and on top of it a wicked-looking knife. There was a man there, but he was not substantial enough to recognise, although she felt his menace. He took her by the shoulders and started to shake her. He kept on shaking her, yelling, 'Where is it?' Terrified she reached behind her and picked up the knife, raising it above her head. And then she woke up to find herself sitting up in bed tangled in the bed curtains. The tears were flowing down her cheeks and her right hand was clenched tightly as it would have been if grasping a knife.

Was she reliving something that had really happened? Had she used that knife on the man? Killed him and fled to the sanctuary of Blackfen Manor? Was that why she was so fearful all the time? Afraid of retribution? Did those two men she had seen know about it? Had they followed her intent on vengeance—or possibly blackmail? But no one had seen the men except her, so perhaps she had dreamed them, too. Only she could not stop herself coming to the conclusion that there was something in her past that was evil. Was she a bad person? Had she done something so terrible she had blotted all memory of it from her mind?

She made herself open her hand and lay it flat, half-expecting to see it covered in blood. There was nothing wrong with it. Feeling along the bed, she pulled the rosemary from beneath her pillow and threw it as far from her as she could. If remembering was going to come back to her through terrifying dreams, she did not want to remember.

She tried to go back to sleep, but could not. She lay tossing and turning, longing for James to come and hold her in his arms as he had before, to soothe her and tell her not to worry, because he would look after her. Not Duncan, her husband whom she could not remember, but James, whose comforting presence she could recall very clearly. That was an added complication. She found herself thinking of him constantly, thinking of his masculine good looks, his warm smile, his gentle teasing, the feel of his touch, the sound of his voice. It was impossible to think of Duncan that way because for her he did not exist.

Morning came at last and she rose early, dressed and went out into the courtyard, but she dared not go beyond the drawbridge. She paced about until she heard the servants stirring and went indoors to help prepare the aunts' breakfast trays, then she had her own breakfast and wandered about waiting impatiently for them to come downstairs. Her dream had lost some of its terror, but it would not go away altogether. It hung over her like that cloud she had drawn on the fen, threatening a storm, a storm of unpleasant recollections she was sure.

Aunt Harriet was the first down and, after commenting on Amy's early rising, disappeared into the kitchen to confer with the cook about the day's menus. It was only when Aunt Matilda came down and they gathered in the little parlour that all three were able to have some conversation together.

'Why were you up so early, Amy?' Harriet asked. 'Could you not sleep?'

'I had a dreadful nightmare and could not go back to sleep after it,' she admitted.

'You should not have eaten that cheese at supper time,' Harriet said.

'I do not think it was the cheese,' Amy said drily.

'What, then? Oh, do not tell me you put that rosemary under your pillow? Foolish, foolish child!' Harriet exclaimed.

'What did you dream about?' Matilda asked curiously.

She told them. Matilda put her hand to her mouth

with a little cry of horror. Harriet simply sniffed and said she would have something to say to Widow Twitch when she saw her.

'But it must have had some basis in truth,' Amy said. 'I did not conjure it out of the air. Did I use that knife? Am I a wicked person? Am I being searched for to be arrested and punished? If I am, then I am putting you both at risk for aiding me.'

'I never heard such nonsense,' Aunt Harriet said, as Johnson, the first footman, came to announce Captain Drymore was at the door.

'Show him in,' her aunt said, then to Amy, 'We shall see what he has to say about your dreams.'

James entered the room and bowed to them. 'Good morning, ladies,' he greeted them, looking from one to the other. Harriet was tight-lipped, Matilda was bright-eyed, but poor Amy looked as troubled as she had when he first met her. 'What is amiss? Have you seen those two men again?'

'No,' Harriet said. 'Our niece has had a disturbed night.'

'Oh.' He turned towards Amy, one eyebrow raised in enquiry.

'It was only a bad dream,' she said. 'Do sit down, Captain. We are forgetting our manners.'

He sat on a chair facing Amy. 'Does that mean you have remembered something?'

'I do not know. If it was a memory, it was so dreadful, it is no wonder I wished to forget it.'

'Memory, pah!' Harriet said. 'Cheese before bed, more like. Amy has a foolish notion she has done something wicked and is going to be punished for it.'

'Tell me about it,' he prompted Amy gently. 'But only if you can bear to repeat it.'

She went over it again and with each telling it seemed to lose some of its terrors, especially now he had come. 'Tell me it wasn't real,' she finished. 'Tell me I did not use that knife. Tell me I am not wicked.'

'I am sure you are not,' he said. If that were the case, she would never have implicated herself by telling him of her dream and putting the idea of a stabbing into his head. 'You did not dream you actually *used* the knife, did you?'

'No…' It was said hesitantly.

'There you are, then.'

'I always did say my niece had too much imagination,' Harriet said. 'And that proves it. What have you been reading, child?'

'Nothing, except some of the papers in the cupboard in the book room. There were documents about the house being sequestered by Cromwell's Parliament and being returned when Charles regained the throne,' Amy went on.

'That happened a hundred years ago. They would surely not have given you bad dreams,' Harriet commented.

'We did touch on the Jacobite rebellion and the possibility of Prince Charles invading again.'

'We?' Harriet enquired with a raised eyebrow.

'Yes, the Captain was with me. It was while you were sleeping yesterday afternoon.' She paused. 'Perhaps I should not have gone to the cupboard.'

'There is nothing there that is not already known. We have nothing to hide.'

'I wonder if we ought to meddle with Mrs Macdonald's memory,' James murmured. 'Perhaps it were better to let sleeping dogs lie.'

All that did was to convince Amy that he knew more than he was saying and it was not good. Oh, when would this torment end? And what was Captain James Drymore really doing in Highbeck? And those two men she had seen, who were they? Everything was closing in on her. She felt unable to breathe. Standing up suddenly, she said, 'I must go out in the air.'

They watched her run from the room. 'Go after her, Captain,' Matilda said. 'She needs reassurance. I will stake my life she has done nothing wrong and you must convince her of it.'

He caught up with her as she crossed the draw-bridge. 'Amy, where are you off to?'

She spun round to face him. 'I do not know. To Widow Twitch. Yes, that is it, to see the wise woman.'

'No.' He grabbed her arm. 'She will fill your head with more nonsense and I do believe your dream was nothing more than a mix of several unrelated matters. The two men who frightened you, Mrs Twitch putting ideas into your head, our talk of sieges and Jacobites, even the big cloud you drew.' He smiled. 'Put it all in a pot and give it a good stir and what do you have but a disjointed dream?'

'Oh, I wish that were so,' Amy cried.

'Of course it is so. Now, my dear lady, you are to put it from your mind and come with me to help me decide where to put my pictures. And we shall leave space for the drawing you did of me. If you would be so kind as to allow me to have it, I shall have it suitably mounted.'

'It is not good enough to be hung.' He had diverted her thoughts and made her relax and she smiled a little tremulously, but it was a smile.

'Oh, it most certainly is. But I want the cloud with the cherub put in first. Now, will you come?'

'Gladly.'

He offered her his arm and she took it and they walked side by side over the drawbridge towards the copse of trees. 'I need my little homemaker,' he said quietly. 'Without her, the Lodge is nothing but a place to stay.'

'You are very good to me,' she said, wondering why he had suddenly said that. To make her feel better, she supposed, and he had succeeded in that. 'When I feel only half a person, you make me feel whole again.'

'Then I am glad.'

'But you must not let my problems divert you from your own business.'

He felt a sharp pang of guilt about not finding his wife's killers and that was unfinished business he must attend to. Once nothing would have deflected him from seeking retribution, but just lately that fury had abated somewhat—because of Amy? 'I have deferred that for a time. I will go back to it when the time is right.'

'Would you like to tell me about it?'

He put his hand over hers on his sleeve. 'One day I will. But now I have some pictures that need hanging.' He took her hand and tucked it under his arm and thus they arrived at the Lodge. Her nightmare was forgotten. Almost. It was an idyll he knew could not last. One day she would remember everything and he was afraid it would bring her more distress.

Chapter Five

'Miss Hardwick, there is a Mr Gotobed at the door,' the footman said. The three ladies were in the withdrawing room, the aunts were discussing a letter they had had from their lawyer and Amy was putting the cherub into the cloud on her sketch before giving it to Captain Drymore.

'What manner of man is he?' Harriet asked.

'A gentleman by the looks and sound of him, madam. Brown silk coat with pearl buttons, close-fitting breeches with ribbons at the knees, and shoes with silver buckles and red heels. He's wearing a full toupee with end curls and a prodigious amount of jewellery, though I can't say that it's real.' All three ladies smiled at this; Johnson prided himself on his powers of observation.

'Did he state his business?'

'Not to me, madam, but he did say he comes recommended.'

'Then you had better show him in. And stay within call, in case we should need to order refreshments.'

The aunts put aside their correspondence, smoothed down their skirts and straightened their wigs, by which time the footman announced, 'Mr Martin Gotobed.'

The gentleman strode into the room, swept his three-cornered hat under his left arm, and executed an elegant leg. 'Ladies, your obedient.'

'What can we do for you, sir?' Harriet asked.

'I am on a tour of the area and I have heard that Blackfen Manor is an exceptional example of a Tudor manor house and hoped that you will do me the honour of showing it to me. I hope I do not disturb you.'

'You do not disturb us, sir, but from whom did you hear about the Manor?' Harriet enquired.

'Why, from Mr Duncan Macdonald.'

'What did you say?' Amy cried, in her agitation dropping her crayon on the floor, where it rolled at his feet. He picked it up and presented it back to her with a bow. 'You have spoken to him?'

'Indeed, yes, we are well acquainted with each other.'

'When did you speak to him? Where is he? Is he coming here?' The questions tumbled from her.

'As to the last, I do not know, madam, nor as to his present whereabouts. I spoke to him, let me see, when was it?' He appeared to be teasing her and she did not like that. 'I do believe it was three months past. It could have been a little longer or perhaps not quite as long. I imperfectly recall the exact date.'

'Was he well? What did he say to you? Did he mention me? I am his wife,' Amy said.

'I had deduced that, madam, from his description of you. He said I might find you here and to convey his everlasting devotion.'

'Why does he not come himself? Is he ill?' Amy asked worriedly.

'He has not been enjoying the best of health,' the man murmured.

'What is the matter with him?'

'Why, madam, I thought you knew.' Mr Gotobed raised an eyebrow.

'No. I…' She hesitated. She was not sure of this man at all and was unwilling to tell him of her own troubles, but she needed to know what had happened to Duncan.

'Our niece has not been well herself,' Aunt Harriet put in. 'She is staying with us while she makes a full recovery. If you know anything about Mr Macdonald, then pray tell us quickly.'

'He and I were together in the infirmary. He had sustained a knife wound.'

Amy gave a little cry of distress and fainted, falling sideways off her chair on to the floor, scattering crayons and sketch book. In the pandemonium that followed Gotobed hurriedly bowed his way out and said he would return at a more convenient time to enquire as to the lady's recovery. The aunts ignored him, being more concerned with bending over Amy, flapping their fans over her face and begging her to wake up.

He had no sooner gone from the room than James arrived. The front door was open and there was no footman in attendance. He could hear little cries of distress coming from the drawing room and hurried there, not waiting to be announced.

He found Amy prostrate on the floor, the aunts kneeling beside her, heads down, wide skirts billowing about them, so they looked like slumbering swans. Susan hovered uncertainly. He rushed over to join them. 'What has happened?'

'She swooned clean away when that man said he had spoken to Duncan. She ought to be put to bed and the physician called, but we cannot lift her.' She looked up and noticed Susan. 'Go and fetch Johnson and one of the other men—'

'No need for that,' James said, stooping to pick Amy up in his arms, which he did effortlessly. 'I will take her.'

They were too distressed to protest and followed him as he carried his burden upstairs and gently laid her on her bed, with her aunts and Susan bringing up the rear. By this time she was stirring and a low moan escaped her lips.

'Lie still,' he said, watching a little colour come back to her paper-white face. 'You have had a shock.'

'That man…'

'He has gone,' Harriet said, as Susan went to the washstand to wring a cloth out in cold water.

'Gone! Oh, no!' Amy tried to scramble up, but a hand from James gently pushed her down again. 'But I have to talk to him, I have to find out…' Did she really want to know that she had stabbed her husband? The knife in her dream: she had used that, hadn't she? Why? Why? Why? How badly was he hurt? Who had taken him to the infirmary? Which infirmary? Was he still there or had he been discharged? No wonder he did not want to come to see her, if she had done that to him. Yet, according to their visitor, he had sent his everlasting devotion to her. And who exactly was Mr Gotobed? A thieftaker sent to bring her to justice? She could not stop shaking.

'If I had known what he would say, I would never have received him,' Aunt Harriet said. 'I cannot have people coming here without a by your leave and frightening you like that.'

'Who was he?' James asked.

'He gave his name as Mr Martin Gotobed,' Matilda said from the other side of the bed, where she had pulled up a stool and was sitting holding Amy's hand. 'He said he was on a tour of the area and wanted to look round the Manor. We did not think anything of it. People are always calling and asking to be shown round. But when he said he had been recommended by Duncan, of course it upset poor dear Amy.'

'I can imagine.' He was looking down at Amy. She was shaking and clearly terrified. 'Did you know the gentleman?'

'I do not think so… I cannot know, can I? He gave no indication he knew me except from my description, which he said came from my husband.'

'I don't believe a word of it,' Harriet said. 'Now, Susan will fetch you one of Cook's remedies and you must rest.'

'How can I rest? My head is buzzing with questions. It is why I must talk to Mr Gotobed…'

'With your permission, I will speak to him on your behalf,' James said.

'And will you tell me truthfully what he says, however bad it is?'

'Madam, I would not lie,' he said coolly. He was not angry with her so much as with the fop who had thrown her into such confusion.

'I beg your pardon,' she said. 'I am not myself.'

'The medicine will help,' Harriet soothed her niece. 'Come, Captain, we will leave Amy with my sister and you and I will repair to the drawing room.'

James followed her downstairs, though he would far rather have stayed and talked to Amy. There was something else in those expressive eyes besides shock at meeting someone who knew her absent husband. She seemed to be shrinking inside herself, just as she had been on the journey from London in the coach. Had the shock finally brought back her memory?

In the drawing room Miss Hardwick offered him a glass of port, which he accepted, not because he particularly needed a drink but because he could see she was nervous and steeling herself to say something to him.

'I met a foppish man crossing the drawbridge as I came here,' James said, watching her pouring the wine with hands that shook. 'That, I assume, was Mr Gotobed?'

'Yes.'

'Tell me what he said to upset Mrs Macdonald.'

After handing him his glass of wine, Harriet repeated word for word what had been said. 'Amy fainted when he said Duncan had sustained a knife wound. Not to be wondered at, is it? Not after that dreadful nightmare she had. She was already half-convinced she had used that knife and when someone arrived who appeared to confirm it…' She shrugged. 'Is it any wonder the poor child swooned?'

He was thoughtful. How much of Amy's nightmare had been the result of a returning memory? How much sheer fantasy? She had been in a state of fear when he first met her and she sometimes jumped at her own shadow. She was certainly afraid of being followed. The state of her house in London bore witness to violence of some kind. Could she, *in extremis*, have mortally wounded her husband? 'No, it is not to be wondered at,' he agreed. 'But do you think she could have used a knife if she had been sufficiently provoked? If she were threatened and desperate—'

'Captain, how could you?' She was clearly outraged and he did not blame her; she adored Amy and would believe no ill of her. 'Surely you have come to know our niece well enough to know she could never do anything so wicked?'

'I beg your pardon. I was simply acting devil's advocate, you understand,' he said in an attempt to pacify her.

'Perhaps you would do better to practise your advocacy on Mr Gotobed, Captain. I believe he is staying at the King's Arms. He said he would call again when Amy recovered, but I shall refuse him admittance. She has been so much better in the last few weeks, I will not have her set back again, not for anything.'

'I will most certainly do that and with your permission will call again tomorrow.' He put down his glass of port, which he had hardly touched, bowed and turned to leave.

'Captain, you have become a staunch supporter of this family,' she said, her voice stopping him as he reached the door. 'But I beg to remind you that you have been employed by Lord Trentham to find Duncan Macdonald. I was not particularly anxious to have him found before, but now I have changed my mind. We must discover the truth as soon as possible. I do not trust Mr Martin Gotobed at all.'

Although he did not consider himself employed, having refused a fee from his lordship, he nodded in acquiescence and left the room. Miss Hardwick had reminded him of his duty. He was not there to amuse himself with a lovely young lady, take her shopping and picnicking, but to unravel a mystery.

And his mystery lady was even more of a mystery than he had supposed.

He returned to the Lodge, musing as he went. He was almost certain that Amy was too lovely, too gentle and considerate of others' feelings to ever harm a living soul, let alone another human being. Look how she had been glad he had not shot the ducks and the compassion she had shown towards poor Joe Potton. Could anyone like that launch a vicious attack on her own husband? Even if she had been provoked beyond endurance, could she have done that? No, he decided, and he would do well to prove it and set her mind at rest.

Which was most important, to help Amy regain her memory or find out what had happened to her husband? Surely one would lead to the other? He wished Sam would come back; he might have news, but he had not heard from his servant since the arrival of the wagon with his belongings, which told him he had executed the first of his errands. But what of the rest? Sam was no scholar and writing letters would not come easy to him, and he would not ask anyone to pen one for him if there was something he did not want anyone else to know.

After sitting over a lonely dinner, instead of dining at the Manor, which he had been doing more and more frequently, he set out to join the carousers at the local hostelry. The newcomer would easily have been recognised for his extravagant clothes and affected manner, even if James had not come across him earlier in the day. He was surrounded by the men from the village enjoying a sup after a hard day's work and the peacock was a source of amusement. James, surveying the scene from across the room, was sure the man was plying them with drink in order to loosen their tongues. He smiled to himself; Gotobed was not from this part of the country or he would know its dour inhabitants were the world's best at keeping their tongues between their teeth.

He strolled over to them and because some of the local men had come to know him in the time he had been in Highbeck, they greeted him and asked him to join them. 'This here's Mr Martin Gotobed, Cap'n,' Dusty Green, the miller, said. 'He's lately down from London.'

James gave Gotobed a perfunctory bow. 'Captain James Drymore, at your service.'

Gotobed beckoned the innkeeper to bring more ale. 'Take a drink with me, Captain.'

'Thank you.'

'Where are you from, Captain?' Gotobed asked him, as the men moved up a little to allow him to take a seat between them.

'I am a man of the world,' James said with a smile. 'I travel.'

'Ahh, but you must have had a beginning somewhere?'

'My life began in Hertfordshire,' he said. 'My green years were spent there. Does that answer your question?'

'Yes, indeed.'

'And where did you have your beginning, sir?' James countered.

'In a house on Piccadilly. I, too, have travelled, but there is nothing like England's rich and verdant landscape and the convivial company of one's compatriots to encourage a man to settle down.'

They were sparring with each other, James realised, each curious about the business of the other, but two could play at that game. 'Are you of a mind to settle down?'

'I am looking for a house hereabouts,' Gotobed confirmed.

'Why here?'

'Why not? It is as good a place as any, better than most, for the inhabitants are most welcoming.' He smiled at the other men who were drinking in the conversation along with their ale.

'The Cap'n hev moved into the Lodge,' George Merryweather told Gotobed. George was the blacksmith, a huge man with bulging muscles, a good man to have on one's side in a scrap.

'The lodge?' One eyebrow was raised in enquiry towards James.

'Yes, the Lodge on the Manor estate.'

'Ah, I collect seeing you as I was leaving the Manor this afternoon.'

'Yes.' Now they were closing in on the crux of James's concern. 'I fear you left the ladies in disarray.'

'Not intended, sir, not intended. I thought felici-tations from her husband would please Mrs Macdonald.'

'When and where did you meet him?'

Gotobed looked sharply at him, making James wonder if he had been a little too direct and that was borne out when the man said, 'And what is your interest in the affair, sir?'

'I am a friend of the family and charged with looking out for the ladies, particularly Mrs Macdonald.'

'Aah.' There was a deal of insinuation in that short exclamation.

James ignored it. 'Where is her husband?'

Gotobed shrugged. 'Under the cold earth by now, I shouldn't wonder.'

'Dead?' His heart missed a beat and then settled

again sufficiently for him to go on listening, but his head was buzzing. Could it be true? And what did it signify? To his shame and consternation his first reaction was relief that Amy was free of the encumbrance of a husband whom he had never met, but had no high opinion of, but that was followed by another thought. If the man had died of his injuries, who had inflicted them?

'He was mortally wounded,' Gotobed revealed.

'By whom?' James asked.

Again a shrug. 'Who knows? He did not say.'

'But he did name his wife to you.'

'Yes. Lying side by side in an infirmary with nothing to occupy us, it is not surprising we exchanged confidences, is it?'

'But not enough for him to tell you who had wounded him.'

'I did not press him.'

'But he did send his devotion to his wife.'

Gotobed laughed. 'No, but I thought it would please her.'

James's spirits sank. The more the man said, the more worried he became. Macdonald had evidently said enough for the man to locate Amy but why would he want to? What else had Macdonald told him? Was Gotobed a real stranger to Amy, or had she met him before and forgotten it?

James finished his ale, said goodnight to the company and walked back to the Lodge, with a full moon lighting his way. He had discovered nothing about what had happened to Amy before she boarded that coach. What he *had* learned was that for some reason as yet unknown it was important for Gotobed to get close to her. And not only Gotobed—there were those two who had been stalking her. James had not seen them, but it did not mean they did not exist. Nor could he be sure her husband was dead as Gotobed had claimed. If Sam did not come back soon, he would have to go to London and find out for himself.

He returned to the Manor next morning, far earlier than would be deemed correct for a social call, but he reminded himself, with a wry smile, of Miss Hardwick's stricture that he was being employed to do a job and if he adhered to that premise it did not matter what time he called.

He was admitted by Johnson and immediately conducted to the small parlour at the back of the house where Amy was sitting alone. She had her sketch book on her knee and a charcoal crayon in her hand, but did not appear to be using it. Did not appear to hear his entrance either, for she jumped when he gave a discreet cough. 'Oh, Captain, you startled me.'

'I beg your pardon.' He bowed. 'If you do not wish to be disturbed, I will go away again.'

'I am thoroughly disturbed already, Captain. You do not make it worse. Please be seated.'

'I understand.' He found a chair and brought it up close to hers and sat down. 'You are finishing my picture, I see.'

'Yes, but I wonder that you still want it, after what happened yesterday.'

'What has yesterday to do with that?' He nodded towards the picture. The cherub, round faced, smiling as he had done when given the sixpence, was the image of Joe Potton. The wings that sprouted from his shoulders blended into the cloud that surrounded it.

'Oh, everything, I should think. One malicious cloud and one benign, watching over what we do. I think the malicious one is in the ascendancy.'

'Surely not?' James said gently.

'I had such a shock yesterday…' She trailed off a little tremulously.

'I know. Has it helped you to remember?'

'No. But I cannot think otherwise than my night-mare was memory, brought to me in my sleep. Mr Gotobed as good as confirmed it.'

'But you cannot be sure, can you?'

She smiled, though it was a little wan. 'Bless you,

Captain, for wanting to believe the best of me, as my aunts do, but we cannot escape from the truth that I may have—no, almost certainly did—take a knife to my husband. I keep asking myself why, what made me do it? And how badly was he hurt? Mr Gotobed did not say.'

'I should not believe everything he says, you know.'

'Have you spoken to him? What did he say?' she asked eagerly.

He hesitated. 'I am persuaded he did not know your husband well, they were simply side by side in the infirmary and talked for want of something better to do. As to why he is in Highbeck now, I have yet to discover.'

'You would do better to wash your hands of me, Captain, and go back to the business that brought you to Highbeck,' she said with a sudden flash of spirit.

She *was* the business that had brought him to Highbeck. He had been commissioned by Lord Trentham to find out what he could, but that was not the only reason he stayed. It was Amy herself. Not since his wife's untimely death had he felt so at peace with himself and he had been thinking that Amy and the tranquillity of the countryside were weaving some kind of magic. He supposed it was because of that he had never told her what had brought him to Blackfen Manor in the first place.

She would not have been so easy with him, so confiding, such a delightful companion if she had known his real errand was to uncover the mystery of her forgetfulness. Mr Martin Gotobed had brought it back to him with a vengeance.

'I perceive from your silence that you agree,' she said, manfully holding back tears. If he could believe her guilty, then what hope had she?

'Not at all. I was simply trying to make sense of everything.'

'And have you succeeded?'

'No. There are too many unanswered questions.'

'Do you know what I think? I think Mr Gotobed is a thieftaker come to take me to a justice. When he calls again, I shall surrender myself to him.'

'You will do no such thing!' He had raised his voice, making her start back in surprise. He moderated his tone. 'God knows there is a mystery here, but it does not call for such drastic measures. He does not look like a man from the judiciary to me.'

'What do they look like? I cannot believe they are all rough looking. Sometimes they must be able to pass themselves off as gentlemen in order to do their work.' She gave a little laugh, though there was no humour in it. 'Why, you might be one yourself.'

This was too close for comfort. 'Do you really believe that?' he asked with a frown.

'No, of course I do not. Are you not known to Lord Trentham, who is an old friend of the family? Besides, would you have spent weeks in Highbeck, when you could just as easily have arrested me the first day you arrived?'

'Thank you for that,' he said drily.

'It does not change anything. I must talk to Mr Gotobed. He is my only link with my husband. He has spoken to Duncan since I last saw him and I must know more, even if it means I learn something not to my credit and am arrested.'

'Amy, will you cease this talk of being arrested! There is no proof, no evidence at all, that you have done anything wrong.' He could not let Amy put herself in jeopardy by letting Gotobed see how vulnerable she was. And perhaps if James pressed him a little harder, he might be more forthcoming.

'No, you must not do anything so foolish,' he reiterated, then rose to take his leave, just as Aunt Matilda came into the room.

'Captain, I did not know you had arrived. How do you find our Amy?'

'Much recovered, but still not quite herself.'

'I do not know who myself is,' she cried. 'Nor what manner of person I am.'

'Ah, but we do, we know you very well,' her aunt said. 'You are goodness itself, a lovely, talented, caring person who would not harm a fly. Is that not so, Captain?'

'It is indeed,' he said, bowing, then turned to Amy. 'If it is not too much for you, perhaps you will go riding with me tomorrow, Mrs Macdonald.'

'The air and exercise will do you good,' Matilda said, when she hesitated. 'Sitting at home brooding will only make you feel worse.'

Amy forced the semblance of a smile to her face. Everyone was so kind to her and perhaps a ride, especially with the Captain, would invigorate her and calm her at the same time. 'Very well. I shall be pleased to ride with you, Captain. Will eleven o'clock be convenient?'

'Perfectly convenient.'

She pulled the drawing from her sketch book and offered it to him. 'Do you still want this?'

'Indeed I do.' He took it and bowed his way out.

'We are so lucky to have him to look after us,' Aunt Matilda said after he had gone. 'He has proved himself to be a very worthy friend. Do you not agree, Amy?'

'Yes,' she said, wishing she had not accused him of being a thieftaker. She had said it without thinking, but it had angered him. It was all because of Mr Martin Gotobed. She had almost given up expecting to remember what had happened before she came back to Highbeck, had simply been enjoying the company of the Captain, conveniently forgetting that she was married and should not be doing so. Then she had had that frightening dream, which had put doubts into her head, and hard on the heels of that came Mr Gotobed with his revelations. She had been living in a fool's paradise, condoned—no encouraged—by her aunts and it was time she woke up to the truth.

Next morning, she packed a basket with food left over from the previous night's meal and set off to visit the poor in the village, as she often did, forgetting she was supposed to have an escort when she went out. She felt more than usually nervous and it was the presence of those two rough men and Mr Gotobed in the village that was to blame. If she saw any of them again, she would not run or faint, she would confront them and demand to know what they wanted of her. She was unsure whether to be glad or sorry when she completed her errand without meeting them.

Perhaps the Captain had discovered something. It was strange how she had come to rely on him so heavily. It was as if she had always known him, that he had always been in her life, protecting her, even though she had been assured that was not so. She looked forward to his visits, the little outings they had. He helped her to forget that she was trying to remember. Until someone like Mr Gotobed came along and upset everything, reminding her she had a husband and should not be spending so much time in the Captain's company. She did not *feel* married. It was one more wickedness to add to what she believed she had already done and must never be spoken of aloud. She was turning into the drive of the Manor on the way home, when she found herself face to face with Martin Gotobed.

He was as flamboyantly dressed as he had been the day before, though today he was in pink-and-yellow stripes. He swept her a bow. 'Mrs Macdonald, your obedient.'

Was such a greeting normal for a thieftaker about to arrest a suspect, she wondered, or was he trying to put her at her ease in order to wrest a confession from her? Her heart began to beat faster. 'Mr Gotobed, how do you do? Were you about to visit us and tell us more about my husband?'

'No, for I know no more. I was coming to warn you…'

She gasped. 'Warn me?'

'Yes. It pains me to say this, but Captain Drymore is not the friend you think he is.'

This was the last thing she had expected to hear.

'Mr Gotobed, it is not courteous in you to speak of a gentleman behind his back in that fashion.'

'I would say it to his face if he were here. Indeed, I had hoped he might be, then you might see for yourself how he received the news that I am on to him.'

'On to him? Mr Gotobed, you are talking in riddles. Pray, explain yourself.'

'That is my intention.' He bowed again before going on. 'Captain James Drymore has been paid by the judiciary to find and arrest your husband. I have it on the best authority.'

'He's a thieftaker?' she whispered, trying not to let him see she was shaking with emotion at hearing this.

'Nothing so straightforward. He is an undercover agent, a man who does his work in secret, worming his way into people's lives to be made free with their confidences, in order to find his evidence. And if he does not find it, he is not above fabricating it and taking up an innocent man and hauling him before a magistrate in order to claim a reward.'

'That is nonsense. I do not believe you,' she said shakily.

'Your disbelief is natural, but it only shows how clever he is.'

'And what is my husband supposed to have done?'

'Ask the Captain.'

'Mr Gotobed, I am afraid I do not have time to stand and listen to this. I am engaged to go out and am in some haste.' She made herself sound as haughty as she could.

'Very well, I will leave you, but you will discover I am right and when that happens I beg you to remember I came in friendship and would help you if I could.' And on that enigmatic note, he turned on his heel.

It was only after he had gone, bowing and smiling his oily smile, that she realised she had not asked him why he thought the Captain was intent on arresting her husband and not *her*. And that was because what he had told her had driven every other thought out of her head. Captain James Drymore, son of an earl, a thieftaker? It beggared belief. The truth was she did not want to believe it. But supposing, just supposing, it were true? How did she know he was who he said he was? He had come to Highbeck armed with a letter from Lord Trentham, but that could have been a forgery. And there was that incident in Ely. Without a moment's hesitation, he had grabbed that boy when others might have stood aside and let him make his escape, and would have handed him over to the judiciary if she had not intervened. Then he had complained she was making him soft, as if that were something of which to be ashamed. Thieftaker or no?

It was not only her memory she had lost, it was her ability to tell truth from fiction, good from evil. Everyone was suspect in her eyes. From the Captain down to two men poaching, from Mr Gotobed to Widow Twitch. She ran up the drive, into the house and up to her bedchamber where she shut herself in.

She was sitting on her bed, staring into the distance while her thoughts tumbled about like autumn leaves, when Susan knocked at the door and came into the room. 'The Captain has arrived.' She stopped suddenly. 'La! Miss Amy, you look as if you had seen a ghost. Are you unwell?'

'No…yes…' She felt sick and so confused she could not face the Captain, much less go riding with him. 'I do feel a little faint. I beg you to tell him I have the headache.'

'Very well. Then I will bring you a tisane and you must rest. You have had a prodigious shock to the system, so a megrim is not to be wondered at.' She bustled out again, leaving Amy once again alone with her thoughts.

James received the message with dismay, not so much that they could not go riding together, though he had been looking forward to it, but that the shock she had received the day before must have been more severe than at first thought. It was all the fault of that macaroni, Gotobed, and he could cheerfully have strangled him. Another evening in the man's company had elicited no more information about Macdonald and how he came to be stabbed, even though he threatened him with the law. The man had laughed at that and only confirmed James in his belief that Gotobed was a muckworm.

'Please tell your mistress that I am sorry she is unwell and will call again to see how she does,' he said, and took his leave.

He paused in the courtyard to set his hat on his head before mounting and in so doing glanced upwards at what he knew to be Amy's bedchamber window. A shadow moved past it and then was gone. He was certain it was Amy and she had been watching him.

How genuine was her headache? How genuine was her loss of memory? Some things she found easy to recall—why not others? Was she afraid of his questions and therefore deliberately avoiding him? Did that mean she was recovering her memory and did not want him to know? Did she truly believe she was guilty? Did he believe she was? No, he told himself firmly, he believed she was perfectly genuine, but that did not alter the fact that Duncan Macdonald was mixed up in something sordid and it was high time he found out what it was. And that meant London.

He returned to the Lodge to find Sam sitting at the kitchen table wolfing down a meat pie Mrs Landis had given him. As soon as he saw James, he crammed the last of it into his mouth and stood up.

'So, you're back,' James said, stating the obvious. It was not a rapturous welcome, but Sam knew him well enough to know he was glad to see him.

Sam swallowed hard. 'Yes, Captain, arrived not half an hour since. Came in all haste, did not stop to eat.'

'Have you eaten enough now?'

'Yes, Captain, sir.'

'Good. Go and change out of those travelling clothes and come to me in the drawing room. I would know what you have discovered. Mrs Landis will show you to the room we have made ready for you.'

'Yes, sir.' He disappeared behind the housekeeper and James went to the drawing room to wait for him as patiently as he could. If Sam had done his work well, some of the questions that plagued him might be answered. He paced the room. If the news was bad, if Amy really had attacked her husband, severely enough to put him in hospital, or even kill him, what would he do? His duty was clear, but something stood in the way of it, something he had not bargained for when he agreed to take the commission, and that was his high regard for Amy and the two old ladies.

He was on his fourth perambulation of the room when Sam reappeared, dressed in a plain brown suit of clothes and a clean shirt. He had evidently dressed in a great hurry, for his wig was awry and his neckcloth only half-tied. James turned towards him. 'Well?'

'Mrs Landis said your belongings had arrived safely—'

'Never mind them. What did you learn about Duncan Macdonald?'

'He's dead.'

'*Dead!* Are you sure?'

'Certain sure. I saw where they buried him.'

So Gotobed was telling the truth! James sat down heavily on one of the new armchairs, indicating to Sam to sit in another. 'Go on.'

'You ain't goin' to like it.'

'For goodness' sake, man, get on with it.'

Sam looked sharply at him, surprised by his tone of voice. It was not like the Captain to snap. 'He died in prison.'

'Prison! Not a hospital?' James exclaimed.

'Well, you could call it that, it was the prison infirmary. Can't see that it matters where he drew his last breath, it's what happened afore what signifies.'

'So? What did happen before?'

'No one ain't exactly sure. A constable was tipped off that a murder was being done at the Macdonalds' house, but when he went there, he found Macdonald alone, lying on a bed, mortally wounded. The constable sent for a doctor who patched him up and pronounced him fit enough to be moved and he was took to Newgate on a cart.'

'Arrested?'

'Yes.'

'On what charge?'

'Theft and murder. Seems he were on the highpad lay. He and two accomplices held up a stage and shot one of the occupants.'

'Good God, a highwayman!' He was reminded of the two who had held up the coach on the way to Highbeck and was convinced they were the same two accomplices of Macdonald's. 'How did you discover all this?'

'Heard it being talked about in the kens where such as they congregate. That's what you wanted me to do, ain't it?'

'Yes.' The man probably would have been dead or dying even as they travelled to Highbeck in that coach. If Amy had known that, it was no wonder she was afraid. But had she? 'Was any mention made of Mrs Macdonald?'

'Not in my hearin'.'

James got up and went to the sideboard to pour them both a glass of ale from a jug. He put one down beside Sam and returned to his seat. It was done in an effort to assemble his thoughts, which had immediately gone to Amy and that coach ride. She had been in a pitiful state and the arrival of the two robbers had set her in such a quake only his arm about her had held her upright. He was prepared to wager they were the same two she had seen in Downham Market and skulking in the grounds of the Manor. How much did she remember? Her nightmares seemed to indicate she knew something. He had been in a quandary before Sam returned; he was in a worse one now.

'When did this happen?'

'Just over three months ago. He might have lived, but you know what a pestilential place Newgate is,' Sam went on. 'His wound went bad and he expired before he could be brought to trial.'

'Gotobed was right,' James murmured.

'What a strange name. Who is Gotobed?'

'A man who turned up at the Manor, full of himself, said he knew Macdonald, frightened Mrs Macdonald half to death. Later he told me the man was dead. I thought he was lying.' Had Amy been right in her conjecture Gotobed had come to arrest her?

'Does Mrs Macdonald know that?'

'No. At least, I do not think so.'

'You goin' to tell 'er?'

'Someone will have to.' He did not know how he was going to do it. If Macdonald was really a thief and murderer Amy was well rid of him, though she might not agree. She might not even believe him. Had she loved her husband, even though he was a criminal? Perhaps she did not know he was of that fraternity. 'I think I must talk to the aunts,' he said. 'What else did you discover?'

'Nothin' more, nor nothin' about Smith and Randle neither. Either they decided not to go back to London or their friends are keeping mum.'

'Ah, they evidently do not believe I have given up looking for them.'

'And have you?'

'Certainly not. I will deal with them in my own good time.' He was surprised at his reaction. Once he would have rushed from the room to saddle up his horse and go after them at full gallop, but nearly a month in Highbeck in the company of Amy had eased his suffering and though he still wanted to see the men punished, it was no longer the core of his existence. How that had come about without his being aware of it, he did not know. He supposed it was the slow pace of life in the countryside and the influence of Amy. She was free of her husband, but not of her fears. More than anything he wanted to allay them, to prove to her, once and for all, that she was innocent of any wrongdoing. It was time he returned to the capital.

Chapter Six

That night Amy had another nightmare. She was running down a road in her soft indoor shoes, fleeing from some unknown terror. Her heart was beating like a hammer and her breath was spent. She did not know how much longer she could keep running and then she stumbled and whoever or whatever it was behind her caught her up and grabbed her arms. She screamed.

It was the scream that woke her. She was tangled in the bedclothes. While she was endeavouring to extricate herself, sobbing all the while, Aunt Matilda rushed into the room in her nightrail and nightcap. 'Amy! Amy! What is the matter? What happened?'

'It was another dream,' she said, breathless and still tearful, though trying to hide it. 'I was running away.'

'What were you running from?'

'I don't know. All I saw was a dark shadow, like that cloud in my drawing. But it grabbed hold of me. I was so terrified I woke.'

'Oh, my dear, what do you think it meant?'

Aunt Harriet came in at that point, having stopped to put on a dressing robe, and sat on the bed opposite Matilda.

'I do not know. I wish I did. It was a street with uneven paving and buildings either side and a church in the distance. Yes, a large church with steps up to the door. It was dark, but there were people about. They did not come to my aid.'

'I wager it was Henrietta Street, near Covent Garden,' Harriet said. 'You lived there with Duncan.'

'That must surely mean my memory is returning.'

'Perhaps,' Harriet said.

'Then if this dream is a true memory, then so was the other. I did stab Duncan.'

'No, you did not, you could not. I will not hear of it,' Matilda said, much distressed. 'Harriet, tell her you will not countenance the idea that she could harm anyone, let alone her husband.'

'Even if you had wanted to, I doubt you would have had the strength,' Harriet told her practically. 'A strong man could easily overcome you.' She went to the window and drew back the curtains, flooding the room with daylight. 'Look, it is fully light now, so let us all dress and go down to breakfast. You will feel more cheerful after that and then we will think about what to do.'

The aunts left her and in a little while Susan came with hot water and helped her to wash and dress. She went downstairs to the breakfast room, but could not eat. The terror of her dream still haunted her and she could not shake it off.

'You must tell the Widow Twitch about your dream,' Matilda said, pushing a dish of hot chocolate towards her. 'She will know how to interpret it.'

'Nonsense!' Harriet put in briskly. 'It would be more to the point to tell the Captain. He will know how to go about finding the truth.'

'The Captain!' Amy cried in scorn. 'The Captain has deceived us all. He is a thieftaker and secret agent come to arrest me.'

Her aunt laughed. 'Yesterday you were convinced it was Mr Gotobed intent on taking you up, when truth be, neither is the case.'

'How can you be sure?'

'Mr Gotobed is nothing but a troublemaker and is probably after money, and Captain Drymore was sent to us by Lord Trentham to uncover the mystery of Duncan's disappearance and see if he could help you recover your memory.'

'He knew!' She was astounded. 'He knew all along about my loss of memory and Duncan being missing before he ever came to Highbeck?'

'Yes. Your mother asked Lord Trentham to find someone to help us.'

'Then why did he not say so? Why didn't you? Why the secrecy? I am out of all countenance with all of you.' She was angry, angry with James, angry with her aunts and angry with Mr Gotobed most of all for being right about the Captain and destroying her illusions. She jumped up and hurried from the room.

'Where are you going?' Matilda called after her.

'To have it out with him.'

She ran to the Lodge and now banged on the door, trying to control her temper, but it flared again when James himself opened it. 'Mrs Macdonald, I was on my way to enquire how you did.' His smile of welcome vanished when he saw the breathless and angry little termagant in front of him.

'I am no better for what I have just learned,' she said furiously. 'How could you? How could you deceive me so, when you knew how much I trusted you? But that is what you wanted, was it not, my trust, my…' She could not go on, unable to find the words for what she felt for him. Instead she pounded his chest with her fists, which had no more effect than a puff of wind on a rock.

He grabbed her wrists, assuming she had somehow found out about her husband's death, no doubt from Gotobed, for she had had no opportunity to speak to Sam and, in any case, he would not have said anything. It was not how he had wanted her to learn about it. 'Amy, please calm yourself and let us talk about it.'

She struggled to free herself. 'Don't you touch me, you…you viper!'

He could not help laughing, she was so furious and so very lovely, but that made matters a hundred times worse. She wanted to hit him, to lash out with fists and tongue, to hurt him, as she was hurting, to make him sorry he had ever come to Highbeck and humiliated her. It put her to the blush to think she had wanted his company, had felt able to lean on him when she was unhappy, had told him things she would never have told anyone else. The trouble was, it was disappointment with him that made her angry, disappointment that he was not the knight in shining armour she had wanted him to be, but a man on a mission and one he had been paid to do. 'Laugh if you must,' she flung at him, 'but I am not laughing.' No, she was crying, crying fit to break her heart.

If he had ever had any doubts about her, they vanished as he took her into his arms to comfort her. 'Hush, my dear,' he murmured. 'I will not laugh again. It was very remiss of me. But you know, you are such a spitfire when you are angry.'

She hated herself for the way she relaxed against him, putting her head on to his shoulder, feeling the strength in his arms, just as if she had not been berating him like a fishwife moments before. They stood, so close their bodies seemed to meld into each other, each curve of hers fitting into a curve of his. They stood like that for several seconds until her tears stopped.

'Better now?' he asked, leaning back from her and lifting her chin with one finger to study her tear-wet face.

She nodded in a kind of trance, unable to maintain her wrath while he was being so careful of her. He took her hand and led her into the drawing room where he drew her down beside him on the sofa, as he had done once before. 'Now, tell me what it is I have done to deserve such a scold.'

Her tears had stopped but, realising she had not solved anything by being a watering pot and allowing him to trade on her weakness, her anger returned and she pulled herself away from him. 'You will not twist me round your thumb ever again,

Captain James Drymore. I know you for what you are.'

'And what is that?' he asked, his voice calmer than he felt.

'A thieftaker. A secret agent, a destroyer of lives…'

'Harsh words, lady, harsh words from someone as gentle as you purport to be.'

'But can you deny they are true?' she demanded.

'I can and I do. I must know from whom you heard such a thing.'

'Mr Gotobed,' she said.

'He is a scurrilous knave. You would believe him before me?' His anger almost matched hers now, but he had long ago learned to control all outward signs of his feelings. Becoming heated did no good at all. Besides, his anger ought to be directed at Gotobed, not her.

'I might not have done, but my aunts confirmed it. I was never so mistaken in a man…' She gave a strangled laugh. 'What a jest that is! How do I know I have not been mistaken before? I cannot remember.'

He smiled over her head. Poor dear, no wonder she was confused. 'What exactly did the Misses Hardwick confirm?'

'That Lord Trentham sent you to Highbeck to uncover the mystery of Duncan's disappearance and to help me recover my memory. You were not here on business. You lied—' She stopped suddenly. 'Oh, but I suppose worming your way into my confidence *was* your business.'

'I do not deny why I came, but I came as a friend to help you, not to arrest you, and I do not accept the term thieftaker.'

'But you *do* arrest people?' She was calmer now, but not yet ready to admit she had been unreasonable.

'I have no power to do that. If I see wrong being done, then I alert the proper authorities and they make an arrest.'

'For a reward?'

'Certainly not for a reward,' he snapped. 'I have no need of blood money.'

'And are you going to turn me in?'

'What for?'

'For stabbing my husband.'

'So, you remember doing that, do you?' he asked mildly.

'Not exactly, but why else would I be tormented by nightmares?'

'Amy Macdonald, you are trying my patience,' he said, taking her by the shoulders, but instead of shaking her as he was about to do, he stopped and looked down at her, feeling an overwhelming temptation to kiss her, to put his lips to hers and taste the sweetness of them. He came to his senses almost immediately and dropped his hands. How could he so far forget himself as to think of such a thing?

She wanted to maintain her anger, she really did, but she had seen how he looked at her. His words were angry, but his expression was not. For a single heartbeat she had thought he was going to kiss her. And for another beat, she knew that she would have welcomed it. How foolish she was! Why was she so weak where he was concerned? She stood up suddenly because her thoughts were taking her along forbidden tracks and letting them have their way would damn her for ever. 'I am going home.'

He stood beside her. 'Then I shall escort you.' He intended to speak to the aunts while he was at the Manor, to tell them that Duncan Macdonald was indeed dead and ask if she should be told and by whom.

'Why? Are you afraid your captive will elude you?' Oh, why was she baiting him like that? It would serve her right if he turned his back on her and her problems. And who would help her then?

She was not the captive, he decided, he was, caught in chains he could never have foreseen. 'Not at all, but I have undertaken to see you safe when you are out and about and that is what I intend to do.' His voice was clipped with the effort of keeping himself under control.

They walked in silence. It was the first time they had quarrelled and Amy could not understand why it made her feel so miserable. It had soured what had earlier been an easy rapport and she blamed herself. She wanted desperately to believe he was still the man who had become her friend—more than her friend, her rock. If only he had denied everything!

His reflections were equally remorseful. It pained him to think he had so nearly fallen victim to temptation. Acknowledging that made him feel guilty not only on behalf of his dead Caroline, whom he had vowed to avenge, but also because kissing a respectable woman was not the behaviour of a gentleman, especially when done in anger and frustration. Even though he had not done it, the wish had been there.

As they crossed the drawbridge they saw a carriage standing at the door, its four horses being looked after by a coachman and a postilion. Amy had come to dread callers, especially of late, and, in spite of her estrangement from James, was glad of his presence as they made their way towards the drawing room.

They found her aunts in conversation with their

cousin Gerald, or rather he was holding forth while they listened, sitting upright in their chairs, their expressions immutable. James, who had not met the gentleman before, was introduced and made the man a bow of acknowledgement. This was received with a perfunctory nod before the man turned back to the aunts and continued his tirade. James, thwarted in his purpose of speaking to the aunts about Sam's revelations, would have taken his leave, but was beckoned to remain by Harriet.

He found the man's attitude to his relations boorish. He was a very fat man in a dark Ramillies wig with the queue tied up with a wide black ribbon. He wore a long black silk coat, the buttons of which could never be fastened over his bulging stomach. His long waistcoat was decorated with swirls of embroidery. Ruffles of lace cascaded from neck and wrist. He flung his arms about and paced the room as he talked.

'Whoever heard of a gaggle of women managing an estate as exalted as this?' he demanded. 'You will ruin it. It needs a man to see to it properly. I cannot think what my uncle was thinking of—'

'So you have said before,' Harriet interrupted him. 'I beg you not to repeat yourself.'

'I would not need to if you would listen and take heed. Accept defeat and move to the Lodge, which is why it is there, for widows and unmarried ladies to enjoy a peaceful existence without the worries of a great house. You cannot like the duties of estate management, even supposing you had any idea how to go about them.'

'We have been managing perfectly well ever since Papa's death,' Matilda told him. 'And the Manor is our home, left to us unentailed.'

'I am persuaded it was entailed and your father ignored the stricture, which is illegal and by that token I am, as the direct male descendant of our grandfather, the legitimate heir. And you have no one to leave it to, whereas I have sons—'

'We have Amy,' Harriet contradicted him sharply.

'Bah! Another female!' He turned towards Amy, who had been standing close to James, listening to this exchange in consternation. She was worried, not for herself, but on behalf of her aunts. 'She is worse than you are, not being in her right mind.'

Amy gasped and the aunts looked furious. James felt it expedient to intervene. 'They are not the words of a gentleman about a lady, Sir Gerald,' he said, taking Amy's arm and giving it a little squeeze. 'Mrs Macdonald has lost her memory, not her wits.'

'I stand corrected.' He bowed perfunctorily to Amy. 'I beg your pardon. But that does not alter my opinion on the will.'

'But can you prove your claim?' James persisted.

Sir Gerald turned on him. 'And who are you to ask such questions? A new lawyer, perhaps?'

'No, a friend of the family. And I ask you again, can you prove what you say?'

'I intend to do so.' He turned back to Harriet. 'That is why I called, to give you due warning and advise you it will save a deal of trouble if you were to move into the Lodge forthwith.'

'I am afraid they cannot do that, even if they would,' James said laconically. 'The Lodge is occupied.'

'Occupied?' Sir Gerald repeated in surprise. 'By whom?'

'By me, sir.'

'Then you had better quit, sir.'

'I have a binding contract, which I shall insist upon,' James countered.

'We shall see.'

Recognising that he would not get anywhere while James was there to protect them, Sir Gerald took his leave in a great huff, muttering they would hear from his lawyers in due course.

As soon as he had gone, Amy sank on to a sofa and, being bidden to do so by a nod from Harriet, James sat beside her. 'Odious man!' the good lady said.

'Does he have any cause to expect to win?' he asked.

'Not according to our lawyer. It is all bluster.'

'I think it might be prudent to draw up a contract between yourself and me,' he said, smiling.

'Do you mean there isn't one?' Amy asked.

'The word of a gentleman was good enough for us,' Matilda said. 'We would trust the Captain in all things.'

'Nevertheless, you are right, Captain.' This from Harriet. 'Prudence will prevail. How long shall this contract be for? Six months from the date you moved in?'

'Oh, I think the Captain's business will be concluded long before six months have passed,' Amy put in sharply. 'In fact, I dare say he is thinking of leaving for London almost immediately.'

They all looked at her in surprise. It was so unlike Amy to be waspish. 'I did not say that,' James protested, though it was exactly what he had had in mind.

'No, but you cannot wish to carry on with your undertaking now your true purpose has been well and truly uncovered. And my memory is coming back slowly of its own accord and what I cannot remember, I am sure Mr Martin Gotobed will supply.'

'Mr Martin Gotobed is a scoundrel,' James said. 'I forbid you to speak to him.'

'*Forbid*, Captain? How so, forbid? You are not my husband that you can dictate to me,' Amy fumed.

'No, more's the pity.'

'*What* did you say?'

He hurried to retract. The conversation was becoming uncomfortably personal and he was not inclined to analyse his own feelings, certainly not admit them to anyone else. On the other hand, it would be a churlish man who denied he found Amy attractive and lovable enough to marry. 'I meant that if I were, you might be more inclined to take heed of what I tell you.'

'Why should I?'

'Now, now, children,' Harriet said placatingly, making James look at her in astonishment. It was a long time since anyone had addressed him as a child. 'Pray do not quarrel. Amy you are not still at odds with the Captain, are you? He has done you nothing but good, as you must allow, and truly we kept his errand a secret only to help you. If I had known you would be so upset by it, I would have told you long ago. Now, say all is forgiven and be friends again.'

James turned to her with a smile and held out his hand. 'Pax?'

Slowly she took it. 'Very well, Captain. I concede you were all thinking of my good, but I wish you to be more open with me in future.'

He smiled and put the back of her hand to his lips, in order to evade answering her request. He had yet to consult the aunts about how to proceed over Sam's revelations.

'Now that is done and we are all as one again,' Matilda said and turned to Amy. 'Did you tell the Captain about that dream you had last night?'

'No, I was too angry with him.'

'Tell him now.'

'Why? It was nothing.' She was aware that James still had hold of her hand and he was looking at her with an expression of deep concern. She felt foolish and drew her hand away.

'Nothing!' her aunt exclaimed. 'You woke up screaming and terrified out of your wits and say it was nothing. These nightmares you have must mean something. What we need is someone to interpret them.'

'Not Widow Twitch, I beg you,' Harriet said. 'I am persuaded she does more harm than good.'

'Tell me,' James said softly.

So she did. 'Aunt Harriet said the road was where my husband and I had our home near Covent Garden,' she finished. 'But if it was, why was I running and who was after me? Was I coming here? Why don't I remember buying my ticket and boarding that coach?'

'Your escort had it.'

'And who was he?'

James looked from one aunt to the other and then at Amy. She was looking at him, entreating him to help her, and in the face of what she had said about being open with her, he decided to tell her some of the truth. 'His name was Gus Billings and I am of the opinion he was not your protector, but your keeper. I do not know what hold he had over you, but you were clearly afraid of him. And he was known to the highwaymen who held up the coach. They had some conversation before allowing us to proceed…' He paused, noting how pale she had become. 'Do you wish me to go on?'

'Yes, please.'

'I believe you may have recognised them, too. I am not sure, but I think they might be the two you saw in the grounds.'

'Captain, that is enough,' Harriet said. 'Can you not see how your words are frightening poor Amy?'

'I do not wish to frighten her. But I am persuaded it was shock that caused the loss of her memory and so perhaps a shock might restore it.' He paused, assembling his thoughts before turning back to Amy. 'Your aunts have always discouraged you from returning to your home in London, but I think the time has come for you to go back. A sight of your home might be enough to restore your memory. If you agree, I will be pleased to take you.'

'Captain!' Matilda protested. 'That is unkind in you.'

'No, he is right,' Amy cried. 'I am in such a turmoil that I am prepared to try anything, even if it is painful. I have to find out what is hidden in my past, whether it is good or evil. I can no longer live with the uncertainty. And perhaps it will not be so bad. I might find Duncan was not so badly hurt and will forgive me.' She did not know why she added that, perhaps to remind herself that she was married, however much she might wish otherwise.

James was tempted to tell her what Sam had told him, but he held back. He wanted to make sure of the facts himself. Henry Fielding would be able to confirm them and, even if all Sam had said was true, he wanted her to remember everything herself. Only then would she be ready to move on, to put the past behind her and consider her future. 'Then when shall we go?' he asked.

'Tomorrow?'

'Too soon,' Matilda said. 'You are not yet recovered from your bad night.'

'I shall recover all the sooner if I am doing something, Aunt. Idleness has not worked, so perhaps action will. Captain, I shall be ready whenever it is convenient to you.'

'I shall need to arrange a post chaise,' he said. 'The public coach will be too slow and too uncomfortable.'

'That will be a prodigious expense, Captain.'

'Think nothing of it, I do not. Shall we say the day after tomorrow, as early as may be? I shall send a man ahead to arrange post horses. If we make good time, we shall arrive in the capital in a little over ten or eleven hours and will not need to rack up anywhere. That is if you can stand to be so long upon the road.'

'Yes, the sooner we arrive the better.'

'Take Susan with you,' Harriet said. 'You will need a maid and a chaperon. It is all very well to go about the country unaccompanied, but in town it is not to be heard of.'

'Very well. I will go and put it to her, and, if she is agreeable, we can spend tomorrow packing. I shall not need to take much with me, for I must have clothes at home.' She jumped up and, bobbing a little curtsy to James, ran off to find the maid, leaving him facing the aunts.

'We shall miss her dreadfully,' Matilda said. 'It is wicked of me for wishing harm to her husband, but I hope she does not find him and comes back to us quickly.'

It was the opening he wanted. 'She may return sooner than you think,' he said, then paused to marshal his thoughts before continuing. 'I have been given some news concerning Mr Duncan Macdonald that your niece will undoubtedly find disturbing…'

'Then do not keep us in suspense, Captain,' Harriet said, giving her sister a disapproving look.

He related everything that Sam had told him, which shocked the ladies so much he feared they might swoon—certainly Matilda looked as though she might—but Harriet was made of sterner stuff and simply urged him to go on.

'I could have told Mrs Macdonald,' he finished, 'but I feared sending her into a relapse and wanted to consult you first. You may wish to break the news to her yourself.'

'This is indeed bad news,' Harriet told him. 'Not that the man is dead, for I never did like him, but because of the effect it will have on Amy.'

'I cannot tell her,' Matilda cried, fanning herself vigorously. 'And why take her to London when there is nothing there but more misery? She had better stay here.'

'Because she knows there is something very wrong,' James explained. 'And until she remembers and can accommodate herself to it, she cannot feel free to carry on with her life. She may have loved her husband.'

'Amy could never love someone as wicked as he was.'

'We do not know that he was especially wicked. He may have been wrongly accused. It is another reason why I wish to go to London, to ascertain the facts for myself. And for her. Until then—' He stopped speaking as the sound of footsteps on the stone floor outside the room told them Amy was returning. 'Shall you then leave all to me?'

'Gladly, Captain,' Harriet said, then, raising her voice slightly, added, 'There is an errand you could do for us while in London, Captain, if you would.'

'An' it be in my power, then I will do it.'

'Mr Smithson, that's our lawyer, has asked us for some papers for his perusal. He already has our father's will, but has asked us to forward other documents, like the Manorial rolls and our grandfather's will. I was in no particular haste to send them, but Sir Gerald's visit has made me think otherwise. We do not want to trust them to the mail, so if you would take them with you and put them into Mr Smithson's hand, we will be much obliged.'

'It will be my pleasure,' he said, turning to smile at Amy as she came into the room.

'Susan is all agog at the idea of a visit to London,' she said. 'And she is quite sure we can be ready by eight o'clock the morning after next.'

James stood up and took his leave. The die was cast. He was feeling more than a little apprehensive about what lay ahead, but they could not go on as they had been doing and something had to be done. For Amy's sake as well as his own.

James, riding in the best equipage with the best team of horses he could find, arrived at the Manor a little before eight on the appointed morning. He meant to take no chances and so Sam sat on the driving seat beside his coachman, with a blunderbuss alongside him. They drew up in the courtyard, but before James could jump down and go to the door it was opened by Johnson. Behind him in the hall, Susan was fussing over two portmanteaux and a hatbox. While the footman was loading the luggage into the basket at the back of the coach, Amy and her aunts appeared.

James went to greet the ladies, noting that Amy, dressed in a simple round gown and a hooded cloak, looked a little strained, though manfully trying not to show it. Matilda was tearful and though Harriet was dry-eyed, she was looking glum. 'I shall be back before you know it,' Amy said, kissing them both. 'With or without Duncan.' She turned to James with a smile that was only a little forced. 'Captain, for good or ill, I am ready.'

He helped her into her seat, followed by Susan. Then Harriet gave him the package of documents and he climbed in himself.

'Goodbye and God speed,' the aunts cried as they began to move.

Amy turned and waved until they passed over the drawbridge and the aunts were lost to sight. Then she sat back, knowing she had a long journey ahead of her and what was at the end of it she could not even begin to guess.

They were silent for some minutes, constrained a little by the presence of Susan and the fact that Amy had not entirely forgiven him for keeping secrets from her. But they could not spend twelve hours in close proximity without speaking and it behoved her to make some effort at conversation. 'This is a very comfortable coach, Captain,' she said, patting the red-velvet padded seat. 'Wherever did you find it?'

'In Downham Market. The landlord of the King's Arms has a brother who deals in carriages and he was able to find the horses, too.'

'It is all very fine. I am much obliged to you.'

'Oh, do not talk of obligation,' he said, understanding her nervousness, for who would not feel nervous given what had happened on her last coach trip? He was a little anxious himself. Those two highpads might be anywhere. 'It is my privilege and pleasure.'

They left Highbeck behind them and took the road to Ely, alongside the river where they had been held up before. 'We should make good time,' he told her. 'The horses are fresh and I have sent ahead for frequent changes, so, all being well, we should reach each stage at the appointed time.'

'All being well,' she murmured. 'You mean so long as we are not held up by highwaymen.'

'Mercy me!' Susan gasped. 'I pray we are not.'

'Sam is up beside the driver with a blunderbuss,' he told her. 'Have no fear.'

But Susan's fear was soon superseded by sickness. However good the horses and however comfortable the coach, nothing could make up for the state of the roads. Before long they were obliged to stop for Susan to get out and be sick. Amy stood by her, rubbing her back. 'Shall we take you back home?' she asked. 'I would not have you ill on my account for anything.'

'No, Miss Amy, I am charged with your care and I am not one to neglect my duty, however uncomfortable it might be. I shall do very well now I have got rid of my breakfast.' She looked pale as a ghost but would not hear of them abandoning the trip to take her back, so Amy guided her back to the coach with her arm about her shoulders.

James was standing at the door, waiting for them. 'Would you feel better in the air?' he asked Susan. 'You could squeeze in between Sam and the coachman.' He looked up at Sam. 'You would not mind that, would you, Sam?'

Sam grinned. 'I'd not mind at all, Cap'n, if Miss Bedson have a mind to travel up here.'

Amy looked doubtful, but Susan brightened at the prospect. 'I think I should like to try it,' she said.

Sam jumped down and helped her up, then climbed back himself, so that the maid was securely seated between the two men. Sam handed Susan a small flask he had taken from his pocket. 'There, take a swig of that, my lovely, I'll wager it will put the roses back into your cheeks.'

'You must tell us at once if you want to come back inside,' Amy said, watching a little colour come back into her maid's cheeks, though she suspected that might have been caused by Sam's familiarity.

She resumed her seat in the coach. James got in beside her, shut the door and bade the coachman to proceed.

'Will she really be better up there?' Amy asked as they moved off.

He smiled knowingly. 'I am persuaded Sam's company will effect a cure, even if the fresh air and the cognac does not.'

'We are half an hour behind now. Will we be able to make up the time?'

'Oh, I think so.' Now he had Amy to himself, he set about allaying any fears she might have by cheerful conversation. He talked of the weather, which was warm and sunny, the state of the roads and where the post horses would be waiting and where they might take refreshments, and the time they might expect to arrive in the capital, to all of which she responded, which he took to mean he had been forgiven.

Even so, he would be in trouble again as soon as she found out he knew about the death of her husband and had not told her. He must find a way of breaking the news to her. Whether that would be enough to bring back her memory he did not know, but what he really wanted was for her to remember everything of her own accord. 'I can understand you are impatient to go home,' he said, 'but it will be very late when we arrive and perhaps we should postpone going to Henrietta Street until the morning when you have had a rest.'

'But where am I to stay?' she asked in alarm.

'At Colbridge House. My parents will make you welcome, I am sure, and tomorrow we will go together to your home.'

'You would come with me?'

'Most decidedly. We cannot know what we will find. You may have need of me.'

'I have needed you a great deal lately, Captain, and I wonder you put up with me,' she said gratefully.

'There is no question of putting up with you,' he said. 'Your company has been an abiding pleasure that I would not have forgone for anything.' He was, he decided, becoming a veritable gallant, but was nevertheless sincere; to say he enjoyed her company was an understatement—he revelled in it.

'But you know nothing of me, except what the aunts have told you on the one hand and what Mr Gotobed has said on the other. The two sides do not marry up, do they? Am I as good as the aunts say or as wicked as Mr Gotobed implied?' she asked.

'I have the evidence of my own eyes and ears,' he said. 'And if it were not important to you to know the answers to that, I would not care if you never regained your memory. You are Amy, my homemaker.'

She laughed. 'Thank you, Captain.'

'Do you not think you could call me James? After all, I have been addressing you as Amy for some time now.'

'So I have noticed.' She smiled. 'I should perhaps have corrected you, but I did not want to stand on my dignity. After all, I do not think I have a right to expect that formality.'

'It is not for want of respect,' he said. 'On the contrary, I respect and admire you for your courage and compassion and the love you bear your aunts, but I have come to know you so well over these last weeks and been privileged to offer you comfort and protection, that the formal address seemed unnatural. To me you will always be Amy.'

'Thank you for that. But if I should turn out to be steeped in wickedness, will you still feel the same?' she asked curiously.

'You are not steeped in wickedness. If there is wickedness it is not of your making, I will stake my oath on it.'

'You mean you are not taking me back in your role as thieftaker?'

'Heaven forbid! Nothing is further from my mind.'

'Captain…'

'James.'

'James, then. How did a man of your rank in society come to be called a thieftaker? Mr Gotobed was scornful when he told me that, as if it were something not quite respectable.'

'The name was not of my seeking,' he told her. 'It happened quite by chance that I came upon criminals and ne'er-do-wells in my travels and was instrumental in handing them over to justice. It is not the same as being a thieftaker. They make a living by arresting people for the reward put out for them and for that reason are sometimes not as scrupulous as they should be about taking up only those who are guilty.'

'Yes, that is what Mr Gotobed said. He talked of you manufacturing false evidence…'

'You do not believe I would stoop to that, do you?' he asked.

'No, I am sure you would not. But tell me, how did it all start? And how did you come to take on my problems?'

He smiled. 'I was asked by Lord Trentham, who had been approached by your mama who was worried about you.'

'Yes, but you could have refused.'

'I might have done, but I remembered we had already met on the stagecoach going to Highbeck. I had often wondered what had happened to you after I left, so I agreed.'

'I see. And glad I am of it. But why were you on that coach? Highbeck is a remote spot…'

'I was going to Downham from whence I meant to proceed to Peterborough,' he told her. 'The coach being held up and then overturning delayed me and my journey was in vain.'

'I am very sorry for it.'

'I have had many such abortive journeys. I am become used to it.'

'You said you were searching for something. Widow Twitch said it was peace of mind and you would find it when you stopped looking for it,' she reminded him.

'So she did. And maybe she was right, I cannot tell. My peace of mind and the dealing out of justice to two murdering thieves have been inextricably entwined. I was, am, determined to see them hanged—' He stopped speaking, putting a hand to the pin in his neckcloth, struggling with barely repressed emotions. 'You see, they killed my wife…'

'Oh, James, I am so very, very sorry.' She put a hand on his arm. 'I should not have quizzed you. It was unkind of me.'

'No. I needed to tell you.'

'And did you find them?'

'No, they had gone to ground as they have done time and time again in the last two years. I was obliged to return to London empty-handed. It was then I met Lord Trentham.'

'Do you mean you gave up the search to help me?' she asked in astonishment.

'I can return to it later,' he said, grimly.

'If it is not too painful, would you like to tell me

about your wife?' she asked. That he had obviously loved his wife was giving her more than a little heartache, but her concern for his unhappiness overrode that to some extent and perhaps talking about what had happened might help to ease his mind.

He had never spoken of how he had felt when he learned what had happened to Caroline, though his family and Sam had seen his violent reaction and no doubt guessed. Now he found that unburdening himself to Amy was like balm to his soul. 'I meant to leave the navy and take up an occupation that kept me at home,' he told her at the finish. 'If only I had done it sooner, she would still be alive.'

'You cannot blame yourself,' she told him, so wrapped up in his story, she forgot her own troubles. 'And when you think about it, it could have happened when you were at home. Your wife needed only to be out shopping when you were busy elsewhere and you would no more have been able to prevent it.'

He smiled, realising quite suddenly that it was guilt which had been driving him the last two years, but, because of Amy, the guilt was finally fading. 'Bless you,' he said, putting his hand over hers in her lap. 'You have made me feel easier with myself.'

'But you are still bent on vengeance?'

'Vengeance,' he repeated sharply. 'Is it vengeance to want to see my wife's murderers hang?'

'Perhaps not, but have you never wondered what she would have thought about it? Would she have wanted you to spend your life chasing after her killers? Would she not have wished you to be happy?' she said gently.

'I shall be happy when I see them hang,' he growled.

He was not yet ready to listen and she did not press her point home, leaving him to muse upon what she'd already said. A few minutes later they pulled into an inn to change the horses and they left the coach to take refreshments. Afterwards Amy asked Susan if she wanted to resume her seat in the coach, but she declined, blushing furiously as she did so. 'I like it up top,' she said. 'You can see so much more of the countryside and, to be sure, the freshness of the air is helpful for my malady.'

Sam winked at James as he helped her climb back up to her seat, making him smile. He and Amy resumed their seats and their conversation became more general. She was glad he had told her about himself; it made him seem less severe and helped her understand what drove him to do what he did. He was a man who could love deeply and feel pain and anger and she could sympathise with him in that, but her story had yet to be told.

Chapter Seven

'Wake up, Amy.' James gently lifted her head from his shoulder. After gallantly trying to keep awake, she had begun to nod off after the last change of horses and he had slipped his arm behind her to make her more comfortable. He had sat very still, cushioning her against the jolting, careful not to disturb her, but it had given him time to think, to look back over the last few weeks and wonder how much his life had changed. And it was all down to the young woman who slept in his arms. She trusted him and he must not fail her as he had failed Carrie. Amy was right in a way; his being away at sea had no bearing on Carrie's murder. But Amy should not have told him he had allowed his pursuit of vengeance to take over his life; it was too close to the truth to be comfortable. But was she right? Would Carrie have wanted that? Very likely not, he acknowledged, but he could not give up—justice ought still to be done. Those two should not be allowed to go free to kill again.

He eased his arm out from behind her as she stirred into wakefulness. 'We have arrived.'

She wondered for a moment where she was. The movement of the carriage had stopped and there were lights outside. 'I was asleep,' she said, surprised at herself. Of late she had been almost afraid to go to sleep for fear of the dreadful nightmares, but this time there had been no dreams.

'Yes.'

'What time is it?' she asked.

'Nine o'clock.' The coachman was opening the door and letting down the step. James got out and turned to hand Amy down. 'Come, let us go inside, you must be tired and hungry.'

The Earl and Countess were away visiting friends in the country, they were told by the footman who admitted them, but James soon had the household running round to prepare a light meal and rooms for Amy and Susan, which they went off to do willingly. Amy, still a little dazed, felt sure they were whispering among themselves about who she might be, but as they had taken Susan with them, she supposed they would aim their questions at her. Susan could be relied upon to be discreet.

While that was being done, James took her into the drawing room. 'Sit down, Amy. Supper will not be long and then you may go to bed. I am sure you are much fatigued.'

'I am not at all sure this is proper,' she said nervously, looking round at the opulence of the furnishings, the collection of pictures and ornaments. Blackfen Manor had some rare and valuable items, but nothing like this. This was on a grand scale. 'I do not think I should be here.'

'Nonsense, where else would you be?'

'But your parents are from home.'

'While I am in London it is also my home. And I am sure they would not mind.' In a way he was glad his parents were away, they would only lecture him about giving up his pursuit of Carrie's killers and marrying again. And they would certainly quiz Amy.

'I ought to go to my own house. My husband…'

He was about to tell her she had no husband, but realised she was too exhausted to take it in. Tomorrow, when they went to Henrietta Street, she might remember what had happened and he might discover she knew it already. If not, he would break the news to her then. 'Amy, you are too tired to face that now.'

That was certainly true. She would have asked if she might go straight to bed, but at that moment the butler came into the room.

'Supper is laid out in the small dining room, sir,' he said, somewhat pompously. Visitors who turned up at this time of night and expected supper without changing out of the clothes they had travelled in were obviously beyond the pale! 'And Mrs Macdonald's maid is having supper in the kitchen and will go immediately afterwards to the lady's room to await her mistress.'

'Thank you,' Amy said quietly as James rose to take her hand and tuck it under his arm to go into the dining room where a lavish meal was laid for two. She was too tired and apprehensive to swallow more than a few mouthfuls.

'Poor dear, you are worn out,' he said, abandoning his own meal and standing up to offer her his hand. 'Let me show you to your room. Tomorrow we will go to Henrietta Street and then call on your mama, but for now you need to sleep.'

She was thankful that he was not going to press her to eat more, or even talk, and she took his hand and allowed him to conduct her up a fine marble staircase to the first floor, which housed the main reception rooms. 'You will see those tomorrow,' he said, as they passed on and up another flight of stairs to the next floor where he stopped outside one of the many doors and opened it. 'Here you are. I hope you will be comfortable.'

'I am sure I shall. Goodnight, Captain.'

'James,' he reminded her.

'James it was when we were travelling, but we are here in London and must now follow the rules of proper etiquette.'

'Very well, Mrs Macdonald,' he agreed, smiling. 'Goodnight.' He lifted her hand to his lips, kissing the back of it and then turning it over to kiss the inside of her wrist. The sensations that coursed through her as he did that did nothing to calm her and everything to set her in a complete quake. In the last twelve hours, coming as they did on top of the weeks of enjoying his company at Highbeck, she had come to know and understand him a little and that confirmed her conviction that her feelings for him were deeper than she ought to entertain, considering she was married to someone else. Without speaking, she pulled her hand away, stepped into the room and shut the door on him, leaning against it breathing heavily. It was only when Susan appeared from an adjoining room that she pulled herself together and tried to act normally.

James stood outside the closed door for a minute, more than a little confused himself. It was becoming harder and harder to stand back from her, to remember his errand and not let his feelings get the better of him. Tomorrow, she would know her husband was dead; tomorrow she might remember everything and when that happened his mission would be accomplished and Amy would go from his life. Instead of making him feel satisfied with a job well done, it made him feel unaccountably low in spirits. He turned abruptly and went back to finish his supper and then went to bed himself.

Amy woke early and lay in bed, staring at the luxurious hangings of her bed. She should not be here, staying with a gentleman when his parents were from home. It was scandalous behaviour for any woman, but especially a married one. Today, she might find out the truth about Duncan; today, everything might be revealed and she would have to say goodbye to James Drymore, for his mission would have been accomplished. But supposing what she discovered was something she did not want him to know, something bad about herself? Suddenly, it was important to go alone.

She left her bed and went into the adjoining room to wake Susan and commanded her to pack. 'We are leaving, now, at once,' she told her.

'Why, whatever has happened?' the maid asked.

'Nothing, but I cannot stay here when the answer to the riddle is so close. Make haste, I would be gone before Captain Drymore realises I am out of bed.'

A few minutes later they were standing in the street outside the house, each carrying a portmanteau. 'Where do we go from here, Miss Amy?' Susan asked. She spoke sharply, being annoyed with Amy for leaving the comfort of a grand house where she could be cosseted and spoiled and thrusting them on to the street with no idea of where they were.

'Home,' Amy said. 'Henrietta Street.'

'And do you know the direction?'

'No, but we shall go to the end of the road and hire chairs to take us.' Amy was very glad Aunt Harriet had given her a small purse of money before she left.

'Pin money,' she had said. 'You cannot expect the Captain to pay for everything, though he is generosity itself.'

Twenty minutes later they were standing outside the house she and Duncan had shared and she did not remember it. It was a vast disappointment. Not because it was so small and squashed between two larger properties, but because she had hoped the sight of the street and the house would make her memory come flooding back. 'Come on,' she said, steeling herself. 'Let us discover the worst.'

But the door was locked and no one came when she knocked. They found a passage at the side that led to round to another door at the back, but that, too, was locked.

'Where are the servants?' Susan asked.

'With no one here to look after and no one to pay their wages, I have no doubt they left. We shall have to break in.' She picked up a rock and hurled it at a window. The noise it made as the glass shattered had her looking round fearfully. No one came, no irate husband, no curious neighbour.

Using her gloved hand, Amy broke more glass until she had made a sizeable hole.

'Miss Amy, you are never going to climb in there, are you?' Susan asked.

'Yes. There is no other way to gain entrance.'

'I wish we'd waited for the Captain. I don't feel good about this at all.'

Neither did Amy, but she was here and she was not going away until the mystery was solved. She had the upper half of her body through the hole she had made and was wondering how to get the rest of her through without cutting herself on broken glass when someone seized her round the waist. 'Susan, let go of me,' she commanded. 'I cannot get in if you pull me back.'

'Come out, you foolish woman.' The irate voice was certainly not Susan's. She withdrew and turned to face James.

'Captain, what are you doing here?'

'Looking for you. Just what do you think you are about?' he demanded.

'I am trying to get into my own house,' she retorted.

'Then allow me.' He climbed in and, a few seconds later, opened the door to admit her.

She stepped inside the kitchen to a scene of chaos. The furniture was overturned, crockery smashed and there were what she realised must be blood-stains on the floor. She stood like a statue, unable to take in what she saw, hardly able to breathe, though her heart was pumping almost in her throat. 'I was right,' she whispered. 'I did this.'

'Rubbish!' He had seen it before and had known it would shock her, but he had planned to warn her a little before they arrived together, and possibly explain about Duncan's death. He had had no idea she would leave his house without telling him; because he had known how tired she was, he had not been surprised that she had slept late. It was not until one of the footmen told him they had not seen Susan at all that morning, that he had sent one of the chambermaids up to check on them.

His initial annoyance that she had seen fit to leave without saying a word had soon given way to worry. He felt sure she would want to go to her old home, but had she any idea how to get there? Did she have any money? If she tried to walk, she would be at the mercy of any footpad or ne'er-do-well who accosted her. He knew he could run faster than he could be carried in a chair and, grabbing his sword and pistol, came hotfoot after her.

His relief at finding her safe was soon supplanted by concern for how she was feeling. She had turned paper-white and her whole body trembled. He went to take her arm, but she shrugged him off and walked slowly through the house and up the stairs, following a trail of blood. It ended in the bedroom with bloodstained sheets. She stood hanging on to the bed post for support, and suddenly a voice was echoing in her head. 'Go to Blackfen Manor. I will join you there. Tell no one.'

'Where is he?' she murmured.

'Who?' James had followed her, ready to catch her if she swooned, while Susan stood in the doorway, unwilling to venture further into the macabre room.

'My husband, of course.'

Now he could delay telling her no longer. But how much to say? How much to leave out? 'Amy, I must tell you something…'

'About Duncan?' she whispered.

'Yes. Come downstairs to the drawing room. You cannot stay here.'

She allowed herself to be led away. The drawing room at the front of the house had not seen the carnage of the rest and he settled her on to a sofa, telling Susan, who was almost as white as her mistress, to see if she could find anything in the kitchen to make a drink.

He sat beside Amy. 'I know a little of what happened,' he told her. 'But not the whole. I hoped that you might regain your memory sufficiently to tell me the rest.'

'Do you know where my husband is?'

He swallowed hard and took her hand. 'Amy, I am afraid Duncan Macdonald is dead.'

'I knew it. I killed him.' It was said flatly, because she had felt for some time that Duncan was no more. Her frequent nightmares seemed to confirm it. She felt nothing. It was as if all her senses had been turned off. Her surroundings were a blur, her brain would not function. All she could do was repeat 'I did it' in a monotone.

'I do not think so.' He had to stay calm for her sake, but his own nerves and emotions were in complete disarray.

'But you are not sure, are you?' But if she had brought about her husband's end, why was his body not found in their house? Had he crawled away to die? She ought to show some signs of sorrow at his loss, but she could not mourn a husband she could not remember and whom she was convinced she had harmed.

How could he answer her honestly? Should he tell her that her husband was a thief and a murderer? Would it make her feel better? Never before had his dealings with criminals given him such soul-searching anguish.

'Your silence is answer enough,' she said dully. 'You must do your duty as a thieftaker and turn me in.'

'You have not asked how you came to kill your husband, nor why. Is that because you have remembered it?' he asked.

'No, I have not remembered. But the evidence is overwhelming. All the blood.' She shivered. 'And my nightmares.'

'Let us suppose you were not the doer of the deed,' he said, trying to reason with her. 'Let us suppose you simply witnessed it. And then let us ask ourselves, who else could have done it.'

'Who else?' she echoed.

'Yes. The man Billings, for one. Or those two men you saw in the grounds of the Manor…' He paused. This had to be acted out to the bitter end. 'Amy, I fear your husband was embroiled with some very unsavoury characters. I do not know how it came about, but he was wanted, along with them, for highway robbery and murder. Someone informed the Watch that a murder had occurred at your address, but when they got there, the only person they found was your wounded husband. He was taken to Newgate, but his wound became infected and he died. Prisons, even the infirmaries, are not the cleanest of places.' He paused to let his words sink in. 'I am very sorry. I would not, for the world, have distressed you and even now I wonder if I should have left you in ignorance.'

'The ignorance was more distressing than the truth,' she said, surprised by how little impact this news had on her. It was as if he were telling her something she already knew. 'But whatever you say about Duncan and his associates' guilt has not proved my own innocence.'

'That will be my next task.' He was more than ever convinced she was a victim, not a villain, but he was also worried that others might not share that view and he was determined to protect her. With his life if necessary.

'Do you think you can?'

'I will do my utmost.'

Susan came into the room, saying she had found some chocolate and a bottle of cordial in a cupboard. 'I am not sure either is fit to drink,' she said. 'There's half a bottle of brandy.'

'Bring that,' he commanded. 'It will be safer than old cordial or chocolate, and do your mistress more good.'

'How did you learn about Duncan?' Amy asked him after Susan had gone to do his bidding. 'Was that one more thing you knew before coming to Highbeck and decided to keep from me?'

'No. Sam Roker discovered it when he returned to town to fetch my belongings. He has been with me on all my adventures and he has a nose for these things. I would have told you at once, but...' he shrugged '...you seemed so content with your aunts and I heard you say on one occasion that perhaps you could live without a memory. If Mr Gotobed had not arrived...'

'Was he one of the gang, too?'

'No, I do not think so, but he claimed he saw Duncan Macdonald just before he died.'

'All this is making my head spin,' she murmured.

'Poor Amy,' he said sympathetically. 'You have been through the mill, haven't you? Now, here is Susan with the brandy. You must drink a little, then I will take you home.'

'Home?' She gave a cracked laugh. 'This *is* home.'

'I meant my home.'

'No, that is not fitting. I will go to my mother.'

'Of course.' Perhaps she was right; she needed her mother at such a time, not a man she only half-trusted. 'If that is what you wish.'

Reluctant to leave her to find chairs or a cab in case she took it into her head to disappear again, he decided they would walk. There had been no rain recently so the roads were dusty rather than muddy and Lady Charron's apartments were only a short step away. 'When you have finished your brandy and feel calmer, we will go.'

But her mother was not at home. The servant who came to the door in answer to James's knock told them she was rehearsing *The Beggar's Opera* at the Drury Lane Theatre. James sent a gutter urchin to fetch a cab and took her and Susan there. He told the maid to stay with the cab, which the driver did not mind in the least, being paid for doing nothing, and then he escorted Amy inside and used his best wiles, including half a guinea, to pass the door-keeper who directed them to Lady Charron's dressing room where they were obliged to wait until the rehearsal was finished.

Amy sat on one of the hard stools in front of the mirror, but she was in such a state of nerves that she could not stop shaking. James watched her, wishing with all his heart he could make matters easier for her. He stood beside her and put his hand lightly on her shoulder and she looked up at him and managed a weak smile.

She was not at all sure what he thought of her, whether he was standing by her in his role of friend or thieftaker, whether he truly believed her guilty or innocent. But she was in his hands and had to trust him to do as he said and uncover the truth, however unpalatable it might be.

They heard the music come to an end and a few minutes later Sophie Charron came in, dressed in the costume she would wear for the performance, the skirt of which was at least two yards wide, forcing her to enter the room sideways. Once inside she turned to face her daughter. 'Amy! Amy, my child. They said you were here. How pleased I am to see you.' She bent to drop a kiss on Amy's cheek. 'But what brings you? I thought your aunts were looking after you.' She was plumper than Amy had expected. Her face was heavily painted and she had three black patches dotted on her cheeks. Her wig was enormous and topped with feathers. Her heavily embroidered stays were very low cut and revealed more of that lady's bosom than was entirely proper.

Amy stood up and bobbed a curtsy. 'Mama?' There was a questioning note in her voice.

'Of course I am your mama, who did you think I was? To be sure you have spent most of your life with your aunts, but I have come to see you from time to time and you visited me at home when you lived in London with Duncan Macdonald. Surely you remember that?'

'No. I have forgotten everything,' Amy said. 'Mama, may I present Captain James Drymore?'

Sophie turned towards James, her wide skirts swaying and brushing against a table on which was a vase of flowers. It would have toppled if James had not been swift enough to catch it and set it upright again. She put up her quizzing glass to see him properly. 'I am pleased to meet you, Captain. Lord Trentham has told me about you.'

'My lady.' He bowed with a flourish.

'Have you been able to uncover the mystery?'

'Only some of it.'

'Duncan is dead,' Amy said, flatly. 'I—'

'He was attacked and mortally wounded,' James put in before Amy could say she had killed him, which he guessed she was about to do. He did not think that was a wise idea.

'Was he? Well, that does not surprise me,' her mother announced.

'Why not?' Amy demanded. 'Do you know what happened?'

'No, I do not, but he did not choose his friends wisely. Gamesters, all of them, not gentlemen either. I saw them once at Almack's, playing very deep. No doubt he was in debt to them and would not pay up. Such men can be extremely danger-ous.'

'I did not know that,' Amy said.

'Of course you did. I remember you coming to me once in tears and asking what you should do about it. I gave you some money because Duncan had left you without any.'

'I do not remember it.' The more she learned about him, the more she wondered if she had ever loved her husband. Why, then, had she married him?

'Do you recall *anything*, Amy?' her mother asked impatiently.

'Little things about when I was a child, nothing recent. But I have had terrible dreams which I think are returning memories, but they frighten me so. They are so violent. I dreamed there was a bag of gold coins and jewels…'

Sophie looked at James, a questioning look on her face. 'Has anyone found such a thing?'

'No, my lady.'

'Duncan Macdonald was like Sir John in many ways,' her mother said. 'They could both be the essence of charm and good manners when it suited them, but both were braggers and both had violent tempers, especially when in drink. We are well rid of them.'

'Is my father dead?' Amy asked.

'Not that I know. He is on the Continent some-where. I have not heard from him these last three years, so I cannot tell you exactly where.'

'Was he a Jacobite rebel?'

'Where did you get that idea? Did Duncan tell you that?' her mother exclaimed.

'If he did, I do not recall it.' Amy was becoming very tired of having continually to say she could not remember. Even the mess in her house had not revived her memory, and if that could not, then she supposed nothing could. 'Susan told me Mr Roker was talking to her about the rebels and how so many of them were forced to flee to France and that some-where there was hidden treasure…'

'Who is Mr Roker?' Sophie enquired.

'He is my servant, my lady,' James put in. 'The story of the Arkaig treasure has tickled his fancy and no doubt he sought to divert Susan with it. She had been sick, you see.'

'Rumours,' Sophie said. 'Nothing but rumours. I never realised they had spread so far. I beg of you, Captain, to set the record straight with your servant and anyone else you hear tattling. It could ruin my reputation and I would be hissed off the stage if it were thought I was connected with traitors and rebels.'

He bowed in acquiescence, though how he could prevent people from talking he did not know, especially as new rumours were flying about that Bonnie Prince Charlie was in London to drum up support for another uprising. Could there be any truth in them? Was the Young Pretender going to cause more trouble? He didn't see how he could; his Scottish supporters had all been subdued by the draconian punishments meted out to them, many of them had been deported to America and the West Indies. They were in no position to rise again. And surely the Prince did not have enough allies in England? France and Spain would not help him unless he could show them he had overwhelming support. And where did Amy's family, particularly her father and husband, fit into all that? As far as he knew Sam had not connected Sir John with the rebels, so why had Amy jumped to that conclusion? Had she known something? Was it all part of the reason for her loss of memory? This mystery just seemed to continually deepen rather than unfold!

They were interrupted by the arrival of a young man who breezed into the room without knocking. 'Oh,' he said, when he saw Amy and James. 'I did not know you had company, Sophie.'

Her mother waved a hand at him. 'Come in, Harry, and be presented to my daughter, Mrs Macdonald, and Captain James Drymore. Captain, Amy, this is my protégé, Mr Harry Portman, son and heir of Lord Portman of Braintree.'

The man was the same age as James, perhaps a year or two his junior, and dressed in a suit of lilac silk. His waistcoat was white, his stockings white, tied at the knee with lilac ribbon. A quizzing glass and watch dangled on two ribbons about his neck. His fingers sparkled with jewelled rings. He was, so James decided, as eccentric a macaroni as Gotobed, but with a little more taste. He bowed to Amy and kissed her hand. 'Mrs Macdonald, your obedient.' Then he bowed to James. 'Captain Drymore, how do you do? Your fame precedes you.'

'Oh?' James queried. 'In what connection?'

'Why, in connection with your thieftaking exploits. According to Lord Trentham, no criminal is safe once you have him in your sights.'

'Lord Trentham is too kind. And also inaccurate,' James said drily.

Harry turned and addressed himself to Sophie. 'I came to say you are wanted on stage for the second act.'

'Then I must go,' she said, preparing to get herself out of the door the way she had come in. 'Amy, bring the Captain back later and you can tell me all about what you have been up to, nightmares and all, and how my sisters do and what is happening at Highbeck. I really must try to pay a visit before too long.'

'Mama, I have nowhere to go.'

'What's wrong with your house in Henrietta Street?'

'I had to break a window to get in,' Amy told her. 'But apart from that, nearly everything in the house has been ruined or plundered. The clothes presses are empty and so are the kitchen cupboards.'

'Well, I am sorry, but I do not see how you can stay with me. I do not have the room and I am never in. You would find it dull in the extreme.'

James could see the disappointment and hurt in Amy's eyes even if her mother could not. He felt like shaking the woman and demanding she attend to her daughter. No one could have been less like the lovable Hardwick aunts. 'It is of no consequence,' he said. 'Mrs Macdonald is welcome to stay at Colbridge House while we are in town.'

'There!' her mother said with satisfaction. 'That is a much better idea.'

'Come, Amy,' he said gently. 'I will take you home. We will come back and see the performance this evening and perhaps Lady Charron will dine with us at Fenton's afterwards.'

'May I be one of the party?' Portman asked. 'I would hear about your exploits as thieftaker.'

The request did not please James, but he could think of no excuse to exclude him, especially as Lady Charron agreed. Having squeezed herself out, she was followed by Portman, leaving James and Amy to find their way back to the street and the patient Susan.

'How can I go back to your home?' Amy asked as they climbed into the cab beside Susan. 'Your parents are from home.'

'They were not at home last night either.'

'That was different,' she said illogically. 'If I am not to be arrested and thrown into prison, then I would like to go back to Highbeck. Susan and I can board a stage.'

Susan gave a little gasp at this, making James smile. The maid was not at all happy with that idea. Did it have something to do with Sam? he wondered. 'That I will not allow. When you go, you go back with me. And there is no question of you being arrested,' he said firmly.

'No?'

'Of course not.'

'How soon can we go?' She was desperate for Highbeck and the restful sympathy of her aunts and wished she had never left. Nothing had been gained and she felt worse than before. Her one consolation was the presence of James, who was determined to look after her and prove her innocence. She wondered why he bothered, but she was very glad of it.

'I have to see some people while I am in town and also deliver your aunt's packet to Mr Smithson,' he told her. 'And we are engaged to meet your mama this evening, though I wonder if you are not too fatigued and ought to rest. You need to recover from the news of your husband's death and the journey here…'

'I never felt less like resting, my insides are churning, my head is spinning and I cannot rest until I have spoken to my mother again and learned all she knows. As for my husband's death, it seems so remote, as if it happened in another life and I suppose, in a way, it did,' she said sadly.

'Very well,' he said. He would have taken her hand but for the presence of Susan. Instead he addressed the practicalities. 'Now, this is what we will do. You will come with me to Colbridge House and have something to eat and drink, since you have had nothing since last night and that was little enough.' He did not add that the brandy he had given her might have steadied her nerves, but it had certainly gone to her head. 'After that you will rest while I go about my business. Susan will wake you in time to dress for dinner before we go to the opera. Tomorrow we will decide about returning to Highbeck. Do you agree?'

'I suppose I must.' The effects of the brandy were beginning to wear off and she was too tired to argue.

Amy was in a quake by the time they arrived at Colbridge House, but James's hand under her elbow steadied her as they were admitted by the butler who seemed surprised to see her again. 'Nuncheon,' James commanded him.

'Very good, sir.' He hurried off to obey and James led Amy into the drawing room. She wished she could escape to the solitude of the bedchamber she had used the night before and reflect on a day that had been full of shocks and revelations. Luckily James understood and though she barely took in what he was saying, he filled the waiting time with tales of his adventures at sea; by the time those had been exhausted, nuncheon was served.

Afterwards James conducted her to her room, but, unlike the evening before, he walked a little apart from her, bowed formally and left. Susan helped her undress and she lay on the bed, not expecting to sleep, but she was so tired, her eyelids closed almost immediately and she was allowed the solace of oblivion…

James went straight to Smithson, the Hardwick lawyer, where he delivered the package, then to his own lawyer where he left instructions about his

Newmarket estate, then off to Newgate prison where a guinea bought the information he needed, that Duncan Macdonald had most definitely died in custody.

'Did he ever have a visitor by the name of Gotobed?' he asked the turnkey.

'Visitor,' the man laughed. 'Gotobed weren't no visitor, he were in Newgate at the same time as Macdonald. Thick as thieves, they were.' He laughed at his simile. 'Well, they *were* thieves. They spent a deal of time whispering together. If the Scotsman hadn't been a-dyin', I'd have said they were plottin' something.'

'Gotobed is a convicted criminal?'

'Not exactly. He was awaiting trial for fraud and was acquitted. He had a good lawyer and money enough to bribe witnesses.'

That answered one question, but there were many more.

After leaving Newgate, he called on Henry Fielding, who was writing at his desk when James was shown into his office. 'Captain Drymore, it is good to see you,' he said, rising to greet him.

'Are you busy?' James asked, surveying the scattered papers on the desk.

'It can wait. I have been drafting a proposal to

recruit a few trustworthy fellows to patrol the streets and root out crime.'

'More thieftakers?'

'No, for these will be paid a wage and not have to rely on rewards for a living. They will be young and healthy and, whenever a crime is reported, will be able to run hotfoot to the scene to apprehend the criminals before they can make their escape. It is my vision for the future, where these men are recognised and respected and criminals go in fear of them.'

James smiled. 'Police?'

'No, the public equate that word with French gendarmes and the Revolution. They would never trust them.'

'Fielding's Runners, perhaps.'

'Not that either, for I hope they will long outlast me. Perhaps Bow Street Runners, since they will be working from this office. But enough of that. You have, no doubt, come about those rascals, Smith and Randle.'

His words brought James up short. That ought to have been his first concern, had always been in the forefront of his mind, behind every action, until he met Amy. Now he was not so sure. 'That, too, but, as you recall, you sent me on an errand for Lord Trentham.'

'Ah, yes. Tell me what you have discovered.'

James told him, though he was careful not to say

anything about Amy's nightmares and her conviction that she was in some way culpable. Confessions were often taken as proof by the judiciary and the thought of his lovely Amy being sent to the gallows made his heart almost stop.

'I had no idea the man was in gaol when I asked you to find him,' the magistrate said. 'But if he had not been brought to trial on account of being too ill, that would account for it. Did he make a deathbed confession?'

'If he did, they were made to a man called Martin Gotobed. He was in Newgate at the same time as Macdonald.'

'Oh, that one. A slippery customer indeed. Got away with his crimes on account of the witnesses changing their story. I have no doubt he bribed them, but I could not shift them and so we had to let him go,' Fielding said.

'He was in Highbeck when we left,' James said. 'And so were two men I'll lay my oath were Macdonald's cronies, though I cannot be certain. If they are, why are all these loose fish congregating at a remote hamlet like Highbeck?'

Fielding shrugged. 'Perhaps you should find out.'

James sighed. 'More thieftaking?'

The magistrate laughed. 'Well, Captain, you are so good at it. And one reason I rely on you is that I know you to be a man of principle and honest in your dealings with them. I wish there were more like you, then men like Gotobed who can afford to bribe and coerce witnesses would never escape justice.'

'It has not helped me to find Smith and Randle.' It was all very well to tell Amy he felt easier about Caroline's death, but murderers should not be allowed to think they could get away with it and commit other devilish crimes with impunity. If there was no longer a thirst for vengeance, there ought still to be some measure of justice. 'But I will run them to earth after I have concluded my present enquiries.'

His next call was on Lord Trentham in Grosvenor Square; as Lady Charron's representative, it behoved him to keep him up to date with his enquiries.

His lordship was preparing to go out, the footman told him, but on being acquainted with James's presence, asked the servant to show him up to his dressing room. 'We will talk while I dress,' he told James, signalling to his valet to carry on with his work. 'Have you come from Highbeck?'

'Yes. I have brought Mrs Macdonald with me. I thought the sight of her house might help, but all it did was distress her. We are going to the opera tonight at Lady Charron's invitation. I hope it will give her a little diversion.'

His lordship smiled. 'You sound convinced she is genuine.'

'Yes, I am.' He went on to describe everything that had happened before adding, 'I met a friend of her ladyship's at the theatre, a Mr Harry Portman. Her ladyship introduced him as her protégé. He invited himself to join the party. A bit of a queer fish, I thought. He mentioned you.'

'Yes, I know him.'

'I wonder how much Lady Charron has told him.'

Lord Trentham laughed. 'All, I should think. And before you condemn her for it, be assured Mr Harry Portman is not what he seems. It is not generally known and I doubt her ladyship is aware of it, but he stands high with the government.' He tapped the side of his nose, getting his hand in the way of his valet who was vainly trying to powder his hair. 'I can say no more, except that if he has anything to say on the matter it would be as well to listen.'

James thanked him and took his leave, striding down the road deep in thought, not about Harry Portman, nor Smith and Randle, but about Amy and her problems, which over the last few weeks had become his problems. He could not shake off a feeling that Blackfen Manor held the key. He was glad they were returning on the morrow.

Hot water had been brought up for Amy to wash and change, though what to change into she did not know. She had not come prepared for opera going. 'I ought to go into mourning, I suppose,' she told Susan. 'But it would be hypocritical to pretend, so what am I to wear?'

She had not cared what had been packed for her and it had been left to Susan to decide what to take. While Amy had been sleeping, she had taken a gown from Amy's portmanteau and shaken the creases out. It was a simple gown in dove-grey silk with only slight padding at the hips and a brocade stomacher finished with a fichu of white lace at its neckline, which could be called half-mourning. Susan arranged her hair becomingly, padding out the side curls and threading black ribbons through the lace cap to signify her widowhood. Slipping into her shoes, Amy took a last look in the mirror and went out onto the landing just as the dinner gong sounded.

James was just coming from his dressing room, dressed in a dark mulberry satin suit, white ruffled shirt and a white neckcloth. 'Good evening, Mrs Macdonald,' he said, bowing. 'Were you able to rest?'

'Yes, I did not think I would, but I fell asleep,' she admitted.

'Good.' He offered her his arm and they proceeded down to the dining room in stately fashion. On the way he pointed out the family portraits hanging on the walls of the staircase, telling her the family's history as he did so. It was an old family, he told her, the earldom went back over a century. This was his father, this his grandfather, this his grandmother and this his brother Edward, Viscount Drymore, who was the next heir. 'You will like him,' he said. 'As my parents prefer to live in London, he lives with his wife and four children on the family's Hertfordshire estate. My father has all but handed it over to him to manage.'

'Do you visit him often?'

'Yes.' He paused. 'Now that is an idea. Shall we break our journey to Highbeck and stay a night with him? It will be less of a trial if we do it in two stages. What do you say?'

She was a little taken aback. 'Are you sure he will not mind?'

'He will be delighted,' he assured her.

'Very well, I should like that,' she said.

'Then I will arrange it. Now, let us go and eat. The meal is only a light one, considering we are to have supper after the opera.'

Even so it consisted of seven dishes and a remove of fruit and tartlets, making Amy wonder what a full meal might be like in that grand household. She was too unsettled to eat much. Afterwards the coach was called up and they rode in comfort to the Drury Lane Theatre and took their seats in the Colbridge box.

The Beggar's Opera was popular with the crowds because it was so different from the usual run of operas. The hero of the piece was a highwayman, the heroine, played by Sophie, a gaoler's daughter, and the chorus was a band of criminals and whores, which James thought ironic, considering everything that had happened to Amy in the last three months. But the music and performances were good and Amy did not seem unduly upset. In fact, she was looking particularly charming and frequently grabbed his arm to point out something amusing she had noticed on the stage. She had evidently made up her mind to try to put her troubles behind her, at least for the evening, and he was determined to make sure nothing cast a cloud over it.

He had hardly paid attention to the opera and was still in something of a brown study when they went to Sophie's dressing room after the performance and were joined there by Harry Portman, extravagantly attired in a spotted silk coat, heavily embroidered waistcoat of silver brocade, frothy muslin neckcloth and pink stockings with bunches of ribbons at the knees.

During supper, James acquainted Lady Charron with the progress of his investigation. After all, she was Amy's mother and the one who had asked for enquiries to be made and would have been his paymaster if he had ever considered accepting imbursement. He told her of the two men Amy had seen in the grounds of the Manor and his conviction they were the two highwaymen and known to Amy's unprepossessing escort. 'I am also of the opinion that they were involved in whatever happened in Henrietta Street before Mrs Macdonald left,' he said.

Sophie turned to her daughter. 'And you really do not remember any of that?'

'No, Mama, nothing before the coach turned over. You see, I banged my head…'

'And it seems to have addled your wits.'

'I say, Sophie, that's doing it too brown,' Harry Portman drawled. James was surprised at his intervention; he had been examining his fingernails and had not appeared to be listening. Now he tapped Sophie on the arm. 'If Mrs Macdonald cannot remember, then she cannot remember. I am persuaded her wits are unaffected. Let us leave all to

Captain Drymore and change the subject. What do you think of our new bridge, Drymore?'

The new bridge over the Thames between Lambeth and Westminster was nearing completion. Until it opened, anyone wanting to cross the river had either to brave the traffic jams along Fleet Street and over the six-hundred-year-old London Bridge or go all the way to Kingston and cross by the wooden Fulham Bridge.

'Long overdue, I should say,' James answered, knowing it had taken twelve years to build. 'It will certainly aid those working in Westminster, not to mention bring in extra trade to both sides of the river, though I hear it does not please the ferrymen.'

'No, but one cannot hinder progress and now, but for a lick of paint, it is finished.'

They went on to discuss the architecture of the bridge and how it would be an extra crossing for troops if they were called to put down any new rebellion which everyone seemed to think might come from the south.

Amy, glad she was no longer the centre of attention, did not join in. James turned once or twice to smile at her, which received a tentative smile in response. She was in her own little world of shadows and he swore to himself that, come what may, one day he would make her happy again.

Chapter Eight

Drymore Hall was a vast mansion set in rolling parkland, with a long carriage drive and a sweeping turning circle at the front door, in the middle of which was a statue of a man on a horse. Its regiment of windows gleamed in the late afternoon sun. Amy began to feel nervous. 'It's a palace,' she breathed.

'Not quite.' James turned to smile at her. 'Old, but not as old as Blackfen Manor. But like the Manor to you, it was my childhood home.'

The carriage rolled to a stop. James opened the door and jumped down without waiting for the coachman to come and let down the step. He ran lightly up the steps and banged on the door, which was opened by a liveried footman. 'Captain Drymore,' the man said, a broad smile creasing his face. 'I will tell the master you are here.'

'Who is here?' said a voice which belonged to a

man in his early forties who had come from one of the many rooms, carrying a book. 'James, well I never! What brings you here? Not that I am not delighted to see you. Come on in. We were never more surprised when Father told us you had decided to stay in the country for a time and had sent Sam Roker to fetch your belongings. You surely did not need to take a repairing lease?'

'Certainly not! I am not in debt, at least no more than a few pounds for my last suit of clothes and a new pair of pistols, which I shall discharge while I am here.'

'The pistols?'

James laughed. 'No, the debt.'

'Then, pray, come in and tell us all about it…'

'Edward,' James interrupted him, 'I am not alone. I hope you do not mind, but I have brought a guest. We need to rack up for the night. Do you think Elizabeth will mind?'

'Of course not. Bring him in.'

'It is not a him, it is a lady.'

'Really?' He did not even try to hide his surprise. James had shown no interest in ladies since his wife died. 'Don't leave her out there, man, go and fetch her.'

Amy was fetched and ushered into the drawing room where the Viscount and Lady Drymore waited.

'Edward, Elizabeth,' James said, as they rose to

greet her. 'Allow me to present Mrs Macdonald. Mrs Macdonald, Viscount Drymore, Lady Drymore.'

Amy gave them a deep curtsy, only to find herself being raised by the Viscount himself. 'Come and sit down, Mrs Macdonald,' he said, leading her to a sofa. 'You must tell us all about yourself.'

This was harder than she could ever have imagined. She did not know all about herself and did not know what to say. She glanced at James, who was smiling encouragement. 'You can be perfectly frank,' he said.

Amy began tentatively explaining who she was and how she had come to meet the Captain and a little of her life at Highbeck. That done, her voice faded to a halt. James came to her rescue and explained how she had come to lose her memory and how he had taken her to London in the hope that it might be restored, making himself sound matter of fact, his part that of investigator, nothing more.

'Oh, you poor thing,' Lady Drymore said to Amy. 'And how brave of you to venture back to that house. I could never have done it, I am sure.'

'It had to be done, my lady,' Amy replied.

They were interrupted by the entrance of the children, two boys and two girls, all boisterous and noisy. Seeing James, they flung themselves at him in delight. It was only when he gently disengaged himself, they realised their parents had another visitor and stood obediently to be presented to Amy. The boys bowed and the girls curtsied. Amy smiled and asked them their names and how old they were, which the eldest answered. 'I'm Edward, called Teddy on account of papa is Edward, too, and this is James, after Uncle James, and the girls are Marianna, who is eight, and Isobel, who is six. We have been on a nature ramble with our governess this afternoon and have collected flowers to draw…'

'You can show them to us later,' their mother said. 'Go back to Miss Wiles now and have your supper.'

They ran off and a maid came to say Amy's room was ready and hot water taken up for her to prepare for dinner. Amy went up behind the maid in a daze. James's life before he met her, before his wife had died, had been very different from hers. He was way above her in every way, but everyone was so kind to her, she did not feel put down, and in any case, her aunts had brought her up to know how to behave in society. She could and would hold her own.

Susan would not hear of Amy wearing the grey again. 'I thought you might want to dress up,' she said. 'So I packed one of your best gowns.'

Amy laughed. 'You are as bad as Widow Twitch,

claiming to see into the future. Which one have you brought?'

It was an open gown in blue silk, beautifully embroidered with sprigs of pink-and-lemon flowers and worn over a quilted cream-satin petticoat. It had narrow side hoops and a modest neckline edged with lace. The lace continued down the edges of the bodice where it met the embroidered stomacher and that ended in a point just below her waist and was finished off with a satin bow. The narrow sleeves ended in a froth of lace. It suited Amy well, as Susan was not slow to tell her.

'Beautiful,' she breathed, standing back with shining eyes to survey what she considered her handiwork. 'How shall I do your hair?'

'Something simple.'

'Then the Dutch style it shall be.'

Amy sat at the dressing table and patiently allowed Susan to brush her fair hair back from a centre parting and pin it into a knot on top of her head, from where she teased the ends into curls and ringlets to fall about her face and neck. There were no unnatural buckles, no powdering. 'There!' she said at last. 'You are ready. And if that does not turn a certain young man's head, I do not know what will.'

Amy ignored her last remark, slipped on her shoes and took one last look in the mirror before making her way downstairs to the drawing room where everyone was gathered before going into the dining room.

James turned as she hesitated in the doorway. She took his breath away she looked so lovely, if a little pale, which was not down to paint or powder—her complexion was devoid of makeup, not even a patch. The word *wholesome* came into his mind, wholesome and innocent. And entirely adorable. He went forwards and led her into the room to join Lord and Lady Drymore, both of whom were looking very elegant.

James, too, had taken trouble with his appearance. His forest-green coat was plain except for the pearl buttons on the sleeves, pockets and down the front. Its elegance lay in its perfect fit, which emphasised his broad shoulders and neat waist. His breeches, of a paler green, met white stockings just below the knee where a ribbon bow held both in place. Only his waistcoat showed any sign of opulence and that was of heavily embroidered brocade, buttoned to the waist. His only jewel was the pin he always wore in his neckcloth. Sam had insisted on arranging his hair in three padded curls over each ear and tying the rest of it behind his head in a queue, but James had drawn the line at smothering it in white powder.

When dinner was announced, they went into the

dining room, where they were served with a feast by the butler and two footmen dressed in pale blue-and-white livery and white wigs. The first course, already on the table, consisted of fifteen separate dishes, including two soups that began the meal, meat and poultry, with mock turtle made from a calf's head as the centrepiece. There were dishes of peas, carrots, mashed swede and broccoli. When all that was removed, the second course was brought in and this consisted mainly of game: pheasant, hare, partridge and fish, together with fruit tartlets and several kinds of pudding. The meal was topped off, after these dishes had been cleared away and the cloth drawn, with fruit and spun-sugar confections.

Amy did her best to do it justice. Did her best, too, to keep up her end of the conversation as it ranged from the weather and the possibility of a good harvest after so many bad ones. She answered questions about Highbeck and her aunts, and then the talk moved on to the rumours flying about concerning Prince Charlie and what the government was doing to prevent another invasion, and she fell silent. James noticed this and quickly changed the subject by asking about his brother's children, who were very close to his heart, and talking about education in general.

But after the ladies had withdrawn, he brought the

subject up again with his brother. 'The Young Pretender has been seen in London,' he said. 'He walked into Lady Primrose's card party in Essex Street as bold as you please, and she did not turn a hair. I had it from Henry Fielding.'

'Is Fielding proposing to arrest him?' Edward asked.

James laughed. 'I am quite sure he would like to, but the man is as slippery as an eel and has disappeared again.'

'Let us hope he has gone back to France.'

'Yes. You do not wish it any more than I do, for Amy's sake.'

'Amy?' Edward smiled. 'You make free with her given name. Does that mean you have at last decided to remarry?'

'No.' James was quick to deny it. 'Mrs Macdonald has only recently learned of her husband's death.'

Edward, knowing his brother, ignored this prevarication. 'That was a bad business, a bad business indeed. Are you sure Mrs Macdonald knew nothing of what her husband was up to?'

'I am positive she is entirely innocent. But there are other matters that need investigating. Macdonald's cronies and what they are planning, for one thing.'

'And you are intent on going back to Highbeck tomorrow?' Edward enquired.

'Yes. There has to be a reason why all the muckworms are gathering there and the aunts are alone, apart from a handful of servants. And Amy is anxious to return.'

'Then let us join the ladies and enjoy the remainder of our time together. We see too little of you, James…'

It was haymaking time in Highbeck when they arrived and the villagers were out in the fields, either scything or raking it. They turned to look as the coach went by and, seeing who occupied it, waved a greeting and Amy waved, too, glad to be back. This was home; it was where she was most at ease and while James was there beside her, she felt content and safe from harm. He had convinced her he had no intention of handing her over to the law, that there was no need of it, but was he endangering his own reputation as a man of honour by leaving her free? Should she be feeling guilty about that, too?

She turned to look at him. He was smiling. 'Home, Amy,' he said.

'Yes.'

'For me, too.'

'Truly?'

'Yes. I cannot think of anywhere else I would rather be,' he admitted.

'But you have an estate in Suffolk, have you not?'

'I never lived there and now I never shall. I have instructed my lawyer to sell it for me. I shall continue to live in the Lodge until I find somewhere to buy.'

She gave a little chuckle, the first real laugh he had heard from her for days. 'The aunts will be pleased about that and Cousin Gerald exactly the contrary.'

'And you? Will it please you?' he asked.

'Oh, yes,' she said immediately and he was immeasurably heartened.

'Over the last few weeks,' he went on, 'you have made me realise that what I was doing before I met you was wasting my life in search of vengeance, believing only that could bring me peace, but you have shown me I was wrong. My life could be put to better purpose…'

So he *had* listened to her! 'What purpose?'

'That I am not sure of. Doing some good, helping people.'

'Like you have helped me, you mean?'

'But I have not helped you, have I? Your memory has not returned and we still do not know why your husband died.'

'But you have been a great help to me,' she protested. 'You make me feel calm and at ease with myself. You tell me you do not believe I killed my husband and I have to trust you are right.'

'I am heartily glad of that.'

'You know,' she said slowly, 'you said you had been wasting your life and it is the same for me, though with me it is not vengeance, but a memory. I should put myself in the hands of God, who will restore my memory if and when it pleases Him. It is time I thought of something more useful to do with my time. You have made me see that.'

Delighted with this, he picked up her hand and cupped it in both of his, forgetting Susan was sitting opposite her, drinking in every word. 'Thank you, my dear. Let us say we have been of benefit to each other.' He lifted the hand he held to his lips. 'We go forwards from here, is it agreed?'

'Agreed.'

He noticed Susan's eyes widen and dropped Amy's hand back into her lap, turning to look out of the carriage. What he saw made him catch his breath in shock.

Standing beside the road, watching them pass, were two men whom he recognised. One was as thin as a rake, the other a beefy fellow with a red bulbous nose. What, in God's name, were Smith and Randle doing in Highbeck? Were they the same men Amy had seen in Downham Market and in the grounds of the Manor? Had they been the men who held up the coach?

The more he thought about it, the more he thought

they might have been. After all they had boarded a coach ahead of him and Sam; they could easily have left it at Ely and hired horses. Perhaps they had nothing to do with Amy at all. But Gus Billings had known them, so there had to be a connection and that connection, he did not doubt, was Duncan Macdonald. He glanced at Amy, but she had not seen them. Should he tell her and spoil their new-found peace or say nothing?

It was a question that occupied him until they rattled over the drawbridge and pulled up outside the main door. Hardly had the wheels stopped turning than the door was flung open and both aunts ran out to greet them. James jumped down and turned to offer his hand to Amy. 'I have brought your niece back to you as I promised I would,' he told them.

Amy ran to be embraced by each aunt in turn. 'Oh, it is so good to be back,' she said. 'I have missed you so.'

'And we missed you,' Matilda said. 'But why did you not send to say you were coming?'

'There was no time, we only decided the day before yesterday,' Amy said.

'Well, come in, come in, and tell us all about it,' Harriet said, ushering them both ahead of her, followed by Matilda. Sam took the portmanteaux from the boot and handed them to Susan, giving her a large wink and a grin as he did so, which made James smile.

'Sam, take the coach to the Lodge, I will walk from here,' he called over his shoulder.

Once they were settled in the small parlour and tea and refreshments had been ordered, Harriet demanded to know all that had happened.

James, who was more than a little preoccupied, left Amy to relate everything. She described the grandeur of Colbridge House and the palatial Drymore Hall, recounted her meeting with her mother and the visit to the opera and her reaction to the dreadful mess at the house in Henrietta Street, drawing a gasp of horror from Matilda. 'Did you remember how it came to be like that?' she asked.

'No, Aunt. It made no difference.'

'You surely do not still think you were responsible for Duncan's death, do you?'

'You knew he was dead?' she asked in surprise. 'I did not know myself until the Captain told me in London.'

'He told us before you left,' Harriet said. 'And do not climb into the tree-tops over it. He asked who should be the one to tell you and we left it to him. It was done for your own good.'

'I know.' She was far more placid about it now.

'And the Captain has convinced me that I am not to blame for Duncan's death, though I may have witnessed it…'

The aunts both turned to James, who had been sitting silent, his mind on how to go about arresting Smith and Randle and making sure they did not slip through his fingers again. Politeness decreed he should sit and take tea, but he was on hot coals to be gone.

'You have discovered who might have been responsible?' Harriet asked him.

'One of Mr Macdonald's associates, I think. It might have been the man, Billings, but as he is dead…' He shrugged without finishing the sentence. Could it have been Smith or Randle who murdered Amy's husband?

'The only thing that came to me,' Amy went on, 'was a voice, which I think must have been Duncan's, saying, "Go to Blackfen Manor. I will join you there. Tell no one."'

'Ah, that is how you came to be on that coach,' Harriet said.

'Yes, so you see, he was very likely alive when I left and most of the mystery is solved. I have decided not to worry about the rest. I can remember being here afterwards and the Captain coming and that is enough.'

'Are you going to stay here with us, then?' Matilda wanted to know.

'Oh, yes. And the Captain is going to stay, too. He says Highbeck suits him.'

'If you would be so good as to allow me to remain at the Lodge until I find somewhere to buy in the vicinity,' he put in.

'Stay as long as you like,' Harriet said. 'Which reminds me, did you deliver those documents to Mr Smithson?'

'I did indeed. He said he would write to you as soon as he has had time to study them, but he is sure you have nothing to worry about.'

'I am glad to hear that,' Harriet said. 'Not that I ever doubted it, but Gerald was here again yesterday, being as objectionable as ever. He insisted on going round the house making an inventory. He said there were repairs that needed doing and we were not up to seeing to them, which made me very angry. I followed him round to see what he was writing down, but he did not seem to make many notes at all. I think he was simply prying. What I cannot understand is why, after years of silence, he has suddenly taken an interest again.'

'Oh, it is the presence of the Captain,' Matilda said, almost smugly. 'He is afraid Amy will marry him and deprive him of all hope of getting his hands on the Manor.'

Amy's face went scarlet and even James was taken aback.

'Tilly!' Harriet remonstrated. 'You are putting Amy to the blush and embarrassing the Captain.'

James felt something from him was called for, but he was unsure what that should be. Should he deny he had ever thought of Amy in that way, which would be a terrible set down for her? On the other hand he did not want to be pushed into proposing. He was not ready for that. 'Until a week ago, we all believed Mrs Macdonald was married,' he said evenly. 'I am sure she is not yet ready to consider another suit.'

Amy was mortified. Not until that moment had she realised her growing regard for James was more than that. She loved him and nothing would have pleased her more than he should love her, too. But he did not and was letting her down as gently as he could. But could she blame him? She might have said she was content not to push at her memory, but there were still matters unresolved and even if she had not been the one to put the knife into her husband, she must have seen it happen and knew the men who did it and that made her an accessory. He had to uphold the law, that was the kind of man he was; he would not marry a woman like her. The happiness she felt in returning to Highbeck seeped away, leaving her as troubled as she had been before.

'Aunts, what have you been doing while we have been away?' she asked, falsely bright. 'Apart from entertaining Cousin Gerald, I mean.'

'Busying ourselves about the estate,' Harriet said. 'Overseeing the haymaking and clearing the barn for the harvest. And we had two more callers. Why the house should suddenly interest visitors, I do not know. We are so out of the way here.'

'Visitors?' James queried. 'What manner of visitors?'

'A Mr Miller and a Mr Wade. London gentlemen, they said. Studying architecture. They asked to be shown round the house.'

This was not good news. James wondered whether to put the ladies on their guard or say nothing. There must be a reason why the house was attracting visitors. Most recently, those two, whom he did not doubt were Smith and Randle, and also Gotobed, seen whispering with the dying Duncan Macdonald; and even Sir Gerald Hardwick, whose interest in the place had suddenly been revived. And there was the voice Amy had remembered. 'Go to Blackfen Manor. I will join you there. Tell no one.' What was she not to tell? Had she remembered that and decided not to enlighten him?

'Did you show the two London gentlemen round?' he asked the aunts.

'No, but they came into the hall and started asking questions about the house and how many rooms there were. I did not like them and when they started to become too inquisitive, almost as if they were interrogating me, I asked them to leave.'

'Good.' He paused. 'Perhaps it would be wise to be a little less hospitable in future.'

Amy, who had begun to understand how his mind worked, looked sharply at him. Was he simply being cautious or did he think there was more to the visitors than appeared on the surface? Did it have anything to do with her? If she had brought danger to her aunts, she would never forgive herself. He saw her looking at him and smiled to reassure her. 'Just a precaution.'

They talked for a few more minutes, then he took his leave, setting off to walk swiftly through the copse to the Lodge.

Sam had seen to the horses and put the carriage away and was busy in James's bedchamber unpacking. He turned as James entered. 'Is all well at the Manor, Captain?'

'I am not sure. Sir Gerald Hardwick has called again and two other men came wanting to be shown round the house. It looks like we have found Smith and Randle.' He gave a grunt of a laugh. 'Or they have found us.'

'You saw them, too, did you?' Sam said. 'I wondered if you might have.'

'It occurred to me they might be the two who held up the coach when we first came to Highbeck. The masks and cloaks made it impossible to identify them.'

'Then they are connected with Mrs Macdonald…'

'It looks like it. Mrs Macdonald has remembered her husband telling her to come to Highbeck, that he would meet her here. Presumably they knew it. And that fellow Billings did, too. They were all on the way to Blackfen Manor.'

'Then undoubtedly there is something there, something they want and it has to be something valuable. Gold and jewels, mayhap.'

'What made you say that?' James asked sharply. One of Amy's dreams had featured something of the sort, though he did not think Sam knew that.

'No reason, but ain't that what thieves are usually after?' He gave a sudden chuckle. 'You never know, it might be the Arkaig treasure.'

James laughed, too, but it set him thinking and thinking hard. Knowledge of the whereabouts of that, or anything like it, could be a threat, not only from criminals who coveted it, but from the government who had been trying to locate it for years without success. Having it amounted to treason. Surely his beautiful Amy could know nothing of it? He wanted to rush back and warn her, to instigate a search for whatever it was, hand it over and free Amy of any stigma of involvement. He sat down heavily on the bed while Sam continued to tidy away his clothes and put out a fresh coat and breeches for him to change into.

His thieftaking had taken on a whole new meaning. Fielding had sent him here—did Fielding know more than he had told him? Was he being used? It made him angry and, for a second—and it was only a second—he thought of abandoning the whole project and returning to London to confront the magistrate. But he knew at once he could not do that. Amy was here and, wherever Amy was, there he must stay. 'I think we would be wise to search the grounds and outbuildings,' he said.

'For the treasure?' Sam gasped.

'No, man, for those two murdering thieves. We must find out where they are staying and keep a watch on them. Gotobed, too.'

'He was at the King's Arms when we left four days ago. Mayhap they are there, too.'

'Then tonight you and I will go and enjoy the hospitality of mine host.'

Amy lay awake. In spite of telling James she would wait until God chose to restore her memory, she found herself going over and over what she had learned about her husband, her mother's statement about the unsavoury characters with whom he associated and the two men she had seen following her in the grounds. James had not said so, but she knew him well enough now to know that he considered they had been her aunts' visitors and that boded no good. His gentle warnings hid a deep concern.

Dear James! How she loved him! He embodied all that was good, whereas the others represented evil. She needed to know there was none of that evil in her, and to do that she must remember everything. She lay listening to the rising wind soughing round the old house and deliberately made herself visualise the house in Henrietta Street, trying to see it as it had been before someone had fought a battle in it.

She had no idea what her married life with Duncan had been like, except from what her mother had told her, nor what had caused the fight in the house. Nor was she sure there had ever been any gold or jewels except in her dreams. But there had been a struggle. It was coming back to her now; mentally she reached out to grasp it, something she had been shying away from until now, too afraid to face it. Four men. Anger. Everyone shouting. Crockery and furniture being thrown. A knife being produced and a great deal of blood. Screaming. Her screaming as she watched. And Duncan's voice, weak from his injuries, telling her to go to Highbeck. How much of that was real memory and how much suggested to her by dreams and what people had told her? Was she dreaming now? And then she remembered being out in the street, running, running as if the hounds of hell were at her heels…

She began to tremble. It was very close now, the revelation she wanted so badly and yet feared so much. Knowing she would not sleep until it came to her, she left her bed and drew back the curtains. It was dawn, but still very early, too soon to dress and go down to breakfast. She slipped into a dressing gown and sat at the escritoire and taking quill, ink and paper from a drawer began to write down all she could remember and had been told in the order in which she thought it had occurred. Slowly more was revealed on the pages in front of her. It was as if her memory were communicating itself direct from her pen to the paper.

She had helped the wounded Duncan to bed, trailing blood all the way, and tended his wounds, while the other three caroused and argued in the kitchen. Duncan had wanted her to leave him. 'Go while you can,' he had said. 'You know what will happen to you if you do not. They will have no mercy. Go to Highbeck. Tell no one where you are going.'

'But I cannot leave you like this!' she had exclaimed.

'I shall recover, never fear, and join you there.'

'What will they do to you?'

'Nothing. I have something they want very badly. They will not harm me further while I tantalise them with it.'

She would never have left him if she had known he would die or if she had felt an ounce of sympathy for him, but all she could remember feeling was anger that his own disreputable behaviour had brought this trouble on them. The sound of drunken laughter coming from the kitchen finally persuaded her to go. She had flung a cloak about her, crept from the house and run down the street, dodging this way and that, not knowing what to do or where to go. Even as angry with him as she was, she could not do as Duncan asked and go to Highbeck, not while he lay wounded and at the mercy of those men. She ought to find a constable or a watchman, but if she did that, Duncan would be in trouble along with those dreadful men. A doctor, then.

She was standing in the street, too confused to go on, when Gus Billings—she remembered him— had caught up with her and given her the choice of allowing him to accompany her to Highbeck, which indicated he had overheard Duncan talking to her, or taking her back to the house and handing her over to the other two. 'And they will not deal so gently with you, my dear,' he had said with a leer, his hand gripping her arm painfully. 'All I want to do is help you, as Duncan wishes me to.'

As she wrote, the journey in the coach came back to her. James and Sam Roker and a parson had all boarded it in London, as she and Billings had done. James had shown some concern for her and had given her his coat for a pillow. He had spoken kindly and at the inn where they stopped had paid for a tisane for her, but he had also seemed impatient, as if anxious to be at his destination. Or had she simply surmised that because he had since told her about his wife? Why was it all such a muddle?

They had been held up by highwaymen; she remembered that now. The robbers had worn masks, hats and cloaks, so she could not positively identify them, but they had been known to her unwelcome escort. They had conferred together while James stood with his arm protectively about her. Even then, even in the first days of their acquaintance-ship, he had been looking after her, protecting her, as he had been doing ever since. The robbers had let them continue their journey and she remem-bered feeling exhausted and trying to sleep and then being severely jolted and James grabbing her as the coach rolled over. He had pulled her from the wreckage and tended to her. She saw again the mangled coach, the frightened horse careering up the road and Billings lying dead. And she had a bump on the back of her head that hurt when she touched it.

That was the beginning of her loss of memory, that was when her poor brain gave up on her, but it was also the beginning of the rest of her life in which James figured largely. He had brought her safely to the King's Arms, nestling like an injured bird inside his coat against his shirt. She remem-bered that ride in fits and starts, the warmth of him, his gentle voice soothing her, arriving at the inn and being put to bed. Everything after that was clear as day; her aunts' efforts to make her remember; James's arrival in the village, her growing depen-dence on him, her burgeoning love for him which now could not be denied, but must be denied until all taint of wickedness had been washed away.

She heard a cock crowing in the yard and then the clatter of milk pails and then Susan going past her door to go downstairs. Another day had begun. Without waiting for the maid to come with her hot chocolate, she dressed and went downstairs to eat her breakfast with the servants in the kitchen, which she often did. Her aunts were still in bed and she did not want to put the servants to the trouble of serving her in the dining room. Besides, she liked their company, had always enjoyed listening to their gossip and hearing news of the doings of the villagers.

After breakfast, she fetched out her sketching materials and took them into the back parlour where the light was good and set about illustrating her memories, trying to capture the likeness of those two men. It was sombre work and made her feel low in spirits. She could be doing something more useful, she told herself, something to make her feel better. Looking at her drawing, she knew she would recognise those men if she saw them again. Did she know their names? Had she ever known them? Her aunts' visitors had called themselves Miller and Wade, but they could easily have invented those along with their claim to be architects. They held the key and she had to face up to them. James seemed to think they were somewhere in the village. Could she find them?

Hearing the door knocker, she thought it was James and was unprepared when a footman came and told her Mr Gotobed desired a few minutes of her time.

She was inclined to say she was not at home, but was curious about what Duncan had said when he lay dying. She bade the footman to show him into the drawing room and, in the absence of her aunts, who were making calls in the village, told him to send Susan down to her.

She had settled herself on a sofa with her hands in her lap, when Martin Gotobed came striding in, swept off his tricorne hat and executed a flourishing bow. He was wearing yellow breeches, a green coat and a yellow-and-brown striped waistcoat. She thought he looked like some strange beetle. 'Madam, your obedient.'

'Mr Gotobed.' She rose but did not curtsy, waiting for him to state his errand, giving him no prompting by asking how he did. Susan slipped into the room and took up a station just inside the door. He seemed unaware of her.

'Madam, I hope you are well,' he began.

'Very well, sir, I thank you.' She did not ask him to be seated and, as she remained standing herself, he could do nothing but stand facing her. He was no taller than she was, which put him at a disadvantage.

'And your journey to the capital? I hope it proved beneficial,' he enquired.

'How did you know I have been to London?'

'Why, madam, this is a small village, everyone knows everyone's business. Captain Drymore was enquiring about carriages and horses, so…' He shrugged.

She allowed herself a twitch of a smile. 'To be sure. In answer to your question, yes, it was of some use.'

'Ahh.' He paused. 'Then you will have learned of Mr Macdonald's demise.'

'Yes.' She was angry now and did not bother to hide it. 'I also learned you were with him when he died. You could have had the civility to tell me that when you first came here.'

'I was not with him at the moment of his death, but he was certainly beyond recovery when I left him. I would have told you, dear lady, but I could hardly get near you for your bodyguard.'

'My bodyguard? Do you mean my aunts?' she asked.

'No, I meant that thieftaking mariner who seems to have attached himself to you like a leech. I did try to warn you…'

'So you did, but as you see, he did not arrest me,' she said tartly.

'Heaven forfend!'

'Mr Gotobed, why have you come?'

'Why, to convey your husband's dying words to you, and to ask you a question,' he said.

'Go on. I am listening.'

'His last words were of you. He asked me to tell you that. He said he had sent you to Blackfen Manor where he hoped to join you…' He heaved an insincere sigh. 'Alas, it was not to be. When he realised he would not live to keep his word, he asked me to come to you in his stead. He desired me to look after you.'

'I do not need anyone to look after me, sir. And if I did, I have friends and relations who take good care of me.'

'Nevertheless, that was his dying wish and I come to keep the promise I made him. He was sure you would be surrounded by unscrupulous men, from whom you would need safeguarding. Therefore, I come in all humility to offer you the protection of my name and my strong right hand.'

She gave a gurgle of laughter, quickly suppressed. 'Mr Gotobed, are you asking me to *marry* you?'

'I am.'

'I cannot believe you are in earnest.'

'Indeed, I am. A promise made to a dying man is a promise that must be kept, and may I add that it is one I shall take pleasure in fulfilling,' he said, smiling at her.

'Then I am sorry to disappoint you, sir, but I have no wish to marry you. I hardly know you, but from what I have learned, you have not always lived on the right side of the law,' she said bluntly.

'I was wrongly and wilfully accused and found not guilty. And to be sure, you have no reason to condemn me, when you are not the little innocent you would have everyone believe. If Captain Drymore has not arrested you before now, it is because he is waiting for you to lead him to bigger fish. Marry me, and you will be safe. When the knot is tied, we will go abroad where English thief-takers cannot touch us,' he urged.

Susan gave a gasp, making him swing round to glare at her. She glared back, ready to defend her mistress, with tooth and nail if she had to.

'Mr Gotobed,' Amy said, smiling at Susan—she looked so fierce. 'I wish you to leave. Now, at once. And please do not return.'

'I am afraid you will come to regret your decision, dear lady. Others will come who are not so careful of you. Remember that, will you?'

He bowed his way out and Amy sank back on to the sofa, shaking like an aspen. Susan ran to her. 'My poor lamb,' she said. 'I never heard such impudence. There, he is gone now, you may be easy.'

Amy found herself laughing and crying at the same

time. 'As if I would contemplate marrying that…that insect! But, he has set me in turmoil again. He seemed to be threatening me and I wish, oh, how I wish, he had not spoken like that about the Captain and bigger fish. Gotobed's up to something…'

They turned, almost guiltily, as James came into the room. He bowed. 'Good morning, ladies.' He tried to sound cheerful, but the sight of Gotobed strolling nonchalantly across the drawbridge had severely strained his good humour. And Amy's tear-streaked face did nothing to make him feel better.

'Good morning, Captain.' Amy rose and curtsied, while Susan hurriedly dipped her knee and disappeared. She evidently did not think it necessary to chaperon her mistress when the Captain called.

'How are you today, Amy?' he asked gently.

'I am well. I was sketching.'

He smiled; she was evidently not going to tell him what that muckworm had said to her. 'More cherubs?'

'No—this.' She reached across the table to pick up her sketch book and handed it to him.

It was of the kitchen of her house in Henrietta Street. There were two men sitting at the table, two easily recognisable men. A third, the man Billings, stood at the door. A fourth, who could only have been Amy's husband, stood before the hearth, brandishing a knife. She had not drawn herself. 'What is this?'

'What I have remembered.'

'Has it all come back to you?' he wanted to know.

'Some of it,' she admitted.

'Is that Duncan Macdonald with the knife?'

'Yes. There was a violent quarrel and he tried to defend himself from the others with it, but he was no match for them and in the struggle to take it from him, he was wounded,' she told him.

He breathed a huge sigh of relief. 'Thank God for that.'

'What do you mean? He died!'

'Yes, and I am sorry for your sake, but now you know how foolish you were to blame yourself for his death.' He drew her down on to a sofa and sat beside her, holding her hand. 'What happened after that?'

'I helped Duncan to bed and bound up his wound,' she said. 'It was then he whispered to me to come here. I did not realise at the time his wound was mortal or I would never have left him.'

'I have been told it would not have killed him if it had not become infected while he was in prison. As I mentioned to you before, they are not the cleanest of places.'

'Oh. I did not know that. I crept out of the house intending to find help, but the man, Billings, followed me.' She went on to tell him what she had written that morning, about the journey and the highwaymen. 'They were all coming to Highbeck,' she said.

'That much we have deduced,' he said. 'The question is why. What do they want? Have you remembered that?'

'No. I was going to look for them and ask them what they were doing in Highbeck.'

He was alarmed. 'Amy, you foolish, foolish girl. Don't you know by now, those men are dangerous?' He tapped her drawing. 'This proves it. If they could do that to your husband…'

'Then I will ask Mr Gotobed. I doubt he would harm me.'

'Amy! Amy, my love, you must not do anything of the kind. It would be madness. He is no less dangerous than the other two. Just because he pretends to be a gentleman does not mean he *is* one.'

Had he really called her his love? Her heart leapt and then subsided. She had no right to hope. 'But I have to know,' she insisted.

'I thought you had decided to let sleeping dogs lie? Go on from here, we agreed,' he reminded her.

'But I cannot go on. I cannot pretend all is well when I know it is not. And neither can you. Do not tell me you were unconcerned when my aunts said two men had been to the house because I will not believe you.'

'I am concerned, but I beg of you, let me deal with it.'

She gave a cracked laugh. 'In your capacity as thieftaker?'

'Yes, if you like.'

'And having got them, what will you do with me?'

'Shake some sense into you,' he said.

'Is that all?'

'No,' he said, smiling. 'But the rest can wait. We are going riding. Go and change. I will wait for you here.'

She was not ready to give up, but he could be obdurate as she knew very well and arguing with him would do no good. She jumped up and left him to do as he asked. He picked up the drawing to study it. She really was a talented draughtsman; the men were easily recognisable. If Smith and Randle saw the sketch, they would assume she had remembered all and that would put her in even more danger. He folded it and put it into his pocket.

Chapter Nine

While out riding with James, under the wide fen skies, surrounded by a countryside she loved, Amy felt more at peace. She knew she had always been happy at Highbeck and that her time married to Duncan was something best left forgotten. She did not think she had ever loved him, certainly not as she loved James Drymore. The realisation of that had come upon her slowly, day by day, as they had spent time together, learning about each other. He was everything she could wish for in a man: handsome without being vain, honest and principled, but not hard. He was also gentle and kind and protective. She knew she could trust him and what Gotobed had said was nonsense. She wished he felt the same about her, but she did not think he did. He had adored his wife, whom his sister-in-law had described to her as very beautiful and good. 'They were so in love,' she had told her. 'I doubt he will ever get over her death. He always wears the cravat pin she gave him.'

James noticed how withdrawn and quiet she was, which was not to be wondered at. Remembering the carnage in Henrietta Street, and then sitting down and deliberately trying to illustrate it, must have taken all her nerve. And then to have that odious Gotobed arrive to pester her was the outside of enough. He wondered if she would ever tell him what the man had said without prompting. He waited until they were walking their horses along the side of the fen, before he mentioned the subject. 'You had a caller this morning.' He spoke lightly.

'Mr Gotobed, yes.'

'Did he upset you?'

She turned towards him. 'Upset? No, I was angry and then amused. He had the temerity to make me an offer…'

'An offer?' he repeated incredulously. 'You surely do not mean an offer of marriage?'

'Yes, I do. He said it was Duncan's dying wish that he should look after me.'

'Do you believe that?' he asked.

'I do not know what to believe.'

'Amy,' he said seriously, 'you will take care when I am not with you, won't you?'

'Take care?' she repeated.

'Yes. Gotobed wants something from you, something you probably do not know you have, but he will do anything to get it.'

She was attentive now. 'How do you know that?'

'I am guessing, just as I am guessing those two men who seem to appear and disappear at will, also want something, if not from you, then from the house. If your husband told you to come here, he might also have told Gotobed why.' The man was lodging openly at the King's Arms, but no one knew where the other two were staying, probably in some hedge tavern somewhere, though they seemed able to put on the appearance of gentlemen when it suited them. He wished he knew where they were and what they planned. He and Sam had searched the grounds and every barn, cart shed, stable, even the tower, although there was nothing there but an empty cone of brick with a winding stair to its top from which they could survey the countryside for miles. They had found nothing and no one.

'Perhaps there was no reason except that Duncan knew I would be safe here,' she suggested.

'I pray to God you are right.'

'You are frightening me.'

'I do not mean to. There is nothing to fear so long as you do not admit strangers to the house and take care to lock all doors and windows when you retire for the night.'

'You will suggest pulling up the drawbridge next.' She laughed to lighten the atmosphere, which had become very sombre.

He responded with a wry smile. 'I doubt you could make it work. It must be an age since it was last used.' He wanted to search the house, but as he had no idea what they would be looking for, he refrained from suggesting it. Sam's idea of the Arkaig treasure seemed too far out to be given credence.

'Do not say anything of that to my aunts,' she said. 'It will alarm them. I will instruct the servants to take especial care and go round myself last thing at night to make sure all is secure.'

'Good. And do not admit Mr Gotobed again.'

Although he had spoken without inflection, she detected something in his voice that made her turn and look at him. He was staring straight ahead, his hands on his reins, apparently relaxed, but his jaw was rigid and she noticed him swallow hard. He cared! Cared enough to be a little jealous, perhaps?

'He spoke of leaving the country when we married,' she said. 'He seemed to think I needed to escape the law and a certain thieftaker.'

He turned sharply towards her and realised she was smiling. Her lovely eyes were looking at him in a teasing manner and he laughed at himself to think that she could roast him into betraying his feelings. Not that he had not done so already, in a hundred different ways, even before he realised it himself. He knew now, without a shadow of doubt, that he loved her and could not live without her, that she was his whole life. But before anything could be said, there were obstacles to overcome and he hoped and prayed they would not be insurmountable.

'Do you want to escape?' he asked quietly.

'Do I need to?' she countered.

He reined in and dismounted, then went over to her and held out his hand to help her dismount. She slid from the saddle into his arms where he held her. 'Not from me, you do not.'

'I am glad of that.'

'Tell me, you did give him his turnabout, didn't you?'

She looked up into his face and smiled because he looked so severe. 'Did you think for one minute I would entertain the idea of marrying that…that creature? He makes my flesh crawl.' She shuddered to prove it.

He laughed and the next moment he was kissing her. He simply could not help it. Her face tiptilted towards his; her shining eyes, which he had seen in all her moods, from joyous to troubled, and her rose-coloured lips, oh, those kissable lips, invited him to succumb. And this time he did.

She knew she had asked for it and could not even pretend to be angry with him. She put her arms up and round his neck so that her fingers teased his hair out of its queue, and wholeheartedly kissed him back. Everything else was forgotten in the wonder of it. His mouth was firm but gentle, his lips teasing hers apart. Her whole body was quivering with unalloyed joy. It was some time before either drew breath and then it was because they heard a cackle behind them and both swung round guiltily to face Widow Twitch, who was standing between their horses with the reins of both in her hands.

'Well, my beauties,' she said, looking from one red face to the other. 'Is all resolved?'

'What do you mean?' Amy asked, straightening her hat, while James endeavoured to tie his queue back into place.

'Why, your searches. Has your memory returned and has the Captain found the peace he craves?'

'Yes,' James said.

'No,' Amy said. She was in a dream. Could a man kiss like that and awaken in her all kinds of strange responses, if there was not something special between them, some spark which would take so little to ignite? She knew it for love, but did he?

'Oh, I see you do not agree.' The old lady chuckled. 'You must endeavour to do so soon or there will be more misunderstandings, more calamities. Did the rosemary work?'

'No, it gave me nightmares,' Amy said. 'I wish I had never put it under my pillow.'

'But the night dreams were necessary for you to move forwards, my dear. There can be no standing still and no going backwards—'

'Away with you, woman,' James put in. 'You state the obvious. There is nothing magic about what you say.'

'I never claimed to deal in magic, only in wisdom. I am a wise woman, not a witch.'

He laughed. 'I stand corrected. Now, if you will excuse us, we will continue our ride.' He took the reins from her and turned to help Amy mount, half-glad, half-sorry they had been interrupted before he lost all sense of propriety. But the woman was right; they had to resolve their outstanding problems before they could go forwards. And he was becoming more and more impatient.

'Those you are seeking can be found in Ely,' the old lady said.

He was about to mount, but turned back. 'What do you know of them?'

'I was told you had been asking for news of them.

I heard them talking outside the King's Arms yesterday afternoon while they were waiting for the stage.'

'Where in Ely?' he asked eagerly.

'I do not know. They didn't mention it.'

'Oh, James,' Amy said. 'You think those men were my aunts' visitors, don't you? And they arc the ones I drew.'

'Probably,' he said, putting his hand over hers as they gripped her reins. He did not say he knew who they were. It would only add to her distress. 'Come, let us go home.'

He mounted and they rode back towards the Manor in silence. If Smith and Randle were in Ely, he would root them out and arrest them; they would not escape again. Amy must not suffer as poor Caroline had done. Amy would take heed of his advice to make all doors and windows secure, but ought he perhaps arrange for someone to be on guard at night?

They entered the courtyard and were surprised to see a mountain of luggage being unloaded from a carriage. Both vehicle and horses were covered in fine dust, as if they had travelled a long distance. Hurriedly dismounting, they went inside to find Sophie and Harry Portman ensconced in the drawing room with the aunts, drinking tea and eating cakes.

Sophie was wearing a wide-panniered gown in yellow-and-green striped taffeta, while Harry's coat was in pale blue satin embroidered in silver. It had rows of silver buttons and must have cost him all of twenty guineas. Both wore white powdered wigs.

'Mama!' Amy exclaimed, running forwards to greet her. 'What are you doing here?' She turned to Harry, who had risen on her entry. 'I beg your pardon, Mr Portman. How do you do?'

He bowed with a flourish. 'Mrs Macdonald, your obedient.' He turned to produce a slightly less formal bow to James. 'Captain Drymore, your servant, sir.'

James returned the bow. 'Good day to you, sir.'

'Sit down, everyone,' Harriet instructed them. 'Captain, you will take tea?'

'I shall be delighted, thank you.'

Everyone found seats. 'Your mother has caught us unawares,' Harriet said, addressing Amy. 'We had no idea she was coming.'

'I have been worrying about Amy,' Sophie explained. 'She seemed so unwell when we saw her and I felt I should have done more for her…'

James thought this sentiment a little late in coming, but supposed it was better late than never.

'I understood,' Amy said. 'And to be sure I was made welcome at Colbridge House.'

'So I discovered when I called there. I did not

know you had decided to return to Highbeck so soon. But no matter—*The Beggar's Opera* has finished its run and I do not start new rehearsals for two weeks, so I decided to come and see how you did. And Mr Portman was so good as to give me his escort.'

'The servants are preparing rooms,' Harriet said. She was a little stiff as if she were not sure she welcomed the visitors. James wondered if she had taken his warning to heart about not being too hospitable and was obeying it to the letter. Or she disapproved of her sister's relationship with Portman. Or perhaps she was afraid Sophie meant to take her niece away. She need not worry on that score; if Amy went anywhere it would be with him. But nothing like that could happen until the whole mystery was solved and everyone safe from harm.

He stayed a few minutes, taking part in the general conversation, the enquiries about how the journey had been, the exchange of news, both of the success of the opera, the visit to Drymore Hall, which made Sophie green with envy, and the doings in the village, without anyone mentioning Amy's loss of memory. Then James took his leave, but not before Harriet had bidden him back to dine with them. 'We shall dine late,' she told him. 'Will six suit you?'

'Certainly, Miss Hardwick. I shall look forward to it with pleasure.'

* * *

'Now, Amy,' her mother said when he had gone. 'Tell me all your news. Has the Captain proposed yet?'

'No, whatever gave you the idea he would?' She felt the warmth rise to her cheeks and knew her face had turned scarlet.

'Why else has he stayed by you so long in this out-of-the-way place? And bringing you to London and taking you to Drymore Hall. Why would he do that, if he did not mean to propose? He wanted his family's approval,' her mother said complacently.

'Mama, you know why he took me to London, and as soon as we had done what we went to do, he brought me back. We stayed at Drymore Hall to save having to put up at an inn. He has lost a wife he loved and I am sure he has no intention of remarrying yet a while and certainly not to me. I have nothing to recommend me. Besides, I have recently been made a widow.' All of which was said as much to convince herself as her mother.

Sophie looked sideways at her and smiled. 'You do not sound very convincing to me.'

'Sophie, leave the girl be,' Harriet commanded. 'The Captain has been doing what Lord Trentham sent him here to do—help Amy remember and find out what happened to her husband.'

'We know what happened to him,' Sophie said. 'As for Amy, I am not at all sure she could not remember if she chose.'

'Mama, I could not. I tried, believe me I tried.' She did not want to speak of her memory of those two men for fear of alarming her aunts. And James had said he would deal with them, though what he had in mind she had no idea.

'Amy has enough to contend with, without you throwing out accusations like that,' Harriet added.

Sophie laughed. 'The mother hen looking after her chick.' She turned to Matilda. 'Two mother hens.'

'It is as well she has us, for you do not seem to care,' Matilda put in. 'If Amy were *my* daughter—'

'What do you know of having children?' Sophie demanded. 'No man has ever looked at you like that.'

Matilda grew very pink and fled from the room.

'Mama! How could you be so unkind?' Amy exclaimed and ran after her aunt.

Matilda had gone to her room, where Amy found her sitting on the edge of her bed in tears. 'Silly me,' she said, wiping her face with a scrap of handkerchief and making an effort to smile. 'I should not be upset by Sophie's remarks. She was always like that, the beautiful one, the one all the beaux wanted to marry. No wonder Harriet and I were left on the shelf.'

'To me you are very beautiful and you do not need paint to prove it,' Amy told her, as she sat beside her and put her arm about her shoulders. 'And if I have had two mother hens, then I have been doubly fortunate.'

'I am so glad you think that. When you were growing up and turning into a lovely young woman, I used to worry that you would decide to leave us and when you married Duncan Macdonald, I found it hard to be happy about it.'

'You did not like him?'

'No. He was altogether too smooth and too domineering. A man should look after his wife, advise her, gently guide her, not order her to do this and not to do that like some nasty dictator.'

'Did Duncan do that?' Amy asked.

'Yes, all the time when you stayed here with us. I could see you were not happy. I cannot be sorry he is gone.' She managed a watery smile. 'Harriet would condemn me for telling you that, though I know she secretly agrees.'

'Mama said the same thing. Perhaps that was why I forgot him. It was easier than facing the truth that I had made a mistake marrying him.'

'But you are young and you will marry again and leave us once more,' Matilda said.

'I do not think so,' Amy replied.

'Yes, you will, but this time I shall not mind so much. Captain Drymore is altogether a different man from Duncan Macdonald…'

'Captain Drymore!'

'Oh, indeed. It is as plain as the nose on your pretty face that he is in love with you,' her aunt said.

'Aunt Matilda,' Amy scolded, 'you must not say things like that. If the Captain were to hear you, he would be mortified. He loved his wife and will not be inveigled into marrying me, simply because you want him to.'

'But you want it, too, do you not?'

'More than anything,' she admitted.

'There you are, then! You must make a push yourself, if he will not.'

'No, I cannot. I am involved with bad men, criminals, and he is a man of the law. The two simply do not mix.'

'Nonsense! You are as innocent as a newborn babe. I will not have it otherwise. And if the Captain does not believe that he needs his eyes and ears seeing to.'

Amy pretended to laugh and stood up. 'Enough.

Let us go downstairs and join the others. Mama will not be unkind to you again or she will have me to answer to.'

Matilda gave one last sniff and rose to her feet, shook out her skirt, straightened her wig, which had fallen over one ear, and accompanied Amy back to the drawing room. Her mother and Mr Portman had gone to change for dinner, they were told by Harriet. It seemed the transformation required two or three hours of preparation for both of them. It was one reason why Harriet had put off dinner until six; the other was to give Cook time to prepare the meal, considering they had not been expecting guests and she would have to begin almost from scratch.

'You must not be outdone by your mama, Amy,' Matilda said. 'You must look your very best tonight. The Captain is coming—'

'Aunt!' Amy warned.

'The Captain has dined with us any number of times,' Harriet said. 'What is so special about tonight?'

'It will be more formal,' her sister explained. 'And you never know, he might be constrained to ask to speak to Amy alone.'

'Tilly, I am losing all patience with you,' Harriet told her. 'The Captain and Amy have spent hours in each other's company since he came to Highbeck. He has no difficulty in achieving private conversation with her if he wishes it. I beg you leave well alone.'

'Yes, do,' Amy said. Her aunt was right. If James had wanted to declare himself he could have done so any number of times—when he had kissed her, for instance. But that had been a spur-of-the-moment thing; making an offer of marriage needed a great deal more thought than that. And if he had ever considered it, he had dismissed the idea. Had he not as good as said so, when Aunt Matilda had dropped hints before? And who could blame him?

She dressed in the gown she had worn at Drymore Hall, knowing James appreciated it, at the same time smiling at her foolishness. Her aunt had told her to make a push to gain his attention and she had rejected the idea, but here she was doing just that. When she was ready she joined her aunts in the drawing room.

They, too, were in sparkling form, dressed in heavy silk sack gowns with foot-wide cages and wearing their best wigs. Amy did not know they had such clothes; they were not usually dressed so grandly. She supposed her aunts had wanted to prove they had not forgotten how to entertain.

A quarter of an hour before the appointed time they were joined by James, who bowed to each lady in turn, kissed hands and obeyed Harriet's invitation to be seated, which he did, on the sofa next to Amy.

'The wind is getting up again,' Matilda observed. 'I believe we shall have rain before long.'

'Let us hope they finish getting the hay in before that happens,' Harriet responded.

'To be sure, I believe most of it is.'

James and Amy were silent during this attempt at conversation. Each was acutely aware of the other, each holding their feelings and emotions in check, wishing they could be alone together, and yet afraid of what that could lead to, a coming together in harmony or outright rejection? Both could feel the tension building, almost as if it were rising with the wind.

They looked up as Harry Portman entered the room. He was all in pink, a beautifully fitted coat, breeches, stockings, ribbons, all in shades of pink. Even the neckcloth at his throat was in a pale rose muslin. He swept everyone an extravagant bow. 'Good evening, ladies. Captain Drymore. I am not last, am I?' He laughed. 'No, of course not, Sophie is always last. She must make an entrance. It is the actress in her.'

He had hardly finished speaking when the lady herself came into the room, moving sideways as she had a habit of doing in order to accommodate her monstrous caged hips, though the doors of the Manor were by no means narrow. She fairly glittered with jewels and silver and gold embroidery, all on a cream quilted gown. There was a heavy necklace at her throat, drops hanging from her ears, a diamond-encrusted quizzing glass on a ribbon about her neck and in her hand a large fan. Her wig was at least a foot high, made even higher by the feathers that dominated it.

'La! Am I last?' she asked.

'You were worth waiting for, my dear,' Harry said, rising to take her hand. 'Such a sight as I never beheld.'

'Away with you,' she said, fluttering her fan. 'You have seen me many, many times, and taken me out to supper and I never look any worse than this.'

'Tonight you excel. Am I not right, Captain?'

James, who had risen, too, bowed in acquiescence, just as a footman came to announce that dinner was served.

'Perfect timing,' Harry murmured to Sophie as he offered his arm to take her in to the dining room behind the aunts. James and Amy followed in stately procession.

In honour of the occasion they were using the state dining room. Its oak panelling was as old as the house itself, almost black but with a high sheen that gave it a certain warmth. The table was laid with white napery. Crystal glasses and silver cutlery glittered in the light from the two huge chandeliers. They took their seats with Harriet at the head of the table and Matilda at the foot, Harry and Sophie on one side, James and Amy on the other.

They were served by the butler and two footmen who brought in two kinds of soup, followed by a dish of eels, roast duck, crayfish and snipe, all local products easily obtained, but beautifully cooked and presented. This was followed by roast pork, boiled ham, chicken and hare, together with individual cherry tartlets and apple pie. Dessert consisted of candied fruits and sweetmeats. Amy feared much of it would be sent back to the kitchen untouched and resolved to collect it up and make sure it was distributed to the poor families of the village.

Sophie and Harry kept the conversation going with tales of the opera and its cast and how well or not so well it had gone, and who was having an affair with whom and the goings on at court where the King was quarrelling with Prince Frederick, who had made his home in a house on the north side of Leicester Fields in order to escape his father's ire. It was all very frivolous and entertaining.

Amy listened, playing with her food, too tense to eat much. James glanced at her now and again and murmured a comment meant to make her smile, which she dutifully did. His nearness and her aunt's comments that he was in love with her echoed in her head. But what did her aunt know of complex men like James Drymore? Aunt Matilda was an unrepentant romantic and real life was not like that.

The time came for the ladies to withdraw and to leave the gentlemen to their port and brandy. 'Have you made any headway with your investigation, Captain?' Harry asked after the door closed on them.

His languid pose was gone; his expression of indifference to anything but his clothes and fingernails had changed dramatically. His bearing was alert; his eyes keenly intelligent. James was reminded of Lord Trentham's comment that the other man was well regarded in government circles and his opinion was worth listening to. Whatever he did, it was not something he wished to be generally known. 'Very little.' James smiled as he went on to explain about Smith and Randle coming to the house and Gotobed's proposal to Amy. 'There is something behind all of this,' he said. 'I fear for the ladies.'

'I am afraid you are right. It is why I am here.'

'At Highbeck?' James asked.

Harry chuckled. 'I thought that might surprise you. I find the disguise useful at times, but do not be deceived. I can handle myself as well as anyone when I need to.'

'I do not doubt it. Lord Trentham hinted as much. But tell me why you are here, if it is not to escort Lady Charron.'

'To help you bring things to a head,' Harry said. 'You see, I have been digging out Jacobites on behalf of the government ever since the end of the '45 rebellion and incidentally trying to uncover the whereabouts of the Arkaig treasure. We must find it before Charlie's supporters find it and send it to him. He needs it if he is to stage another uprising.'

'Do you have any idea where it is?' James asked.

'None at all, Captain, but we think Duncan Macdonald might have done.'

'What makes you think that?'

'Amy's father, Sir John Charron, was a well-known Jacobite. He sought shelter here in Highbeck in 1746, but with the government troops closing in, he did not dare stay. Duncan Macdonald helped him to escape on a fishing boat out of Lynn. Before Charron left he boasted about knowing the whereabouts of some of the Arkaig gold.'

'Was it an idle boast?'

'We cannot be sure. Sophie believes he told Duncan and Duncan may have told his wife. Sophie is convinced Sir John hid the gold at

Blackfen Manor, probably in the house, but perhaps in the grounds.'

'You think Amy knows?' James did not want to believe it, but he could not help thinking of her dream of a bag of gold and jewels. Had she known? Was that what Duncan had meant when he said, 'Do not tell anyone'?

'Possibly. Possibly unwittingly. Suffice to say, others have learned of it, probably from Macdonald himself.'

'And they are all here, gathering like bees round a hive,' James said. 'I knew there was something in it for them, but had no idea the lure was so significant. What do you propose we do?'

'Find it before they do,' Harry said simply.

They talked a little about how that could be achieved and then joined the ladies in the withdrawing room, where Harry Portman became once again the affected fop.

While Sophie sang for them, accompanied by Amy at the harpsichord, James mused on what Harry had told him. He kept looking across at Amy and wondering just how much she had known. It would certainly account for her fear on the coach with Billings, her indifference to his death and her subsequent terror when those two ruffians turned up, ruffians for whom James had spent two years searching. He wanted to go over to her and shake her, make her tell all, to put his mind at rest, but his overriding feeling was one of protectiveness. It always had been, always would be. And Harry Portman could be wrong. Gotobed was perhaps only after Amy's inheritance, and Sir Gerald Hardwick, the other man who'd shown an interest recently, was certainly a resentful man who felt he had been done out of his rightful inheritance. As for Smith and Randle—he might be their target and not Amy. Please God, tonight would see the end of it and perhaps the beginning of something infinitely more pleasurable. He was itching to be gone and was glad when the evening came to an end and he could politely take his leave.

Back at the Lodge, he changed out of his finery into riding breeches, a fustian coat and low-crowned hat while Sam saddled their horses. As James had arranged previously, they were joined at the cross-roads in the village by George Merryweather and Dusty Green, both big burly men, armed with bludgeons and not afraid to use them.

Ely, though a small town, had its fair share of courts and alleys where the poverty-stricken inhabitants dwelt. Those who could not afford lodgings slept in doorways, in the shadow of the Cathedral's ancient walls or down by the river. They scoured the streets and poked their heads into inns and taverns. 'Smith?' James queried. 'Randle?'

'Never 'eard o' them.' The reply was always the same—even when they tried the other aliases the two men had used to gain entrance to Blackfen Manor: Wade and Miller. This was going to be a long night. They moved on, making their way downhill towards the river.

'Hallo, mister.' The voice came from what appeared to be a bundle of rags in the doorway of a chandler's.

James swung the lantern round. The rags stirred and a face appeared, the face of Joe Potton, the boy who had stolen the pie. 'What are you doing there, young 'un?'

'Tryin' to get some sleep,' he said.

'Have you no home to go to?'

'Not goin' back there. Ma's new feller's too handy wiv 'is fists. Did I 'ear you say you was lookin' for a cove called Randle?'

'Yes, do you know of him?'

'He's Ma's new man.'

'Take me to him.'

'Not likely. 'E'll do fer me.'

'Then show me where I can find him.'

The boy evidently decided he owed James a

favour. He rose and set off at a trot with James and his three companions following, keeping a watchful eye about them. After two or three minutes, he stopped and pointed to a tavern door. 'In there.'

'Are there any other ways in?' James wanted to know.

'Yes, round the back, across a yard.'

'Right. Now, boy, if you want a reward for your night's work, you'll go back to where we found you and wait for me.'

'Rather 'ave it now, if yew don' mind. Yew might not come back…'

James laughed, gave him sixpence and watched him disappear at a run.

The two villagers were dispatched to guard the rear entrance, while James and Sam with pistols cocked burst into the room. Four men sat at a table playing cards. Others, scattered about on chairs or on the floor, were in various stages of drunkenness. Some stirred when they saw the intruders, some ignored them. James was not concerned with them, but with two of the card players. One was as thin as a lathe, the other had a red bulbous nose, which sported a wart. Here were Randle and Smith at last. 'The place is surrounded,' he shouted. 'You are under arrest.'

They did not stop to ask why, but turned the table

over and rushed for a door at the back of the room. While everyone else scrambled for the money that was rolling all over the floor, James and Sam took up the chase. It took them down corridors and through other rooms where the sleeping occupants, being rudely awakened, yelled at them, then out into a courtyard, which had an archway large enough for a vehicle to pass through, and the men were running towards that, only to be confronted by Merryweather and Green. They dodged sideways, one going one way, one the other. James could not shoot for fear of hitting one or other of his own men, so he dropped the gun and hurled himself at Randle, bringing him to the ground. The man squirmed out of his way and produced a knife. James dodged it, but he was not quite quick enough and felt a stinging cut to his cheek. Ignoring the blood, he threw himself on top of the man, struggling for possession of the knife. It was a struggle that ended when James groped for his gun and, having retrieved it, put it to the man's head. 'Surrender or I fire.'

'All right, you've got me.'

James got to his feet, to allow the man to get up, but Randle was not done yet. He dived for James with his knife. A shot rang out and the man crumpled at his feet. James spun round to see Sam with his pistol smoking. 'Thanks, Sam, but I wanted him alive.' That surprised him. A year ago he would have been more than tempted to put an end to their existence himself, but now, thanks to Amy, he knew that was not the way. Justice must be done, but it must also be seen to be done.

'My pleasure, Captain. And I only winged him,' Sam said.

That was evident because Randle was sitting up holding his hand over his upper arm. Blood oozed between his fingers. James was glad the man was not dead; he wanted him to stand trial, along with his accomplice, who had been caught by the villagers. 'A good night's work,' Merryweather said. 'What do you want us to do with them?'

'We'll take them to the lockup for the night. Tomorrow, they must be taken to London.'

'You ought to have that cut seen to, Captain,' Green said.

James dabbed at it with his handkerchief. ''Tis only a scratch. I'll see these two safely in custody first.'

They manacled both men, ignoring Randle's yells of pain, and drove them before them to the town jail. On the corner of the High Street, they came across Joe, eager to know what had happened. His eyes widened at the sight of the manacled men. 'What you goin' to do with 'em?' he asked.

'They are going to stand trial for murder,' James told him.

'Murder!'

'Yes. You deserve a reward for helping us turn them in.'

'A reward?' His face lit up. 'Do that make me a thieftaker?'

James laughed. 'I suppose it does.' He paused. The boy looked thinner than ever and he did not doubt he had little enough to eat. And what sort of mother was it who let her child sleep in the streets because she wanted to be with her new man? 'Do you want to work?'

'What kind o' work?' he asked warily.

'Stable boy. You aren't afraid of horses, are you?'

'Course not.'

James turned to Sam. 'Go and find his mother. If she agrees, take him home with you and get Mrs Landis to give him something to eat. And make sure he washes.'

He watched Sam and the boy go, then followed Green and Merryweather with the prisoners. By the time he had completed a report on the circumstances of the arrest for the magistrate and a doctor had seen to Randle and declared him fit to be locked up along with Smith, it was almost dawn. It had been a long and eventful night, but it was over now.

The door to the past had been shut with the banging of that cell door on those two murderers; the way to the future finally lay open. He fetched his horse from where he had left it and rode back to Highbeck.

In the navy he had become used to long hours of wakefulness, especially when in action, and the night just gone had been one of those. It left him keyed up, restless, and yet bone weary. He needed to sleep, but more than anything he wanted to see Amy. Every minute in her company was precious, every minute apart one of anxiety.

Chapter Ten

It was dawn when Amy was awakened by a tapping sound and sat up in fright, only to realise it was a branch on the tree outside her window, tap-tapping on the glass, as if someone was asking to come in. She had personally checked every door and window after everyone had gone to bed, but every creak of the old building, every rattle of the window pane, startled her. It was as if the very wind was a threat, and that she knew was foolish. She could not help thinking of what Widow Twitch had said about the men James was seeking being in Ely. Had she been right? Were they in Ely? She felt sure James would go looking for them, but supposing he did not find them? Supposing he found them and they had put up a fight? Supposing he had been hurt? She could not lie still and decided to get up and dress.

Her aunts, her mother and Mr Portman were still

in bed and would probably stay there until noon. She dressed, ate her breakfast with the servants and hurried to the Lodge.

James was crossing the yard from the stables when she arrived. He looked exhausted. His face was muddy and caked with blood, although she could clearly see a nasty cut on one of his cheeks. There was a bruise on his brow and another on his chin. His hair was matted and his coat, a fustian frock such as artisans wore, was torn. She ran to him. 'James, what happened? You are hurt.'

Even in his weary state his heart beat faster at the sight of her. She was dressed very simply in a pink-and-white striped gingham gown and a cottager hat, which had fallen down her back on its ribbons. Her expressive eyes told of deep concern. He gave her a crooked smile. 'It is only a scratch.'

'It looks more than a scratch to me. It needs attending to.' She took his arm and pulled him into the house, where Mrs Landis clucked around them like a worried hen. 'Oh, mercy me, what has happened to you, Captain?'

'It is nothing. All I need is a wash and some sleep.'

'Can you find some salve?' Amy asked her. 'A bowl of warm water and some clean cloths. Bring them to the Captain's bedchamber. I must tend to his wounds and then he must rest.'

'Amy, what are you about?' he protested, as she led him upstairs to his room and pushed him down into a chair.

'Giving succour. It is no more than you did for me.' She turned as Mrs Landis appeared with the items she had asked for and stood the bowl of water on the washstand. Amy dipped a cloth in it and began gently bathing his wounds. He suffered this without speaking. 'It is not so bad now it is cleaned up,' she said when it was done. 'You look almost human again.'

'Thank you for that,' he said wryly, as Mrs Landis left them, murmuring something about making him some breakfast.

'What happened? Do you want to tell me?'

'Last night I finally closed a chapter on my past,' he told her.

'*Your* past?' she queried in surprise.

'Yes. It transpires your aunts' visitors were the two murderers I have been chasing these last two years.'

'The men who killed your wife? Oh, James!' She paused. 'You mean they have nothing to do with Duncan after all?'

'No, I do not mean that. They were also your husband's tormentors. I realised that when you sketched them. They turned out to be the men who held up our coach, too.'

'Did they not know you?' she asked.

'There was no reason why they should. They knew they were being sought, but I doubt they had ever known my name, or Carrie's. When I went to the stews and haunts of such men looking for information, I used an alias. They will not be troubling us again. They are safely under lock and key.'

'And they did this to you?'

'We had a little struggle. One of them attacked me with a knife.'

'Oh, James, you could have been killed!' she cried.

He smiled crookedly and put his arm about her waist, drawing her closer to him. 'You sound as if you care?'

'Of course I care.' She could feel the warmth of his hand on her flesh through her thin bodice; it sent waves of desire flooding through her. It was wrong. The time and the place were wrong. He had just come back from avenging the death of his wife whom he had loved. She drew away from him. 'You need to rest.'

He could not deny that. 'Yes. Go home, my dear. I will call on you later. Perhaps we can complete the ride we began yesterday.'

Yesterday. Was it only yesterday? She coloured at the memory of that kiss and the way she had responded to it. If Widow Twitch had not arrived, she would have been lost to all reason and told him she loved him and left herself open to rejection and more heartbreak. She was doubly glad she had not, considering that the two men who had been skulking in the grounds had been the two who killed his wife. Had he known that before she showed him her sketch? 'Do not come if you do not feel up to it,' she said. 'I can forgo my ride.'

He rose, opened the door for her and then raised her hand to his lips. 'I will come.'

As soon as she had gone, he went back to fall across his bed where he fell immediately into a deep and healing sleep.

Amy spent the rest of the morning sketching, trying not to show her impatience for James to come, though her ears were attuned to the sound of horse's hooves. But perhaps he was not well enough, perhaps the effects of the struggle were worse than they thought. He might not come at all. In that case, she would go and see for herself how he did.

He arrived a little after one o'clock, dressed for riding. His bruises were a colourful mix of red, yellow and purple, but he appeared in good spirits.

'Are you well enough to ride?' she asked him.

'Of course. Are you ready?'

'Yes, I have only to put on my boots and hat. Would you be kind enough to ask for my mount to be saddled while I am gone?'

He bowed. 'Of course. I will wait for you in the stable yard.'

'I knew as soon as Widow Twitch said those men were in Ely, that you would go chasing after them,' she said, as they rode. 'It kept me awake most of the night.'

'Is that why you were up betimes?'

'Yes. I could not rest until I knew you were safe.'

'Thank you for that.' He smiled wryly. 'But there is still Mr Gotobed to deal with.'

'Perhaps when he hears the other two have been captured, he will go away and leave us in peace.'

'Let us hope so.' But he did not sound very optimistic.

They stopped to greet the workers in the field and exchange a few words with them about the haymaking, then rode round the open water of the fen and looked at the windmills, which were spaced along the dykes and turning frantically in the rising wind. Completing the circuit, they returned to the Manor. James helped Amy to dismount and accompanied her inside. He did not want to leave her.

She ran up to change while he made his way to

the drawing room where Sophie and Harry were talking with the aunts. 'I hope I do not intrude,' he said, bowing to them.

'Not at all, Captain, you are always welcome,' Harriet told him and then, seeing his bruises, added, 'Whatever has happened to you? Did your horse throw you?'

He grinned crookedly. 'No, it was not a horse.'

'You look as though you have been in a scrap,' Harry said.

'So I have.' He turned back to Harriet. 'You will be pleased to hear you have seen the last of those two unwanted callers.'

'Oh, mercy me!' exclaimed Matilda, putting a plump hand to her heart. 'Whatever have you done?'

'I tracked them down to Ely. They put up a fight, but I had Sam and the miller and blacksmith to help me and they are now under lock and key.'

'I am very glad to hear it,' Harriet said. 'We are in your debt.'

'Nonsense. I have been looking for those two for an age, they are known criminals. With them behind bars, everyone can sleep more safely in their beds.'

'Thank the good Lord for that,' Matilda said. 'Did Amy know about it?'

'Not until she saw me returning when it was all

over.' He grinned ruefully. 'I am afraid I presented a sorry sight.'

'I see you were not so incapacitated you could not ride,' Sophie put in.

'No, 'tis but a scratch and a bruise or two, which will soon be gone.'

'Did you enjoy your ride?' Sophie went on.

'Yes, indeed. We looked at windmills and spoke to the villagers anxiously trying to get the hay in before it rains.'

'I've a mind to go and watch them,' Harry said. 'Will you bear me company, Captain?'

James hesitated. He knew Harry wanted to talk to him. 'You are hardly dressed for a country stroll, sir.'

'Then I shall change.' He jumped to his feet and disappeared.

Sophie laughed. 'I cannot think what has got into him. He is not usually so energetic. But if he is going out, then I shall go to my room and practise my scales.' And she, too, left.

'How is Amy this morning?' Matilda asked James, after they had both gone. 'I heard her creep downstairs very early this morning and feared she could not sleep.'

'I believe she went out to take food to the villagers.'

'She is very naughty,' Harriet said. 'She knew she should not go out alone.'

'But it is just like her to think of the poor,' Matilda added. 'Such a kind heart as she has.'

'Indeed, yes,' he agreed. 'But I did admonish her.' He paused. 'I believe her memory is finally returning. She was able to give me an account of what had happened in London to send her flying to you.'

'Thank goodness. I hope it means she can put it all behind her now and be happy again.'

'You do not wish it any more heartily than I do,' he said.

'I knew it,' Matilda said, smiling broadly. 'You have more than a passing interest in our niece. I knew it weeks ago.'

'Then, madam, you were ahead of me,' he said, more amused than annoyed by the lady's romanticism. 'I would not be such a rakeshame as to allow myself that indulgence. Until a se'ennight ago I believed Mrs Macdonald to be a married woman.'

'But now she is a widow nothing stands in your way,' Matilda pointed out.

'Except the lady's own inclinations,' he said, drily. He had no intention of admitting anything until he had spoken to Amy herself.

'Oh, she will,' Matilda said complacently. 'Depend upon it, she will have you.'

He turned as Amy came into the room dressed in a flower-embroidered gown in a blue that matched her lovely eyes. She was followed by Harry Portman in the rough cloth coat and breeches very similar to those James had donned the night before. James smiled; it would not for a moment deceive the villagers who could spot a foreigner from half a mile, foreigner being the name attributed to anyone from outside the area, but his garb would attract less ridicule than his usual finery.

James left Amy in the care of her aunts and he and Portman left. While on their walk he reported on his adventures the night before and the capture of Smith and Randle.

'You might have told me what you were about, Drymore,' Harry said, aggrieved. 'I could have come with you.'

'I did not think it was something you would enjoy,' James remarked.

'Why not? I can handle myself in a fight, I promise you. And you knew I wanted to talk to those men.'

'You can still talk to them, though I doubt they will tell you very much.'

'What about the treasure?' Harry asked. 'Did they tell you anything about that?'

'No.' James laughed. 'I am persuaded that is a fiction, invented by Duncan Macdonald.'

'I pray you are right. But I am told there is another

man skulking about who might be on the same errand.'

'Gotobed. He was in prison at the same time as Macdonald, but he was found not guilty and, as far as I am aware, has not committed a crime since being released. I have no reason to arrest him.' James chuckled. 'Not that I would not enjoy doing so. He seems to think the way to riches is through Mrs Macdonald, but it might be nothing more than the Manor estate he is thinking of. It will be hers one day.'

'And you, of course, have no interest in that direction, have you?' Harry laughed and punched James playfully on the arm, making him wince when he found one of his bruises.

'The Manor? No, definitely not,' James said.

'I did not mean the Manor, man, and you know it. The lady herself is delectable. And free now.'

James was inclined to be annoyed. Why was everyone trying to throw them together? Was he so very transparent? He would have to do something about it before Amy became the butt of their jokes. Darling Amy. He could not imagine a life without her.

'Do you have a gig?' Harry asked suddenly.

'Yes. Why do you ask?'

'I would borrow it to go to Ely to talk to those men.'

'Then I will take you.' James would not mind

asking Smith and Randle a few questions himself. He had not had the opportunity to interrogate them the night before.

They turned and went back to the Lodge where they found Joe Potton at work cleaning out the stables. He stopped when James appeared. 'I am going to take the gig out, Joe,' he said.

Joe rushed to help harness the horse. James stood and watched him for a minute. The boy was cleaner now, his hair a shining gold halo, and he worked deftly, backing the pony into the shafts and fastening the straps. 'Who taught you to do that?' he asked.

'Sam. He's a real gentry cove, is Sam.'

James smiled. 'Yes, he is. So you think you will be happy here?'

'Oh, yes, 'tis better than sleeping in doorways and being kicked about by coves like those two you nabbed yesterday, tha's for sure.'

'What do you know about them, boy?' Harry asked.

Joe glanced at him and then turned back to James. 'What d'yew want to know?'

'Anything you can tell us.'

'They used to come into the tavern where Ma worked. That's 'ow they got to know her and I 'eard them talkin'.'

'Go on,' James said quietly.

'They said they ha' heard there was treasure hidden at the Manor, but they didn't know 'ow to get at it and then they heard about Sir Gerald being related to the ladies at the Manor and went and talked to 'im about it. 'E got real excited, they said, and dashed off to Highbeck. Didn't do no good, so he bought those two a new suit of clothes each, so they could call on the old ladies and pretend to be interested in arch…' He hesitated over the word.

'Architecture,' James supplied for him.

'Tha's it.' He grinned suddenly. 'They old ladies were too fly for them and they didn't get past the door. They told Ma the ol' fellow was furious he'd wasted his money on their rigs. But they meant to 'ave another try.'

James gave heartfelt thanks that he had caught them before they could harm anyone at the Manor. 'Thank you, Joe, you have been a great help.' The gig was ready and he and Harry climbed in and drove off.

'What was all that about?' Harry demanded.

James explained about Sir Gerald's sudden recently revived interest in the Manor and now he understood why. 'Smith and Randle followed us to Highbeck after they held up our coach, convinced Mrs Macdonald knew where the gold was, but they had no idea how to get into the Manor, nor where to look when they did. Somehow they discovered Sir Gerald was related to the Hardwick ladies and had been trying to claim the estate, and they set out to make his acquaintance. It would have been easy enough to play on his greed by talking about gold being hidden there. I am only guessing, but I am fairly sure that is what happened.'

'And the boy?'

'Joe? I once did him a little favour. He heard I was searching for them and helped us track them down.'

'So for that you have taken him under your wing?' Harry commented.

'Yes. He didn't exactly say so, but from what he told Sam, I am persuaded his mother is a lightskirt and not particularly careful of her son. I would give him a better start in life.' James turned the gig into the yard of the jail and pulled up. 'We shall soon see if my guess is right.'

Amy woke that night to see a dark shadow pass across the window. She thought at first it was a branch of the tree, moving in the blustery wind, but then realised with a start that it was inside her room. There was someone creeping towards her bed!

She sat up and screamed at the top of her voice and kept it up until the intruder dived at her and clapped his hand over her mouth. 'Be quiet, can't you.' She recognised Gotobed's voice and bit his hand but, though he cursed loudly, he did not release her. 'Where is it?' he demanded. 'Tell us where it is, and I will not harm you.'

She could not answer him for the hand over her mouth; the only sound she could make was a series of grunts as she tried to wriggle free of him.

'Come on, tell us where 'tis hid.' He twisted her arm behind her back, but took his hand from her mouth, holding it over her, ready to put it back if she began screaming again.

She gasped air into her lungs. 'I do not know what you are talking about.'

'Course you do.' He jerked on her arm, making her cry out. 'The gold. The gold your no-good husband promised me.'

'I...I know nothing of any gold,' she told him.

He raised his hand to strike her, but suddenly released his hold when Susan burst into the room in nightgown and nightcap, brandishing a poker. Behind her was Harriet in a dressing robe and without her wig. Gotobed dived towards them, pushing them roughly aside as he passed them and took to his heels.

Harriet turned to Amy. 'Are you hurt?'

'No, Susan stopped him.' She could not stop shaking. 'But how did he get in? I checked on all the doors and windows before I came to bed. Where has he gone?'

'We must rouse the menservants,' Harriet said, picking up Amy's warming pan and, taking the poker from Susan, beat it loudly. 'Come on, men,' she shouted, banging away near the open door. 'He cannot be far away. Have at him.'

Amy, realising what her aunt was trying to do, picked up her candlestick and a metal tray and joined in the commotion. Soon doors were opening all along the corridor. Harry was the first to appear, followed by Sophie and her maid, who had stopped to put on dressing gowns. From the rooms above, the footmen tumbled down in their nightshirts. 'Intruders,' Harriet shouted. 'After them.'

But no one knew in which direction to go. Then they heard footsteps running along the corridor, making for one of the turrets. Harry gave chase with the footmen close behind him.

Harriet turned back to Amy, who had slipped a robe over her nightrail and was standing looking bewildered. 'Are you certain you are not hurt, sweetheart?'

'No, shocked, that's all. I knew that dreadful man would not take no for an answer.'

'He has gone now. Go back to bed and Susan will fetch you a tisane.'

'I do not want to go back to bed. I know I shall not sleep,' Amy said.

Harry returned without the fugitive. 'What a rabbit warren this place is,' he said. 'You could hide an army in here.'

'You mean you did not catch him?' Amy whispered, eyes wide with fear.

'Could not. He ran into the room above the drawbridge. Got out through the gap where the chain emerges. Went down it like a monkey.'

It was the one place Amy had not thought to check on her nightly rounds. 'Will he come back?' she asked.

Harry shook his head. 'Not tonight.'

'We must send for the Captain,' Susan said promptly. 'If anyone can catch him, he can.'

But James was already on his way.

Sam had spent the evening patrolling the grounds as the Captain had instructed him to do, pacing round the moat, and he had seen the man come down the chain and run across the grass. He had given chase, but had lost him in the copse and decided to wake James. 'I never saw him enter,' he said. 'I reckon he went in earlier in the day and hid hisself.'

James had sent Sam to rouse the village men and institute a search while he ran to Blackfen Manor.

The house was in an uproar, with everyone trying to talk at once, and it was some time before he could make sense of what had happened. 'Amy, are you hurt?' he asked, putting his arm about her and drawing her towards him.

'Shaken, but not harmed,' she said, feeling infinitely better now he had arrived. 'It is thanks to Susan. She was so brave. If she had not heard my screams…' She was shivering like an aspen. He took off his coat and put it about her shoulders, then led her to a sofa where he sat down beside her. 'Better now?'

'Yes, thank you.'

He blamed himself. He could have asked to stay in the house and would have been on hand to do some good, instead of taking Harry to Ely, where they had learned nothing more than they knew already; the prisoners had simply refused to speak. He had left Harry outside the Manor and gone home to his bed. Nothing would persuade him to leave her again until that miserable cur had been caught and arrested. He might not have had anything to charge him with before, but he did now and he would make sure the man felt the full weight of the law. 'Did he say what he wanted?'

'Gold, so he said. He kept asking me where it was. He said Duncan had promised it to him,' Amy revealed.

Harry was looking smug. 'I told you so,' he said.

'Gold!' Matilda gasped. 'We have no gold. Whatever was the man thinking of?'

'The Arkaig treasure,' Sophie put in. 'Sir John hid it here.'

'Nonsense!' This from Harriet. 'We would never have allowed it.' She ushered the servants out to the kitchen to make a hot drink for them all.

'I know nothing of any gold,' Amy said, looking from one to the other. 'Truly I do not.'

'But there was a bag of gold in your dream,' James said, his heart in his mouth. The last thing he wanted was for Harry to be right.

'But that was not treasure nor anything like it,' she cried, looking from one to the other. 'It was the proceeds of highway robbery. Jewellery and sovereigns taken from travellers. I remember now. It was what the men were quarrelling about. Duncan had been entrusted with looking after it, but he had disposed of it. It made the others very angry.'

'But you said it was on the table in your dream.'

'So I did.' She paused as her brain suddenly cleared and she knew she had remembered everything. 'But it was not there on the night Duncan was stabbed. I found it in the house several days before that and confronted him with it. It was only then I learned the truth about what he had been up to. My dreams were so confusing, they merged the two events.'

James took her drawing from his pocket and smoothed out the creases. The men were there and the table, but there was no bag. He handed it to Harry.

'Hmph,' he said, tapping it with a well-manicured finger. 'But those two evidently believed in the treasure and so did Gotobed. Now, why was that, I wonder?'

'Because Macdonald teased them with it,' James said, hugging Amy to his side.

Harriet returned with a servant carrying a tray containing a jug of hot chocolate and a pile of dishes and poured a drink for everyone. After that, Sophie announced her intention of going back to bed.

'Yes, I think we all should,' Harriet said.

'I do not think I could,' Amy said. 'I should lie in that room imagining all manner of horrors and will never be able to sleep.'

'Then you shall stay here,' James said. 'I will sit with you. Tomorrow we will decide what is to be done.'

Harriet gave him a disapproving look and Matilda smiled broadly. He did not care. Amy was safe in his arms and that was all that mattered. And if Gotobed was so foolish as to come back, he would find James waiting.

After a blanket had been fetched for Amy and

everyone had left them, he sat at the end of the sofa with her head in his lap. 'Go to sleep, sweetheart,' he said. 'You are safe now.'

'I know. The trouble is I am wide awake.'

He pulled the blanket up to her chin and bent to kiss the top of her tousled head. 'Do you want to talk?'

'Yes. You see, my memory is as clear as day now.'

'No gaps?'

'I do not think so.'

'Do you want to tell me about it?'

'I must. You have been so good and kind and it is important you know everything…'

'No, it is not. I do not need to learn anything more if it distresses you to recount it. I know I love you without that, and will do so to the end of my days. It is the future, not the past, that concerns me.'

Startled, she tipped her head up to look at him. 'Love me?' she whispered.

'Yes.' He was looking down at her with an expression of such tenderness, her heart leapt with joy. 'Can you doubt it?'

'Oh.' What she had been about to say fled from her mind at the wonder of this. 'I did not think you could.'

'Could not love you?' He chuckled. 'How could I not? You are adorable and I adore you.'

'But I am not good enough for you. I have been

tainted by wickedness. My husband was a robber, an accomplice to murder and those men… They killed your wife. You cannot possible want anything to do with me.'

'None of that was your fault, was it?'

'No, but when I finally found out about Duncan's stealing, I did not turn him in,' she confessed.

'Because you loved your husband?'

'No, of course not. I doubt I ever did. I was taken in by his good looks and charming manners. I did not even know he was a gambler, until I found we were becoming very short of money. And then he always had an excuse. His patrons had not paid him and he needed canvas and paint in order to do his work and they were more important than food and clothes. Like a fool, I believed him. My jewels went first, then my best clothes…'

'Poor darling. You do not need to go on.'

'But I must. One day when I was cleaning the house—the servants had all been let go—I found a carpetbag full of jewellery and sovereigns in the back of a cupboard. I hauled it out and put it on the table in the kitchen. Then I sat and waited for Duncan to come home. He was very late and the worse for drink, but I confronted him. He blustered and said he had been given it to look after by a friend who feared being robbed, but for the first time I realised he was lying. I told him to take it away, I would not have it in the house. I swear I knew nothing of Randle, Smith and Billings until they came to the house and demanded their share of it.'

'Oh, Amy.' He bent to put his lips to her forehead. 'This can wait until the morning.'

'No, it cannot. Don't interrupt, James, please, or I shall never finish.' He was dedicated to keeping law and order, to handing criminals in for the law to take its course. She had to tell all and give him the chance to turn his back on her if he wanted to. 'What I did not know, until after he was wounded, was that he had gambled the entire proceeds of the robberies and lost. He said he had hoped to recoup and begin a new life and was sure the cards had been marked for he should have won. Even lying there bleeding, he could only think of the game.

'When I asked him how he had come to such a pass, he said it was something he could not help. He had met those three men at a gambling den and was soon heavily in debt to them. When he could not pay, they offered him a way out—he must become a thief and pay them that way. He agreed and he used me to do it. He would take me to extravagant balls and concerts, where the wealthy gathered. I used to enjoy those occasions and assumed the money to pay for them came from selling his pictures. I never asked myself how it came about that at every function we attended someone lost valuable jewellery.' She paused to look up at him, but his expression gave nothing away. 'So you see, it makes me an accomplice.'

'You did not know what was going on. I will fight to the death anyone who says otherwise.'

She smiled wearily. 'Thank you, dear James, but that is not the worst of it. Duncan also confessed to me as he lay there wounded that one night, the four of them decided to hold up a coach on Hampstead Heath. What they did not know was that the coach had an escort. There was a fight and shots were fired. One of the guards was killed. Duncan and his friends fled in different directions, and because Duncan was the only one without a criminal past, he took charge of their loot, which was the bag I found. They waited until the hue and cry had died down, then came for their share. Duncan said he had hidden it for safety. They did not believe him and turned the house upside down searching for it. He taunted them, told them that that paltry bag of gewgaws was worth nothing, that he knew where there was a cache of gold bigger than they could ever imagine and it was all his for the taking. They demanded to know where it was and when he refused to tell them, there was a fight. Duncan picked up the knife to defend himself, but he was no match for them and they turned it on him. Afterwards they let me tend to his wounds while they played cards and drank themselves insensible.

'It was then he told me to come to Highbeck, that he would give them the slip and follow me. If I had not been so angry with him, I do not think I could have left him but, God forgive me, I did. I slipped from the house and ran as hard as I could, intending to find help, but Billings had been listening to us and caught up with me. He said he did not want to hurt me, that if I helped him find the gold, he would make sure I was never troubled by the other two. He would not believe me when I said I knew nothing about it and forced me on to the coach to Highbeck.' She gave a huge sigh. It had taken a great deal of courage to tell it all, reliving it as she did, and she was exhausted. 'Now you know it all.'

'My poor brave darling,' he murmured. 'You have been through the fire, haven't you? But it is all over now. No one will ever frighten you again, not while I have breath in my body.'

'Oh, James.' She reached her arm out of the blanket to put her hand to his face. He took it in his own and kissed the palm. It had the same devastating effect as it had before. She made herself think of something other than her undeniable desire for this man, this wonderful man who had said he loved her and had not condemned her. 'But Gotobed is still free.'

'Not for long. By now Sam will have the village men combing the whole village looking for him. They might even have found him.'

She sighed and leaned against his chest and shut her eyes. He put his arm about her and held her, remembering with a slight smile when he had held her like that on a horse, walking it daintily over the rutted road so as not to jolt her. He had had no idea at the time where that ride would take him and where it would end. He leaned over and gently put his lips to hers. 'Go to sleep, my valiant one. Tomorrow we will talk of the future, not the past.'

'Tomorrow,' she murmured, half-asleep. 'It is already tomorrow.'

He smiled, but did not answer. He might have dozed a little himself, but not for many minutes at a time; his ear was attuned to sounds from outside. But there was nothing except the rain beating on the windows.

When he heard the servants stirring, he woke her with a light kiss. 'Wake up, sweetheart.'

She stirred and turned a sleepy smile on him. 'James. Have you been here all night?'

He gently eased her into a sitting position and withdrew his cramped arm. 'Yes, but now you must go upstairs and make yourself respectable before everyone swoons with shock at the sight of you.'

She turned to kiss him. 'Did I dream it or did you say…?' She stopped, overcome with shyness, which was not at all like her.

'That I loved you? Yes, I did.' He gave her a wry smile. 'But I do not remember you reciprocating.'

'Oh, but I do, dear James, I do.'

'Does that mean you will marry me?'

'I would, but…' She paused. 'Caroline…'

He thought carefully before answering. 'Caroline I loved and shall not forget, but she is no more, and you were right, she would wish me to be happy. I have accepted that what happened was God's will, just as I am sure it was His will I should meet you when I thought there could not be two such lovely and loving women in the world. I make no comparisons. Carrie is part of my past, part of my memory, while you, my sweet, are here and now and I will be the happiest man on earth if you will consent to become my wife.'

'Oh, James, you know I will.' She kissed him on the end of his nose and then scrambled to her feet. 'I shall go and dress at once, then we can tell everyone the good news.'

He watched her go, rubbing his nose, then got up and stretched his cramped limbs, before leaving the house to go to the Lodge to change and to see if Sam had any news for him. The rain had stopped, but the trees in the copse dripped water down his neck and he was glad enough to find Sam there, ready with hot water and a change of clothes. 'Well,' he said, as he stripped off. 'What have you to report?'

'All shipshape and Bristol fashion, Captain. The muckworm has been caught and is tied up in the tower with Merryweather on guard on the door. He can't get out of there less'n he can fly.'

'Good. Where did you find him?' He poured hot water from a jug into a bowl to wash.

'He tried to steal the ferryman's boat, but what he didn't know was that the ferryman had taken the bung out of the bottom as a precaution. It sank twenty feet from the shore. He was just scrambling out, covered in weed, when we came upon him. He didn't put up much resistance.' He watched James finish drying himself and climb into a fresh pair of breeches. 'What happened at the Manor?'

James told him about Gotobed attacking Amy. 'Susan was prepared to have a go at him with a poker, but he pushed past her to escape.'

'She never did!'

'In defence of her mistress, I believe she would face the devil himself.'

'That's my girl!' James looked sideways at Sam, and he hurried to change the subject. 'Gotobed talked.'

'I hope you did not hurt him too much.'

Sam grinned, handing him a clean shirt. 'Not too much, Captain. He's a coward.'

'So what did he tell you?'

'He said while they were in prison, Macdonald told him about his wife and her connections with the Hardwick family and the fine house they had, which would be his one day through his wife. He also boasted he knew the whereabouts of some of the Arkaig treasure and if he helped him escape, he would share it with him. Macdonald died afore any plan for escape could be put into action, if'n Gotobed ever meant to help him, which I doubt. He might have helped him on his way to eternity for all we know. He bribed the witnesses at his trial and was found not guilty and on his release set out with the intention of wooing Mrs Macdonald and laying his hands on her inheritance and the treasure, too.'

'So he had no connection with Smith and Randle?'

'No. They were just rivals, both after the same thing.'

James laughed, running a hairbrush over his hair and handing a ribbon to Sam to tie it back for him.

'Greed makes men do strange things, Sam. I'll wager Macdonald did not tell any of them where to look for the gold.'

'Hinted it was in the house, but nothing exact.'

'Mr Portman seems to think it is there, too, but he is working for the government.'

'Is he?' queried the astonished servant. 'Well, I'll be damned!'

'It is clear the crooks believe the gold exists, but supposing it was a lie invented by Duncan to get them off his back?'

'What a turn up for them if it was!'

He smiled as Sam helped him into his coat, a dark green silk with silver braid edging the front, the flaps of the pocket and the deep cuffs. 'I am going back to the Manor. We shall have to institute a search.'

'Is all well there now?'

'Yes. And you may congratulate me. I am to marry Mrs Macdonald.'

Sam did not even pretend to be surprised. 'That I do, sir, that I do.'

Chapter Eleven

Order had been restored to the Manor by the time he returned and everyone was at breakfast. He was invited to sit down and share it with them. He did so, but he had eyes only for Amy. She was wearing the blue gown he liked so much and Susan had done her hair, but she was looking strained, which was no wonder, poor thing. What she had been through was enough to crush the strongest constitution. But it was over now and he meant to make sure she never suffered another moment's anxiety. He smiled at her and she smiled back, her lovely eyes lighting up with pleasure at seeing him.

The conversation was all about what had happened the night before. James told them all he had learned from Sam, that Gotobed had been caught, and that Randle and Smith had been staying with Sir Gerald. It was they who encouraged him to revive his claim to the Manor.

'Cousin Gerald was involved!' Harriet exclaimed.

'Yes. He thought if he could drive you out, he could search the house at his leisure. When that failed, he told them the best way to get in.'

'I knew he was a muckworm,' Harriet said. 'Now all their plans have been thwarted.'

'Was Gotobed one of the conspirators?' Amy asked. 'I never saw him before he came to Highbeck.'

'No, they were rivals.' It was difficult to remain composed and tell his tale when all he wanted to do was whirl Amy off somewhere and kiss her and go on kissing her until she cried for breath. 'Your husband set one against the other. I imagine if he could see us now, he would be laughing fit to burst.'

'Is there any gold?' she queried.

'I doubt it very much.'

'I intend to search for it,' Harry said, then turning to Harriet, added, 'With your permission of course, Miss Hardwick.'

'Search all you like,' she said. 'I doubt you will find anything.'

'You must search the Lodge, too,' Sophie said. 'John was there.'

'Tell me about it, Mama,' Amy begged. 'I

remember seeing my father here when Duncan and I came to visit…'

'I knew you remembered more than you told us.' Her mother's voice was triumphant. 'You could have saved us all this upset if you had said so at once.'

'Madam,' James said, covering Amy's hand with his own on the table, a gesture not lost on his listeners, who gave a little gasp. He ignored it. 'Amy's loss of memory was genuine and if you knew what she had been through before that, you would not question it.'

Sophie turned to her daughter. 'It seems you have a champion in Captain Drymore, Amy,' she said. 'I wonder if it is a little more than that.'

Amy looked from one to the other and thrust her chin out. She would not be cowed by this woman who had been less of a mother to her than her aunts. She turned to James. 'Shall we tell them?'

'Why not?' He smiled at her and then faced the company. 'You may congratulate me. Amy has been so good as to agree to become my wife.'

'Oh, good,' Matilda cried, clapping her hands. 'I knew it! I never saw such a perfect match of two individuals in my whole life.'

'Aunt,' Amy admonished, blushing furiously.

Harriet reached across the table and put her hand over James's and Amy's clasped hands. 'Bless you both.'

'My felicitations to you,' Harry Portman said.

Sophie got up and went round the table to kiss her daughter. 'I am pleased for you, Amy. Once we have found that gold, you can put the whole unpleasant episode behind you.'

'You are sure it is there for the finding?' James asked her. The woman seemed as obsessed by the thought of riches as Smith, Randle and Gotobed.

'Yes. Sir John was on the run after the '45 rebellion failed. The government forces were closing in on him and he came here in the summer of '46.'

'I sent him away.' This from Harriet.

'He only went as far as the Lodge,' Sophie went on. 'But Duncan, who was here on a visit with Amy, found him and helped him aboard a ship in Lynn to take him to the Netherlands. John told Duncan he knew where some of Prince Charlie's gold was hidden but would not tell him where, saying he intended to return for it when the search for the Prince had died down. But he never did, so it follows it is still here somewhere.'

'Then we must settle it once and for all,' James said. 'Amy and I cannot make plans for our future with that hanging over us. Then I shall take our prisoners to London and hand them over to the proper authorities. With the gold, if we find it. Personally I doubt we shall. How could Sir John have conveyed it to Highbeck when he was fleeing for his life? Gold is heavy and not easily carried or concealed.'

'Quite right,' said a voice.

They all turned in astonishment to see a strange figure in the doorway. His once fine clothes were dirty and torn. His beard was tangled and he had lost his wig. A battered low-crowned hat with a large brim covered his wispy hair.

'My God!' Sophie exclaimed. 'What are you doing here?'

'A fine greeting,' he said, advancing into the room and removing his hat to bow to the company. 'Are you not pleased to see me, wife?'

'No,' she said. 'You are an embarrassment. You went to France to share your idol's exile, you said you would not return. So why are you here?'

'I will tell you later, but I am tired and hungry...'

'Papa!' Amy jumped up to fling her arms about him. 'I remember you, yes, I do. You taught me to fish and to ride and draw. I am so pleased to see you.'

He smiled. 'At least my daughter gives me a welcome.'

'You had better sit down and eat,' Harriet said. 'And then be off. We do not give succour to traitors here.'

'Who is the traitor, madam?' he said, sitting down and helping himself to the breakfast dishes. Most of it had gone cold, but he heaped a plate with it and attacked it with relish. 'Those who toady to the Hanoverian or those who support the true king?'

James looked at Harry. Sir John had condemned himself out of his own mouth. He ought to be arrested and taken with the others, but, seeing Amy's delight, he knew he could not do it. 'Never mind that,' he said. 'Tell us why you are here. I assume you are Sir John Charron.'

'Yes. And who are you?'

'My name is Captain James Drymore. I have the honour to be betrothed to your daughter.'

'What happened to Duncan Macdonald?'

'He died, Papa,' Amy said. She found it difficult to equate this vagabond with the father she had known. That man had been exquisitely dressed, beautifully mannered, affectionate; this man looked more like a tramp.

'Pity. He was a great help to me.'

'He was a thief, a liar and a gambler.' This from Sophie.

'That, too,' he said evenly. 'You might also add greedy. The promise of a few *louis d'or* and he would sell his own grandmother for it.'

'Speaking of *louis d'or*,' Harry put in, 'where is it, this cache of gold?'

Sir John shrugged and laughed. 'Still in Scotland, Mr Portman, for all I know.'

'You know my name?' Harry queried.

'Yes, you were pointed out to me as one to watch particularly.'

'Do you say you never had the gold?' James asked.

'Oh, I had some of it, as much as I could conveniently carry. How do you think I managed to evade my enemies for so long? It came in very handy. What was left I took with me…'

'So why are you back?' Sophie demanded.

'There has been an amnesty. I came to see my wife and my daughter. Is there anything wrong with that?'

'An amnesty for prisoners,' Harry said. 'I doubt it applies to those who chose exile and have suddenly decided to return, especially with the Young Pretender back in London.'

'Is his Highness back in London? Well, I am surprised.' Everyone knew by the way he spoke he was lying.

'But you will not be surprised when I arrest you,' Harry said.

'Very surprised.' He finished eating and pushed his plate away. 'You are too fond of my wife to risk injuring her or her career.' He turned to James. 'And you would never compromise my daughter.'

'Then take yourself off,' Harriet said. 'There is nothing for you here. Go and do not come back.'

'That I intend to do, sister, as soon as I have had some sleep. I have been on the road this last twenty-four hours and am exhausted.' He stood up and walked nonchalantly out of the room. James rose to go after him, but Amy stayed him with a hand on his arm. 'Let him go, James.'

He sat down again. Damn it! The man was right. He could not let Amy's reputation be ruined by a public arrest and trial of her father and the inevitable execution that would follow. Mud had a habit of sticking. On the other hand, he had always maintained that no one should be above the law… It was a dilemma he did not want to face.

'He is a traitor,' Harry said. 'It is my duty to arrest him.'

'After he has slept,' Amy said. 'I shall go and make sure he has been found a bed.' And with that she left the room. As soon as she had gone, a babble of excited conversation broke out. James left them to it and followed Amy.

He found her coming out of one of the unused bedrooms along the corridor towards the turret. She ran into his arms. 'Oh, James, will it never end? I thought once we were sure I had nothing to do with Duncan's death, we would be free of scandal, but this is just as bad.'

He held her close, stroking back her hair and tipping her face up to kiss it. 'It is going to end here and now. We have a future to look forward to, my darling…'

'Not if I am tainted by this wickedness. There will be a dreadful scandal. I cannot subject you to that. I cannot. And I do not want my father to die in disgrace…'

One of the footmen came along the corridor. 'I have been ordered by Mr Portman to stand outside the prisoner's door,' he said.

'Then you must do so,' James said, drawing Amy away. They wandered, arms round each other, towards the turret and climbed the stairs to the top. She was crying silently, the tears rolling down her cheeks. He mopped them up with his handkerchief. 'Do not cry, my dearest one. We will find a way.'

'Why did we come up here?' she asked, bemused.

He grinned at her. 'So that I could be alone with you.'

'Oh, James, I love you so, but I am afraid…'

'No need to be,' he said more lightly than he felt. Come what may, he had to bring this affair to a resolution without Amy's name being dragged through the courts and made the subject of tattle, though how to do it without compromising his own integrity, he did not know.

They stood there a long time, with their arms about each other, looking out at the grounds of the Manor, the trees, the dykes and lanes of Highbeck, her childhood home. What idiocy had made her leave it for London and a smooth-tongued flatterer? Now there was nothing for it but to settle down here once more and, once James had taken his prisoners away, she would not, could not, see him again. Ever. To wish for it to be otherwise would be to wish dishonour on someone who had dedicated his life to upholding law and order, who must do his duty, as he saw it, no matter what the personal cost, but who was dearer to her than life itself. Slowly she turned from him and made her way downstairs. He followed, not speaking.

In spite of Sir John's assertion the gold had never been brought to Highbeck, everyone, except Amy, her aunts and James, busied themselves making a search of the house. James went back to the Lodge to confer with Sam. Harriet and Matilda insisted the searchers were wasting their time and continued with their usual daily tasks; Amy spent her time in the parlour, drawing swift sketches of James by which she hoped to remember him: the thoughtful man, the gentle man, the laughing man who played with children, the angry man, the horseman and the fenman in plain coat and felt hat, James dressed in all his finery at Drymore Hall. She sketched until her fingers ached and all the time wondering how she could help her father to escape.

The searchers found nothing. Harry gave up and arranged secure transport to take the prisoners back to London the following day: an enclosed cart pulled by four sturdy horses. It would be escorted by riders recruited from the villagers, who were more than willing to do it, believing they had saved Amy and her aunts from harm. James, who had returned to the Manor for dinner, approved these arrangements.

It was a strained party, where everyone tried to pretend it was a normal evening. They played music and sang, recited poetry, played cards for buttons and talked of everything and anything so long as it had nothing to do with Jacobites, gold or fugitives. Amy was glad when it came to an end. It had been purgatory trying to behave coolly towards James and keep her distance. A kind word, a gentle touch and she would have been undone.

James noted her distraction and knew the reason for it. When he left he hurried back to the Lodge, changed from his evening clothes into a dark fustian coat and brown leather breeches, then ran back and stationed himself in the shadow of the drawbridge and waited. It seemed an agonisingly long time before a figure appeared at the opening from which Gotobed had escaped. The man climbed out and made his way down the chain, awkwardly, hand under hand. 'All well?' James queried as Sir John landed breathlessly beside him. 'Did anyone see you?'

'No. The sentry was fast asleep at his post.' It was Sam who had suggested Susan should be the one to administer the drug. The footman would not be suspicious if she pretended to feel sorry for him having to stand guard all night, and brought him a drink. It was done, she had told Sam, for Miss Amy's sake and to get rid of Sir John, once and for all.

'Come on, then.' James led the way through the copse towards the Lodge. It was not the shortest way out of the grounds, but it gave the most cover. At the Lodge they were joined by Sam, who took them to the dyke that ran beside the moat and from which the water of the moat had been diverted. There was a rowing boat moored under a rickety bridge.

'It is the least likely way to be spotted by the villagers,' James told Sir John as they scrambled in and Sam began to row. 'The sound of horsemen riding through the village would certainly alert the inhabitants and after the excitement of bringing in Gotobed they would love another capture.'

'I assume you are helping me on account of my daughter.'

'Your assumption is correct. For no one else would I lay aside my scruples, but for that I require something from you.'

'I have nothing. If you are talking about that gold…'

'Gold!' James was contemptuous. 'I have something worth more than all the gold in the kingdom—the love of your daughter. No, what I need from you is a solemn promise from you that you will never return to England, nor do anything to aid the Pretender or the Young Pretender to return. I assume Prince Charles has already left the country.'

Sir John laughed. 'Yes. He came thinking his supporters would flock to him, that if they pledged their assistance it might persuade King Louis to invade. It was a foolish notion, as I told him, no one would give money and weapons to a man who had been so roundly defeated before, even if they were sympathetic to the Cause. We had the devil of a job to get him back to his ship. Once he had been seen, everyone in the capital was on the alert.'

James was vastly relieved. He did not think he could have gone through with this escapade if the

Prince had still been on English soil. 'Why did you not go with him?'

'I wanted to see Amy. Contrary to what you may think, I love my daughter very much.'

'I am sure you do. Who could not help loving her?'

The older man smiled. 'I am glad she has you. I commend her to your care. I am only sorry I cannot be at your nuptials.'

'Rest assured, Sir John, Amy will have all the love and care I can give her. And she will be happy to know you are safe out of harm's way.'

'There is no gold?' Sam queried.

'If there is, I do not know where it is. Sorry to disappoint you.'

They had passed through the village and the dyke gave way to the river. Sam shipped his oars and they disembarked. Two horses stood tethered to a bush on the towpath, neither of which were James's black stallion. 'Sam, what were you thinking of?' James asked. 'Where is my mount?'

'Beggin' your pardon, Captain, but you ain't comin' any further. If I'd had my way, you wouldn't have come this far. For Mrs Macdonald's sake, I will see the gentleman safely on board a ship to take him to the Dutch coast and I will stay until it sets sail, just to make sure he goes. You go back.'

'No. I go on. You go back.'

'Sorry, sir, but we can't stand here arguing all night.' And with that he punched his master so hard on the jaw, James went down like a stone.

When he came to his senses, both Sam and Sir John had gone. Without a mount there was no way he could catch them. There was nothing to do but to return to the boat and row back the way he had come.

It was not yet dawn when he arrived at the Lodge. He crept up to his room, but instead of going to bed, he sat at the window and looked out on the moonlit landscape, fearful for Sam. He would have no peace until he was back safe and sound, but that did not mean he would not have some hard words to say to him when he did. And then he chuckled. No one but Sam would have dared to put him out like that. If he had been aware of what was coming, he would certainly not have succeeded.

He could see the roof and turrets of the Manor and wondered if Amy were awake and thinking of him, as he was thinking of her. He was impatient for the last of the night to go so that he could go back to her. Had Sir John already been missed? What would they do? According to Susan, nothing. 'They'll be mighty glad to see the back of him,' she had said. Susan would be worrying about Sam, too.

The sun came up over the horizon, a great golden ball in a lilac-and-pink sky. He washed, shaved and dressed without Sam's help, ate a leisurely breakfast, careful not to appear hurried, though inside his impatience was making him jittery. He sat at his desk and wrote a report for Henry Fielding about the capture of Smith, Randle and Gotobed, though he wondered if they could make any charge stick on that slippery customer. Just as he was finishing it, Sam came into the room.

James looked up at him, immeasurably relieved to see him, but hiding behind a severe expression. 'Well, what have you to say for yourself?'

'Sorry, Captain. It had to be done.'

'I ought to send you packing.' He watched Sam's jaw drop, then laughed and stood up to clap the man on the back. 'But if he has gone, I will forgive you.'

'He has gone. We arrived just as a vessel was leaving. It sailed before daylight.'

'And you galloped your horse to exhaustion to get back, I suppose.'

'I had two horses, as you recall, Captain. Rode them turn and turn about across country. I reckon I must ha' broke all records.'

'Then go and find some sleep. I am going to the Manor,' James said.

* * *

He arrived as Harry and Sophie were setting off back to London behind the prison wagon with its three prisoners and mounted escort. The fourth, so James was told, had disappeared in the night. 'You would not know anything about that, Drymore, would you?' Harry asked.

'Me? Why would you think that?' He affected innocence, while searching out Amy among those come to see them off, which seemed to be half the village. She was not there. 'How did he escape?'

'I have no idea. The guard swears he did not pass him.' He paused. 'You seem to have a sore jaw, Captain Drymore.'

''Tis nothing. I ran into a tree in the dark.'

'Hmm. Strange tree, one with legs, I fancy.'

James grinned back, but did not enlighten him.

'I am glad he has gone,' Sophie said. 'I could not have borne the scandal. Let us go, Harry. I cannot wait to get back to London.'

'Are you coming with us?' Harry asked James.

'No, I have unfinished business here. But you can take this report to Henry Fielding, if you will.'

He watched the cavalcade set off, then turned to go indoors. As he did so, he looked up and saw Amy at the window of her room. He bounded up the stairs two at a time and burst through the door, much to the dismay of Susan. 'Go and find Sam,' he told her, as Amy turned from the window to face him. She was in a cream dressing robe, her fair hair loose about her shoulders. She looked altogether delectable.

They were unaware of the click of the door latch as Susan left them, but simply stood looking at each other, not speaking. He had expected her to run into his arms, but when she did not, became bewildered and anxious, and also a little annoyed.

She saw the upright, honourable man whom she loved above everything looking like a boy waiting for praise for what he had done. But she knew he had compromised his integrity for her sake. Whether to be furiously angry or grateful she did not know and was as perplexed as he was.

'Sweetheart,' he said. 'How are you?'

'I am well. Did you burst into my room only to ask me that?'

'It is important to me. You saw them go?'

'Without my father, yes. Where is he, James?' she asked.

'Halfway to Holland, I imagine.'

'You helped him.' It was a flat statement and he did not deny it.

'What else could we do? Did you want to see him dragged off to London and tried for treason?'

'You know I did not.'

'I could not let it happen, Amy. Right or wrong, he is your father, after all.' He stroked his hand over his jaw. It had been a powerful blow and still hurt.

'Did he do that to you?'

'No. Sam did. He did not approve of what I was doing. Wanted the glory all for himself.'

She smiled then at the idea of the faithful Sam doing his best to prevent his master doing something he knew to be unlawful, if not traitorous. 'Does my mother know? Does Mr Portman?'

'If they have guessed, they are keeping their suspicions to themselves. I think Lady Charron is relieved there is to be no scandal.' He took a step towards her. 'Amy, why are we sparring when all I want to do is hold you close and tell you how much I love you?'

She could hold out no longer and ran into his arms to be kissed long and passionately until she had no breath left. 'Oh, James, I have been so worried,' she said, when at last they drew breath and found themselves sitting side by side on her bed. How they got there he did not know, but it made him realise that they would have to be married very soon or he would never hold out. 'When Susan told me what you were doing, I was frightened to death. I imagined all manner of dreadful things happening to you…'

'As you can see, nothing did. It is over, my darling, all the worry and heartache. The country remains at peace, the criminals are under arrest, you and I have a bright and happy future before us.'

She realised quite suddenly that what he and Sam had done, though legally doubtful, had helped to preserve peace without any more loss of life. 'Tell me about this future of ours.'

'Well, for a start, there is to be a wedding…'

'Where?'

'As long as there is one, I have no preference as to where it takes place.'

'Then here, in Highbeck, with all our friends about us. What next?'

'We need a home, a small estate with a farm where we can bring up our children…' He kissed her again, but this time, he curbed his passion and it was a gentle kiss of abiding love, a love that would last a lifetime. 'I intend to make sure you have no more bad dreams, no more unhappy memories.'

'Oh, James, that sounds like heaven.' She paused. 'But that will never be enough for you. I remember you saying you wanted to do something to help people.'

'Yes, I did and so I shall. My interest is in law and order. Mr Fielding is setting up a body of men dedicated to doing that and has asked me to help, though in what capacity I do not yet know.'

'You could stand for Parliament,' she suggested.

'So I could, but there is no hurry to decide. I want to spend some time with my wife first.'

She jumped up as footsteps sounded outside the door. 'I must dress. We shall be the scandal of the household…'

He laughed and stood up as Susan came into the room. 'Thank the Lord he is safe,' the maid said. Then, seeing James standing by the window, 'I beg your pardon, Captain. I did not know you were still here.'

'I am about to go.' He grinned at her. 'Are we to offer felicitations?'

She blushed furiously. 'Yes, though we were not going to say anything until after you were married.'

'Oh, Susan, I am so happy for you,' Amy said and ran to hug her maid. 'You deserve all the happiness in the world.'

James smiled and left them. All was right with his world.

They were married six weeks later at the church in Highbeck. It was the soonest Harriet said they could be ready and even that, she said, was rushing it. But the day they waited for came at last. Amy woke to the clatter of servants putting the finishing

touches to the decorations and the feast, superin-
tended by her aunts, whose shrill voices she could
hear contradicting each other's orders. She smiled
and leapt out of bed and went to the window. The
sun was shining in a cloudless sky, the birds were
singing; it was all going to be perfect.

Susan, who had married Sam the week before, but
had promised she and her new husband intended to
stay in the service of their master and mistress,
came into the room followed by two other servants
who trooped in carrying a hip bath and jugs of hot
water. 'Time to dress, Miss Amy,' she said.

Amy laughed. 'You have always called me Miss
Amy,' she said, as the water was poured into the
bath. 'Even when I was married.'

'Oh, that did not count. You are Miss Amy until you
leave the church this morning, then you will be Mrs
Drymore and I shall take pride in calling you madam.'

'Mrs Drymore,' Amy murmured. 'Yes, I think I
shall be proud to be that.'

The other servants disappeared and Susan helped
Amy to bathe and dress. She did not want to have
hoops so wide she could not stand close to her
beloved James, so her gown was a sack dress over
a slightly padded underskirt. In figured brocade in
forget-me-not blue, it had a long train from the
shoulders and lace edging to the square neck and

round the sleeves at elbow level, which fanned out over her wrists. Her stomacher was a deeper blue embroidered with swirls of flowers and leaves. Susan wanted her to wear a white wig, but she would not. 'My own hair, done simply,' she said.

By the time the hair was coiled and curled and threaded with ribbon and Susan had fastened a necklace of pearls and sapphires, which had been James's betrothal present, around her throat, the carriage was at the door. She slipped into her satin shoes and went slowly downstairs. It was strangely quiet as they were helped into the carriage; all the guests who were staying and as many of the servants as could be spared had already gone to the church.

James's parents, brother and sister-in-law and the four children had all made the journey to see him married, so the Manor was bulging with guests. The Misses Hardwick had made them welcome and shown everyone they had not forgotten how to entertain. But afterwards they were going to move into the Lodge, leaving James and Amy to take over the Manor.

Their decision had shocked Amy, who had protested against it. 'You love the old place, you know you do. You fought Cousin Gerald tooth and nail to keep it, so why have you changed your mind?'

'We have not changed our mind. Letting Gerald have it was one thing, giving it you and James is entirely another. And in one thing our cousin was right—it is becoming too much for us. The Lodge will do us very well and we shall be close to you.'

Travelling in the flower-bedecked carriage to her wedding, she could not believe this was happening to her. Her marriage to Duncan had been a very muted affair, with only a handful of guests, mostly friends of Duncan and her mother and father. And her life afterwards had been far from smooth. But that was behind her. She knew, as surely as night followed day, that James would never do anything to hurt her. He loved her. And she loved him. Nothing and no one could alter that. Her life would be spent making him happy. She stepped out at the church door and waited patiently while Susan straightened her gown, then took a deep breath and then walked sedately up the aisle. The whole village packed the church to see 'Miss Amy' married. To them, Duncan Macdonald had never existed.

James, dressed in a cream satin coat, cream silk breeches and gold-and-silver embroidered waist-coat, turned and watched her come towards him and his heart seemed to jump into his throat. She was so lovely, but her loveliness was not only on the outside; the inner core of her was serenely beautiful.

He smiled at Amy and held out his hand to her. She grasped it and stepped up beside him. 'All's well?' he whispered.

'All's well,' she responded with shining eyes.

Epilogue

March 1754

James, pacing the hall at Blackfen Manor, heard the baby's first cry, and bounded up the stairs to Amy's bedchamber. He did not bother to knock, but burst in to cross the room and fall on his knees beside her bed. She was drenched in sweat, her lovely hair was slick with it, but her eyes were bright and she was smiling. 'Are you all right, my darling?' he asked, ignoring the disapproving noises of the woman who had come in to help with the confinement. She was new to the village or she might have known Captain Drymore would never stand on ceremony, especially where his beloved wife was concerned.

'Yes, I feel wonderful,' Amy assured him. 'Are you not going to look at our son?'

'A son?' With a delighted smile, he turned and took the infant from the nurse. He was swaddled tightly, but his tiny fingers peeped over the edge of the cloth. He had huge blue eyes which seemed to be studying his father's face, as if to say, 'Who are you?'

'You have given me a son,' James said in wonder. 'Oh, my darling, I am so proud of you.'

'I did not do it alone,' she said, laughing. 'You played your part.'

The nurse fairly snorted at this and went to take the child from him. He refused to relinquish him. Instead he sat on the edge of the bed and began unwinding the infant bindings. 'I want to see him,' he said. 'All of him.'

Freed from the tight wrappings, the child lay on his back across James's knees and kicked his little legs. He did not cry. 'John,' he said, giving him the name they had decided on, should they have a son. He ran his hands gently all over the tiny body, deep pink with the exertion of making his way into the world.

'John James,' Amy said, reaching out and touching the child's hand. Immediately he gripped her finger. 'He is going to be strong, like his father.'

'Mrs Drymore must rest,' the nurse said, exerting her authority. 'And the boy must be fed. Where is the wet nurse?'

'There is no wet nurse,' Amy said. 'I shall feed him myself.'

'Really?' she asked in astonishment. 'It is most unusual for ladies…'

'Nevertheless, that is what I intend. I fed Amelia without any trouble and she is strong and healthy.' Amy turned to James. 'Where is Amelia? She will want to see her little brother.'

James left her to fetch their two-year-old daughter. He was bursting with love and pride. He was a father twice over and he adored his wife and his children. Was ever a man so blessed?

He soon returned carrying Amelia Harriet. With her blue eyes and fair hair she was the image of her mother. When he put her down, she climbed on the bed beside Amy and stared down at her brother, who had been wrapped up again, but this time more loosely. 'He's very little,' she said.

'He will grow, but until he does, you must be very gentle with him,' Amy told her. 'His name is John, after your grandfather. Would you like to touch him?'

Amelia put out a tentative hand which was gripped by the little fingers. 'Oh!' she said, and laughed.

It was later, when the children had both been taken off to the nursery and the midwife was busy sorting linen in an adjoining room, that James sat holding his wife's hand and voiced his thoughts. 'I have everything I want here,' he said. 'A darling wife, a lovely home, two beautiful children and the respect of the villagers. I thank God for it every day.'

'But?' she queried lightly.

'I think I should give something in return, put something back…'

'But you do. You are an example to every estate owner for miles around. The land has never been in better heart, the villagers are contented and, as a magistrate, you dispense justice fairly and moderately, better than most.'

He smiled at this catalogue of virtues. 'Amy, it is not enough. You remember before we were married, I said I would help Henry Fielding in some way?'

'Yes, but he died.'

'His brother, Sir John, has taken over where he left off. The Bow Street Runners are becoming a body to be reckoned with. They are rapidly gaining stature, but we are no nearer a police force. Before you can arrest anyone, you have to seek them out and prove their guilt, which is often beyond the power of the Runners.'

'I know.' She sighed a little, but she knew him through and through. He loved her and their children, she did not doubt it, but he was the sort of man who felt he had a duty to society and he would never shirk his duty. 'What does Sir John want you to do?'

'It is not what Sir John wants exactly. You know in the last three years he has asked me several times to employ my skills to track down a criminal who has been causing mayhem and no one else able to bring him to book for lack of evidence or because he hides himself too well. I have obliged him a few times.' He smiled suddenly, a smile that could always melt her heart. 'I am rather good at it, you know.'

'I know you are. So, go on.'

'The government is not disposed to fund an extension of the powers of the Runners and local constables, so I was thinking—only with your support, of course—that I would gather together a group of like-minded gentlemen prepared to give their time and resources to the catching of criminals—'

'Thieftakers,' she interrupted him with a laugh.

'You could say that. I think of them as crime solvers.'

'Crime solvers,' she repeated, attentive because he was obviously serious about it and had been mulling it over for some time. No doubt he had wanted to wait until after John was born before mentioning it to her. 'How would you make it work?'

'We would be approached by the public who have been the target of criminals, or by reference from

Sir John or Lord Trentham to take on sticky cases. I spoke to them about it and they are in favour. We would meet somewhere perhaps once a month to start with.'

'Here?'

'No, definitely not here. I do not want my family involved in any way. This is a haven of peace and must remain so. I suggested Bow Street, but though Sir John said it was possible, he did not think it would do to be too closely allied to the Runners. We need to be an entirely independent organisation.'

'I agree, my darling. If—no, when you are successful, they might want to take you over, dictate how you work and that would never do.'

'So you have no objection?'

'No, my darling. After all, it was how we met, in a manner of speaking, and for that I shall be eternally grateful.' She smiled, as she spoke. 'But do you think you could wait until after the christening?'

He detected a teasing note in her voice, but chose to answer seriously. 'I did not mean I was going to rush off tomorrow. I need to find somewhere to hold the meetings first. And I need to speak to one or two others. Harry Portman, for one. I am sure he could be useful. And there is Sir Ashley Saunders. He is the son of one of my father's friends, just down from Cambridge. I met him last time I was in

London and he was idling his time away, flirting with the Season's débutantes. He could do with something useful to occupy him. And no doubt there are others.'

'You have thought it all out, haven't you?'

'It has been on my mind, I admit,' he said, raising the palm of her hand to his lips. 'Crime is a scourge and is growing rather than diminishing. Something needs to be done.'

'Those you have named are wealthy members of the aristocracy,' she said, noting that only hours after having a child this wonderful husband of hers could still rouse her with a kiss; she had a feeling John James would not be the last of their brood. 'You need one or two others, the kind that can go into places where gentlemen would be too conspicuous.'

'Ever my practical wife,' he said, laughing. 'So you support the idea?'

'Of course. My only concern is that you should be safe.'

'I will take no unnecessary risks, I promise. And you are right, about the men. Shall I ask Sam Roker?'

'He would be ideal. He is entirely honest and understands your ways.' She had had Sam in mind from the beginning; he was a faithful servant and would do anything for James and help to keep him from harm.

'I will put it to him.' He rose and bent to kiss her lips. 'Now, you must rest.'

'I will, but, James…'

'Yes, my darling?'

'You will sleep with me, won't you? You will not take any notice of the nurse and that fussy old doctor. I want you at my side.'

'Wild horses would not keep me away.' He kissed her again and quietly left the room to go up to the nursery and take a peek at his children as they slept. 'I pray you grow up in a trouble-free world,' he murmured. 'And if I can do anything towards that, I will.'

And so, a few weeks after the christening of John James, which everyone in the village attended, including Amy's aunts and mother, James's parents, his brother and their ever-growing brood, the Society for the Discovery and Apprehension of Criminals was born. They met in a room in Lord Trentham's Piccadilly home where they undertook commissions, interviewed victims, decided which cases to pursue and reported on the outcome of their enquiries. The success of this venture was confirmed when a communication was brought to James one morning telling him he had been ennobled for his services to law and order, and was now Baron Drymore of Highbeck.

* * *

James realised their fame was spreading when he was approached by several young titled gentlemen asking if they might join the Society—which had come to be known as the Piccadilly Gentlemen's Club by the public, a tongue-in-cheek reference to the mainly aristocratic members of the group.

'Some are simply looking for adventure and some, I think, will not deal well with sensitive issues,' he told Amy. Wherever he was and whatever he was doing, his heart remained at Highbeck and he was never away from home for long. Leaving his associates to pursue whatever cases they had on their books, he would rush back to Amy and his children. It was a time-consuming journey and he often thought about leasing a London home, at least for part of the year, but that might put his family too close to his work, which could put them in danger. Besides, Amy loved Highbeck and it was a perfect place to bring up children. He had bought a new steel-sprung carriage to make the journey more comfortable and spent the time reading papers about the cases they had on hand and mulling over the latest requests. 'We need to weed them out. And they need to be of independent means. We charge only expenses and sometimes not that if the supplicant is poor. There must be no hint of taking rewards.'

'Is that what you have been doing this week?'

'Yes. There is one who looks promising. Jonathan, Viscount Leinster, heir to the Earl of Chastonbury. He has a good head on his shoulders. I have said I will give him a trial.'

The children had been put to bed and she was sitting on his lap, her arms about his neck. They often sat like that when they were alone, but she was heavy with their third child and his legs were becoming numb. He tipped her off him on to the sofa beside him and stretched his legs. 'Darling, I do think you might be giving birth to an elephant this time.'

She laughed and kissed him. 'Which should you like, a male elephant or a female one?'

'I do not mind in the least which it is. All I want is for you to be safely delivered.'

'There is no reason why I should not be. The other two were perfectly straightforward. Are you going to forget the Piccadilly Gentlemen's Club for a few weeks to stay with me until this elephant is born?'

'Most decidedly I am.'

Two weeks later, Charlotte Matilda made her presence felt at seven o'clock in the evening. She was a plump, healthy baby, but very far from being an elephant. The midwife knew better now than to try to bar James from the room. He was there as soon as he heard her cry. She was noisier than the other two had been, screwing up her face and letting out a wail that could be heard all over the house. He picked her up and laughed, walking about the room with her until she stopped. 'Let's get the other two in and see what they make of her,' he said, handing her back to her mother.

All five were soon spread across Amy's bed. 'Do you think we could be the happiest family in the kingdom?' Amy asked softly.

James reached over to kiss his beloved wife. 'In the whole world,' he smiled.

Author Note

I hope you enjoyed reading *The Captain's Mysterious Lady*, which is the first in a series of books with the same theme: how law and order was (or was not) kept in Georgian times. There was no regular police force, the streets were patrolled by the watch, appointed by the parish. Above them were unpaid parish constables, who could arrest suspects and bring them before a justice. The justice could try and punish minor crimes or decide to send the accused to the assizes for trial. When Henry Fielding was appointed Chief Magistrate of Westminster in 1749 he set up the Bow Street Runners and after he died his brother Sir John, the blind magistrate, continued his work, but their remit was limited. There was no such thing as a detective force.

My heroes, beginning with James Drymore, are

all honest gentlemen, who have formed themselves into the Society for the Discovery and Apprehending of Criminals known as the Piccadilly Gentlemen's Club. Its members are all rich enough not to require payment for their services but if a client is particularly wealthy, then any fee they offer is given immediately to charity. Not for the Piccadilly Gentlemen the taking of bribes as other thieftakers were known to do; they do it for the love of adventure and to make the country a safer place for its inhabitants.

In solving the mysteries I have set for them, each finds the love of his life. James is now happily settled with his Amy and in the next book, Jonathan—Viscount Leinster, one of the Piccadilly Gentlemen—finds himself on the trail of a young lady who has gone missing after overhearing a shocking secret about her birth.

Look for Viscount Leinster's story. Coming soon.

HISTORICAL

Large Print
THE RAKE AND THE HEIRESS
Marguerite Kaye

Any virtuous society lady knows to run from Mr Nicholas Lytton. But he's the one person who can unlock the mystery surrounding Lady Serena Stamppe's inheritance. Accepting Nicholas's offer of assistance, Serena soon discovers the forbidden thrills of liaising with a libertine – excitement, scandal…and a most pleasurable seduction!

WICKED CAPTAIN, WAYWARD WIFE
Sarah Mallory

When young widow Evelina Wylder comes face to face with her dashing captain husband – *very* much alive – she's shocked, overjoyed…and so furious she's keeping Nick firmly out of their marriage bed! Now the daring war hero faces his biggest challenge – proving to Eve that his first duty is to love and cherish her, forever!

THE PIRATE'S WILLING CAPTIVE
Anne Herries

Instinct told her that Captain Justin Sylvester was a man she could trust. Captive on the high seas, with nowhere to run, curiously Maribel Sanchez had never felt more free. Now she had to choose: return to rigid society and become an old man's unwilling wife or stay as Justin's more than *willing* mistress…

HISTORICAL

Large Print

THE VISCOUNT'S UNCONVENTIONAL BRIDE
Mary Nichols

As a member of the renowned Piccadilly Gentlemen's Club,
Jonathan Leinster must ensure the return of a runaway.
Spirited Louise has fled to her birthplace, hoping to find
her family – but charming Jonathan stops her in her tracks!
His task is simple: escort Louise promptly home. Yet
all he wants to do is claim her as his own!

COMPROMISING MISS MILTON
Michelle Styles

Buttoned-up governess Daisy Milton buries dreams of
marriage and family life in order to support her sister and
orphaned niece. But Viscount Ravensworth shakes up
Daisy's safe, stable existence. Could a tightly laced miss be
convinced to forgo society's strict code of conduct…and
come undone in the arms of a reformed rake?

FORBIDDEN LADY
Anne Herries

Sir Robert came in peace to claim his lady honourably.
But Melissa denied their love and her father had him
whipped from the house. Embittered, Rob sought his
fortune in fighting. As the Wars of the Roses ravage England,
Melissa falls into Rob's power. He should not trust her –
but can he resist such vulnerable, innocent beauty?

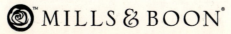 ™ MILLS & BOON®

HISTORICAL

Large Print

PRACTICAL WIDOW TO PASSIONATE MISTRESS
Louise Allen

Desperate to reunite with her sisters, Meg finds passage to England as injured soldier Major Ross Brandon's temporary housekeeper. Dangerously irresistible, Ross's dark, searching eyes warn Meg that it would be wrong to fall for him… But soon sensible Meg is tempted to move from servants' quarters to the master's bedroom!

MAJOR WESTHAVEN'S UNWILLING WARD
Emily Bascom

Spirited Lily is horrified by her reaction to her new guardian, Major Daniel Westhaven. He's insufferably arrogant – yet she can't help longing for his touch! Brooding Daniel intends to swiftly fulfil his promise and find trouble-some Lily a husband. Yet she brings light into his dark life – and into his even darker heart…

HER BANISHED LORD
Carol Townend

Hugh Duclair, Count de Freyncourt, has been accused of sedition, stripped of his title and banished. Proud Hugh vows to clear his name! Childhood friend Lady Aude de Crèvecoeur offers her help – after all, turbulent times call for passionate measures…

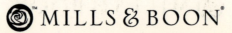 MILLS & BOON

HISTORICAL

Large Print

THE EARL'S RUNAWAY BRIDE
Sarah Mallory

Five years ago, Felicity's dashing husband disappeared into
war-torn Spain. Discovering a dark secret, she had fled
to England. Still haunted by memories of their passionate
wedding night, Felicity is just about to come face to face
with her commanding husband – back to claim
his runaway bride!

THE WAYWARD DEBUTANTE
Sarah Elliott

Eleanor Sinclair loathes stuffy ballrooms packed with fret-
ful mothers and husband-hunting girls. Craving escape, she
dons a wig and disappears – *unchaperoned!* – to the theatre.
There she catches the eye of James Bentley, a handsome
devil. His game of seduction imperils Eleanor's disguise –
and tempts her to forsake all honour…

THE LAIRD'S CAPTIVE WIFE
Joanna Fulford

Taken prisoner by Norman invaders, Lady Ashlynn's
salvation takes an unexpected form. Scottish warlord Black
Iain may be fierce, yet Ashlynn feels strangely safe in his
arms… Iain wants only to be free of the rebellious, enticing
Ashlynn. But then a decree from the King commands
Iain to make his beautiful captive his *wife*!

HISTORICAL

Large Print

RAKE BEYOND REDEMPTION
Anne O'Brien

Alexander Ellerdine is instantly captivated by Marie-Claude's dauntless spirit – but, as a smuggler, Zan has nothing to offer such a woman. Marie-Claude is determined to unravel the mystery of her brooding rescuer. The integrity in his eyes indicates he's a gentleman…but the secrets and rumours say that he's a rake beyond redemption…

A THOROUGHLY COMPROMISED LADY
Bronwyn Scott

Has Incomparable Dulci Wycroft finally met her match? Jack, Viscount Wainsbridge, is an irresistible mystery. His dangerous work leaves no space for love – yet Dulci's sinfully innocent curves are impossibly tempting. Then Dulci and Jack are thrown together on a journey far from Society's whispers – and free of all constraints…

IN THE MASTER'S BED
Blythe Gifford

To live the life of independence she craves, Jane de Weston disguises herself as a young man. When Duncan discovers the truth he knows he should send her away – but Jane brings light into the dark corners of his heart. Instead, he decides to teach his willing pupil the exquisite pleasures of being a woman…

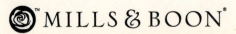

MILLS & BOON